# Love at
# Christmas Inn

# Collection 1

# Christmas Bells are Ringing

## Tanya Stowe

# Bells at Midnight

## Marianne Evans

# With Bells On

## Mary Manners

# Bells on Her Toes

## Delia Latham

# Table of Contents

## Christmas Bells are Ringing ............................................ 3

    1 ...................................................................................5

    2 .................................................................................13

    3 .................................................................................19

    4 .................................................................................27

    5 .................................................................................37

    6 .................................................................................45

    7 .................................................................................53

    8 .................................................................................63

    9 .................................................................................73

       ~ About Tanya ~ ...................................................81

       ~ More Titles by Tanya Stowe ~ .............................82

## Bells at Midnight ....................................................... 87

    1 .................................................................................89

    2 .................................................................................97

    3 ............................................................................... 107

    4 ............................................................................... 117

    5 ............................................................................... 129

    6 ............................................................................... 137

    7 ............................................................................... 145

    8 ............................................................................... 153

       ~ About Marianne ~ ............................................. 157

       ~ More Titles by  Marianne Evans ~ ..................... 158

## With Bells On ............................................................ 163

    1 ............................................................................... 165

    2 ............................................................................... 171

    3 ............................................................................... 177

    4 ............................................................................... 185

    5 ............................................................................... 195

    6 ............................................................................... 203

    7 ............................................................................... 211

    8 ............................................................................... 217

    9 ............................................................................... 225

    10 .............................................................................. 229

~ About Mary ~...................................................233
~ More Titles by Mary Manners ~ ...............234
~ Connect with Mary Manners ~ ................236

*Bells on Her Toes*...................................**241**

1 ...................................................................243
2 ...................................................................253
3 ...................................................................261
4 ...................................................................269
5 ...................................................................279
6 ...................................................................287
7 ...................................................................297
8 ...................................................................307
9 ...................................................................317
10 .................................................................325
~ About Delia ~.............................................331
~ More Titles by  Delia Latham ~ ...............333

# Love at Christmas Inn

# Christmas Bells are Ringing

# TANYA STOWE

# Christmas Bells are Ringing

## Tanya Stowe

*Remember how the Lord your God led you all the way*
*in the wilderness these forty years to humble and*
*test you in order to know what was in your heart,*
*whether or not you would keep his commands.*
*~ Deuteronomy 8:2 (NIV) ~*

# 1

**THE TENNESSEE COUNTRYSIDE ROLLED OUT** before
Ariana Christmas as the highway topped the crest of a small hill,
providing a stunning view of Hope Creek. Early October, and the
trees had turned. Bright orange, russet and golden leaves created
an amazing patchwork of colors on the panorama below.

Beautiful. Even if it was in the back of beyond. She tamped
down on the anger and resentment that threatened to raise ugly
heads again. Those emotions were useless. When her father first
sentenced her to this imprisonment, she'd tried sarcasm, rage and
finally tears. All to no avail. He'd cancelled her credit cards and
her phone account. He'd even taken away her lovely little sports
car with its leather interior and told her she had to earn her own
way. Her ailing Aunt Lizzie needed help. Ari's new job was to
take care of Lizzie, and oh, by the way, oversee the renovations
of the family's historic Christmas Inn.

So not fair. What did Ari know about running an inn? OK, so
she did have a master's degree in hotel management. But she'd
never worked a day in her life. She didn't need to. Her older
brother Ian took his place beside their dad to manage their hotel
empire long before Ari left school. Ian was a natural leader and a
great asset to the business. She should know. Her father told her

so enough times.

She sighed and focused her gaze back on the road. She shouldn't resent Ian. It wasn't his fault he was a natural born leader and IT genius while Ari was good at…Parties. She was the best at partying. In fact, that's what got her into this trouble. A video had surfaced on the Internet and gone viral. OK, so she'd had too much to drink. And yes, her little impromptu dance on top of the table was a bit suggestive. Well, maybe more than a bit. At least it wasn't a strip tease. Still, her parents would probably be shocked to find out she was as pure as the day she'd been born.

*And who's fault is it they'd be shocked?*

There it was again. That nagging little voice she'd been hearing more and more frequently. She didn't much like the constant, niggling reminder of too many things she'd like to forget, or drown out.

She stabbed at the button on the dash, hoping to find a station with some music. All she got was dead air.

The radio in her newly purchased, semi-ancient economy vehicle didn't work. Neither did the air conditioning or the heater. In fact, the engine seemed to resent the need to turn over. Her mother had tried to convince her dad that he should give her a dependable car. But Dad had refused stating, "It's time Ariana learned to appreciate what she has."

Fortunately, she *had* just enough in savings to cover the price of a car and gas from New York City to Tennessee. She'd purchased a throw away phone for emergencies and hit the road. Of course, fuel had cost a great deal more than she anticipated so she'd skimped on lunch and dinner yesterday and completely skipped breakfast this morning, as evidenced by her tummy's angry grumbling. She'd eat when she got to the inn, after the meeting of course. Her father had scheduled a meeting for her with Paulina Kovacs, the inn's manager, and the contractor hired to do the renovations. Ari was already fifteen minutes late. Fortunately, her family's historic inn was just around the corner.

*Chug. Chug.*

Great. There was that funny sound in the engine again. The car stuttered, lost power and slowed almost to a stop. At the last minute, it choked back to life and picked up speed. Ari released her breath in a sigh.

OK. So maybe she should have spent a little more and bought a newer used car. But her favorite designer purse had released their winter addition and she just had to have it. So she'd splurged on the accessory and settled for the cheaper vehicle.

She turned down the drive to Christmas Inn. Her great-great grandfather, Angus Christmas, had been one of the first to settle in the township of Hope Creek. He and her great-great grandmother lived in a small log cabin while Angus built the beautiful white chapel that still stood at the back of the property. Its steeple and bells had earned Christmas Inn a reputation. Legend had it that the bells rang whenever a couple was destined to fall in love.

Even though Ari had heard the story since she was little, she wasn't sure she believed it. Wasn't even sure she believed in true love. But her mother believed. She'd repeated often enough how she and her family had come to spend their summer vacation at Christmas Inn. Ari's dad was home from college for the summer to perform lifeguard duties. The minute her mother saw the handsome son of the inn's owners, she fell in love. The first time he kissed her, near a park bench outside the chapel, the bells had tolled, startling everyone within earshot.

They didn't marry right then, not until three years later when Ari's mother finished college and returned with her family for another summer at Christmas Inn. By that time, the young man she'd been infatuated with on the last visit was managing the place. As soon as he saw her familiar face, he set out to claim her as his own. The rest was history.

Ari had loved hearing the story when she was little. But time and experience had taught her love didn't come that easy or stay so true. Still, Christmas Inn was their home and even after her father purchased more hotels and her family left to manage them, they'd returned to spend every Christmas in Hope Creek.

Aunt Elizabeth and her husband Dale managed the inn. Uncle Dale had passed almost a year ago. According to her parents, Lizzie had not handled his passing well and now her own health was failing. Her oldest friend, Roberta, had moved into the suite to help out.

Ari knew nothing of her aunt's condition personally. Somehow she hadn't managed to return to Christmas Inn for the holidays since she'd left for college. This was her first visit in years and she had to admit, she was a bit excited. She'd always loved Christmas Inn with its quaint, old-fashioned decor and Christmas-themed rooms. She couldn't wait to see it.

The Tudor gables appeared through the trees just as the engine sputtered again.

"Come on. Come on. You can do it."

The vehicle responded with a small explosion. Ari jumped and gripped the wheel as the car coughed and fell silent. It coasted to a stop just short of the front entrance. She released another heavy sigh.

Close enough. The valet could take care of the vehicle from here. Turning off the ignition, she grabbed her purse, checked her makeup and hair, then climbed out. A young man of seventeen or eighteen came out of the inn's front entrance.

"Wow. Sounds like you've got engine trouble."

"Yes. Thank goodness I made it this far. I have no idea what's wrong." She held out the keys.

He stared at her extended hand for a few moments before finally taking them.

"I'm Ariana Christmas. And you are?"

The young man looked flustered. "I…I'm Jason."

"Pleased to meet you, Jason. Just have the car serviced then park it in my place. I'll arrange payment later. Thanks."

She shouldered her purse and headed in to her meeting, even later than her usual fashionably late appearance. The door slid open and a rush of warm air flowed over her. She closed her eyes as familiar smells surrounded her. Smoke from the massive fireplace. Pine boughs and cookies. And maybe just a little dust.

Wait…dust?

Her eyes popped open. That wasn't familiar here. In fact, now that she was inside, the dusty odor was stronger, more like musty old carpet.

Ari halted. The entryway tile had multiple cracks—not to mention the dirt clogged in the corners. The carpet edges were badly worn, and tiny fingerprints caked the sliding doors. A fine layer of construction dust rested on the table beside the entrance, where cookies and hot cider usually resided. Leather divans posed in the square conversation area looked ragged, and black soot marred the large fireplace directly across. The clock above was impressive as ever, albeit in need of a good polishing.

Hammer blows echoed in the distance and the zing of electric drills made her teeth rattle. Obviously the renovations had already begun. Still, how had her favorite place in the world fallen into such a sad state?

At that moment, the elves on the cuckoo clock above the mantel marched out of their little home to chime forty-five minutes after the hour, reminding Ari that she was late. She hurried toward the reception desk, where a young woman greeted her with a sweet smile.

"Hello, I'm Ariana Christmas and I'm very late for a meeting with Ms. Kovacs. Can you send me in the right direction?"

The receptionist pointed to the hall on the left. "She and Mr. Knox are in her office."

Was it her imagination or did the receptionist's voice soften when she said 'Mr. Knox'?

"Thank you. Who exactly is Mr. Knox?"

The girl's smile grew bright and her eyes took on a glazed look. "Why, he's the general contractor hired for the inn's renovations."

No mistake. The girl's eyes glazed over at the mere mention of Mr. Knox.

Well, Ari dealt with dreamy types all the time. She wasn't going to lose her focus. This meeting had taken on new importance. Christmas Inn needed saving.

She knocked on the door. Then, not waiting for a reply, Ari turned the knob and sailed in.

Paulina Kovacs, employee of Christmas Enterprises and current manager at Christmas Inn, sat behind the desk. Dressed in a black pantsuit, her hair pulled into a tight roll and black-rimmed glasses perched on her nose, the woman looked so much like a caricature of a businesswoman, Ari almost laughed out loud. Then she caught sight of the man sitting in front of her desk and caught her breath.

Dreamy was the perfect word. Light brown hair fell over his forehead in just the right casual but controlled wave. A rather thin nose with a perfect slope. Strong lips, the lower fuller than the upper. On any other man, the five o'clock shadow above his lips might have seemed grungy, but on him it looked just rugged enough. And those eyes. Hazel. But she couldn't tell for sure because as she walked forward, they changed with the light. At a distance they'd seemed green but up close they were light brown. Almost yellow. Incredible.

Ari only realized she was staring when Ms. Kovacs cleared her throat. Gathering herself, Ari flashed her trademark smile, guaranteed to conquer any male over the age of five and extended her hand.

"I'm Ariana Christmas. You must be Mr. Knox, our contractor."

"Yes...yes, I am." His handshake was warm and comfortable. Rough fingers. Working man's hands. Quite a change from the male hands she was accustomed to. One side of his mouth curved in a perfect half smile and Ari found herself staring again. She could watch the way his upper lip tilted all day.

But that wouldn't do. Turning, she smiled at Ms. Kovacs and offered her hand. "So pleased to meet you at last, Paulina. I've heard so many wonderful things about you."

One very black eyebrow arched upwards. "Really?" She gave Ari's hand a quick shake then looked down to fiddle with a stapler on her desk. "Well, I'd like to think so, but if that's true, why did your father send you down here to supervise my efforts?"

Ari smiled to cover Paulina's surprisingly honest response. Truth was, her father probably wanted Ms. Kovacs to supervise Ari, but somehow she didn't want to admit that out loud–at least not in front of Mr. Knox.

"I'm really here to watch over my aunt. But now that I'm here, I have to say I'm shocked at the condition of the inn. How did things get so bad so quickly?"

Paulina drew a slow breath. Ari could almost visualize the woman mentally counting to ten. "It hasn't been quick. I've been here for almost two years and I've been asking for funds to renovate since the first month I arrived. It simply hasn't been possible with the budget." Paulina's tone dripped pure frustration.

Ari wasn't sure what to say. "Oh, I see."

The family business couldn't find a way to finance upgrades in their hereditary home? That jarring thought made her father's frustration with Ari's spending habits a little more understandable. Why hadn't he told her? Hadn't he known she'd be only too happy to curtail her activities if it meant Christmas Inn could be brought back to its previous beauty?

"Well, now that the renovations have begun, we absolutely must do something about that entrance. The tile and carpet have to go."

Paulina's eyebrow quirked again but she never said a word. She simply handed Ari a list of budgeted items. Tile. New carpeting. Furniture. Windows replaced. Ari gazed down the list and almost gasped at the total.

No wonder her father was cutting costs where he could.

She swallowed hard and licked her lips. "It seems you and Mr. Knox have the situation well in hand." She flashed Mr. Dreamy a quick smile that had no doubt lost its previous pizazz and met the manager's definitely disdainful stare. "It seems I'm interrupting.

I didn't mean to. I would have been on time but I had car trouble. I barely made it here and handed it over to the valet."

At that moment, a knock sounded at the door. Paulina answered and Jason, the young attendant, peeked around the corner.

"Excuse me, Ms. Kovacs." He glanced at Ari. "Ms. Christmas's car is blocking the drive. It needs to be moved but it won't start. I'm not sure what she'd like me to do with these." He held out Ari's keys.

Paulina drew in a slow, frustrated breath. This time Ari didn't have to visualize the woman counting to ten. She could hear it. "I'll take them, Jason. Thank you."

The young man handed the manager the keys, then quickly stepped out and closed the door. Paulina smiled but her lips had a tight, strained look, hardly a smile at all. "We don't have valet service. And we have a very narrow drive and entry. Your vehicle will need to be towed as soon as possible."

Heat crept into Ari's cheeks. "Of course. I'll take care of that right now." She took the keys and hurried to the door. Just as she reached for the handle, a thought occurred to her. Cheeks flaming, she stood for a moment more, gritting her teeth but knowing she had no other choice.

She turned back around. "Uhhmmm…exactly how do I do that?"

# 2

**TAYLOR CHUCKLED BEFORE HE COULD** stop himself. Normally, behavior from a helpless, pampered New York-type like Ms. Ariana Christmas would not have elicited a laugh. Not even a smile. He disliked her type of "entitled" people.

He'd been earning his own way since he was twenty and his dad was diagnosed with cancer. Taylor left college to study for his contractor's license and took over the family business to support his four sisters and brother. In his line of work, he'd dealt with enough people who thought he and his workers beneath them because they swung a hammer for a living. He had no patience or time for those attitudes.

But Ariana seemed different. There was something engaging about her. Of course she was beautiful, and not just in a pampered way. Makeup and expensive procedures could take care of most flaws. But the woman didn't seem to have any. She appeared totally natural. Long, shoulder-length, dark brown hair with golden highlights. Dark, shapely brows over a pair of warm, chocolate-colored eyes. But it was her bright smile that garnered the most attention. When Ariana Christmas smiled, you couldn't help but smile back.

Why, he didn't know. How could a woman who didn't even know how to call a tow truck win anyone's empathy?

Maybe it was because she seemed to understand how silly it was. When she smiled at you, it felt genuine, like she really liked the world…maybe even really liked you. Right now, her dark eyes were wide, honest, open…seeming to say, "I know. Can you believe me?"

OK. That was a seriously crazy thought. Shaking his head, he looked at Paulina. She didn't seem at all engaged by Ms.

Christmas. In fact, the ever-efficient manager seemed about to blow her top. Her cheeks were flushed bright red. Her lips sealed into a tight line that trembled with her effort to keep them closed. Taylor got the distinct impression she was about to say something she would later regret.

"I can help you with that." In an effort to stem a gathering storm, he lunged to his feet, gathered his notebook and hurried to the door. "Paulina, I think we're finished here. I need to get back to work. I'll give you a call when that supplier gets back to me, but like I said, we're on track to finish early."

Taking Ms. Christmas by the arm, he hustled her out before Paulina had a chance to speak. Once the door had closed behind them he gestured down the hall, encouraging the socialite to take the lead. She started forward and he followed, trying not to notice the shapely legs tucked into knee-high black boots, or how her hips swayed beneath a knee-length black jacket.

Taylor shook his head. Really? One smile and he was following her like a puppy dog—never mind that spoiled little rich girls were not his type. Honestly, Paulina Kovacs with her no-nonsense and practical manner was more to his liking. Maybe that was the real issue. He was fond of the manager and didn't want to see her lose her composure. He would like it even less if she got herself into trouble with her employer over something as silly as a stalled car.

He'd just convinced himself that was the issue when little Miss Socialite stopped in her tracks and turned to face him. Those warm eyes settled on him and captured his gaze in a velvet vice.

"Thank you." Her voice was low and rich, like the melting chocolate of her eyes. Not silly or affected. Sincere. "I really appreciate your offer to help. I've never done anything like this. My family has a valet service for all of our people. Whenever I have a problem, I call the head of our service. Only now…I can't call him." Her tone faltered, wobbled just a little. Then she flashed that smile.

"Anyway, most of the time I walk. You don't really need a car in New York."

Perfect teeth. Full, pink lips. He couldn't seem to take his gaze off her mouth. He didn't know how long he stood there before her smile faltered, kind of faded. Only then did he realize he'd been staring.

"No problem." Taking her elbow, he guided her back down the hall. The sooner he got her car fixed and the woman well on her way, the better. "Usually your insurance will cover the towing."

She stopped again. "Uhhhmm…I don't know my insurance info either. I bought the car just before I left. My dad added me to his policy over the phone so I don't have any paperwork. Just a number."

Taylor sighed. "I know a great mechanic in town who does his own towing. We'll call him and you can sort out the payment later."

"Great. Thanks."

*Don't smile. Please don't smile at me again.*

But she did and her perfect lips hadn't lost any of their impact. If anything, her sweet smile hit his stomach like a punch. She didn't notice what was surely another glazed look on his face because she'd opened the huge bag looped over her shoulder. It was the size of suitcase and sported a designer logo on the side. Probably cost more than one of his workers earned in a month.

That dulled some of the effect of her smile.

She rummaged around inside the bag for several minutes before pulling out a cell phone…a small flip phone that looked like it would fall apart as soon as she opened it.

"If you'll just give me the number of your friend—oh." A frown creased the space between well-shaped brows.

Taylor shook his head. "Let me guess. Your phone's not working either."

She held it up. "It needs to be charged. I don't have anything like that in my car. It's a throwaway phone. I bought it…"

"Just before you left. I get it. Let me call Dan for you."

He pulled out his phone and hit Dan's number. As he began to speak, Ms. Christmas spied Jason walking across the lobby.

"I'll be right back." She hurried across, softly calling Jason's name. Just before Dan picked up on the other end, Taylor heard Ariana Christmas apologizing to the young bellhop about her assumption.

Another surprise. Entitled folks usually never apologized. For anything.

He gave Dan the information and put his phone in his pocket just as Ariana returned with Jason in tow. "He's going to get my bags out before the tow truck arrives."

"Good idea. Dan said he could be here in fifteen minutes."

"That's really quick. I guess it pays to know people in Hope Creek."

Was she being sarcastic? Is that how she got things done in New York, using the people she knew? He studied her expression, trying to discern the hidden meaning. But all he saw was an open, far-too-beautiful-for-his-well-being face.

*Enough.* "Well, you should be set now. I have to get back to work."

Before he could move, she grasped his forearm. Her fingers were slender with perfectly white-tipped nails. No marks. No callouses. Just lovely, white, unused hands...with slender gold bands full of chipped diamonds on three fingers. Definitely a month's worth of salary for a Knox construction worker.

"Thank you."

Just like that, she did it again. Disarmed his rising irritation with a textured, sincere voice.

"No problem. Glad to help."

He started to move away. But she grasped him arm more firmly.

"No, I mean for all your work on Christmas Inn."

That caught him off guard.

"I know I interrupted your meeting with Paulina and came on pretty strong. It's just...well, I hadn't realized how bad the conditions were here. I haven't been back since...since high school."

That was true enough. Paulina had told him Ariana hadn't returned when her uncle passed. Apparently her social calendar had been too full even to visit when her beloved Aunt Lizzie took ill and needed care. Fortunately, her aunt's best friend Roberta Cutler, also recently widowed, moved into the suite to provide her care.

As far as Taylor was concerned that action added another black mark against Ms. Christmas. Family was everything. He'd put all his hopes and dreams on hold to take care of his family. She couldn't even be bothered to attend her uncle's funeral.

He was beginning to better understand Paulina's resentment. She'd tried to hide it but Taylor had worked with the manager long enough to know when she was off her mark. When she relayed how Mr. Christmas had cut off his daughter's funds and sent her south, Paulina couldn't contain her disgust. "I have enough on my plate without having to babysit a prima donna. It's like they're punishing me for her bad behavior."

Taylor'd thought Paulina was exaggerating but after what he'd seen today, she'd hit the mark. Ariana Christmas needed babysitting. He and Paulina had a strict time schedule and enough to do without the added stress of a helpless, clueless socialite…even if she did have the prettiest smile he'd ever seen.

He gave a short, curt nod, making sure it was just a step above rude.

"Just doing my job, Ms. Christmas." Then he turned and walked away.

# *3*

**JASON WAS AN ABSOLUTE SWEETHEART.** After Dan the tow guy drove away, Jason carried her five suitcases and multiple carry-ons to her room. Ari wished she had a decent tip but all she could manage was pocket change dug out of the bottom of her bag. Her suite was in her aunt's house, adjacent to the inn, but it had its own entrance so she was able to slip in without disturbing Aunt Lizzie.

As soon as Jason carefully placed her bags in a pile, she poured the coins into his hands. "I'm so sorry this is all I have. I promise when I have cash, I'll do a better job."

A slight flush tinged his cheeks. "No problem, Ms. Christmas."

She rewarded him with a bright smile. Blushing more, he almost stumbled over her bags on the way out the door.

As soon as he was gone, she unbuttoned her jacket, threw it to the bed and hurried to see Lizzie.

Sunlight flooded the living room of her aunt's suite. Everything was just as Ari remembered. Old-fashioned sheers and 60's style gold, pinch pleat curtains on the windows. An overstuffed sofa and chair in gold brocade sat in a half-circle around the fireplace. Colonial style, dark wood end tables with claw foot legs. A grand piano tucked in the corner and pictures on the mantel. Everything spotless and certainly not showing the wear and tear of the furniture she'd seen in the inn. Still, none of the furnishings had changed since Ari was a little girl.

All of Ari's memories of her aunt were swathed in images from the past…classic sheath dresses modestly cut at the knees, a single string of white pearls around her neck and her white hair pulled back in a French roll, a la Audrey Hepburn or Grace

Kelly.Ari had never noticed her aunt's outdated possessions or fashion—outdated even then, let alone twenty years later. All she remembered was her aunt's loving arms. The scent of her flowery perfume and her smiling face…that most of all. With no children of her own, Aunt Lizzie had always called Ari her "special girl." Ari'd spent every Christmas and most of the summer here while her parents traveled for business.

Her aunt would push back the sofa so Ari could dance like a ballerina. Aunt Lizzie played the piano, classic for her ballerina moves, Big Band for her jitterbug and of course, rock and roll. She would dance for hours and Aunt Lizzie never seemed to tire of playing.

One summer, her aunt set up paint easels in the garden for Lizzie and all the younger guests. The next summer she had a local swim teacher give lessons in the pool. Lizzie even bought a child-sized potter's wheel and placed it beneath the gazebo one summer. Ari and Lizzie's rooms were filled with misshapen mugs, bowls and pitchers for years.

Of course, Aunt Lizzie claimed the lessons were for all the guests but Lizzie knew they were for her. She had many happy memories of Christmas Inn. After such a long time away, all Ari wanted to do was wrap her arms around her aunt and hold her forever.

"Aunt Lizzie?"

Roberta came around the corner from the kitchen with a tray in her hands.

"Bertie!" Ari ran across the room. Her aunt's best friend barely had time to set the tray on a nearby table before Ari rushed into her arms, nearly knocking the older lady backwards.

Bertie hugged her back and Ari squeezed her tighter. "My goodness! I think you're glad to see me."

Ari held her at arm's length. Bertie had cut her salt and pepper hair into a fashionable bob that suited her no-nonsense personality. She had a few more wrinkles but other than that, the older lady looked exactly as Ari remembered.

"I was beginning to worry. You should have been here an hour ago."

"I had car trouble, but let's not talk about that now. Where's Aunt Lizzie?"

"In her room. She didn't feel well enough to get up today."

That didn't sound good. Ari turned to hurry away but Bertie grasped her arm.

"Ari, you've been gone a long time. Things have changed."

"I know, Bertie. Too long."

"Your aunt…" The older lady paused then motioned her to move ahead. "Go on. You'll see for yourself."

Ari spun and ran to the bedroom door, barely knocking before bursting into the room. Her aunt lay in the bed, turned toward the windows. Bright sunlight fell through the open curtain, spilling onto a pale, fragile creature Ari barely recognized.

Aunt Lizzie wore a white nightgown. Her slender arms hid beneath long sleeves, and a high neck covered an even more slender throat. Her once-thick, lovely hair lay in thin wisps around her face and dangled raggedly to her shoulders. Her cheeks were gaunt and she had dark circles under her eyes. A tightness about her skin made the paper-thin flesh look about to burst.

Ari could hear Lizzie's breathing from across the room. Shock halted her footsteps. The raspy, wheezy gasps for air tore at her heart.

"Aunt Lizzie?"

"Ari?" Her aunt held out her hand. "Come closer. I may look like a monster but I promise I won't bite."

Ari hurried to the bedside and grasped her aunt's cool hand. "You don't look like a monster. Don't even say that."

A brief, smile flitted over Lizzie's mouth. "Maybe not a monster but I don't look good. You on the other hand, you're as beautiful as your mother."

Her aunt closed her eyes and leaned back into her pillow. "What a beauty she was. She stole your father's heart the minute he saw her. She was only sixteen, here for the summer with her parents. Of course, he didn't marry her until they were older. He'd finished school and returned that summer to find her visiting with her family once again. I remember hearing the bells toll and I knew…just knew your father had kissed her for the first time."

Ari had heard the story many times, but now, hearing it through her aunt's labored breathing turned Ari's blood to ice. The wonderful story that used to bring her such joy now sounded like an echo in an empty tomb. She blinked rapidly and looked down, hoping to hide her fear from her aunt.

"That's enough talking now." Bertie had followed Ari into the room. "Save your energy for eating your lunch. Let Ari do the talking. I'm sure she has a lot to tell you."

"I'm not hungry."

"You need to build up your strength for your doctor visit tomorrow."

"Don't fuss at me, Bertie. I said I'm not hungry."

"You are going to eat this soup even if I have to sit on the bed and spoon feed you. Ari, why don't you get your things settled while Lizzie's eating."

Ari stepped back and allowed Bertie to pull down the legs of the tray and set it across Lizzie's lap. Then she fluffed the pillows and helped her aunt rise. All the while, Lizzie complained and fussed at Bertie. Ari felt useless and helpless and continued stepping back…all the way out of the room.

She stood at the living room window, shock still sweeping through her in waves, and watched the wind wash golden leaves across the grounds. Bertie came to stand beside her.

"I knew she was ill. But not 'can't walk from the bed to the door' ill. She's dying, Bertie.

"Not quite yet. Her heart's not pumping as it should so it's not pushing the fluids out. She's retaining water and now it's affecting her lungs. Tomorrow we're going to the doctor and I suspect she'll need a hospital stay so they can drain the fluids and get her medications adjusted. She should improve after that."

"I should have been here. I've been gone too long."

"Yes, you have. Why did you stay away?

An image of her family sitting around a Christmas tree, placed right where they were standing, floated into her mind. A good memory. Then another of Ian loading his bags into the back of a car, headed for college after a fun-filled summer here at the inn. A not-so-good memory. Then her aunt's frail body flashed into her mind and she closed her eyes.

"I don't know, Bertie. I just don't know."

Another minute here beside Bertie and she was going to burst into tears. "I'll be back."

She turned and hurried to her room. But even that place seemed too confined, too full of memories. She ran back downstairs and through the breezeway. Stalking across the deck toward the grass, she kicked through the brittle orange and gold leaves that minutes ago had seemed so beautiful. Now they were a sharp reminder of death and dying. The cool crisp autumn breeze brushed over her cheeks. Only then did she realize she was crying.

She hurried down the walk. Everywhere she went she saw signs of disrepair and neglect. Like her life. How long had she been running? Ignoring the truth. She remembered snatches of conversations between her father and brother about cutting their losses and selling the inn.

Ari hadn't really paid attention because she never believed it would happen. They couldn't sell the inn. It was their heritage. Their blessing from God.

As if they had a will of their own, her feet carried her to the white chapel, across Candy Cane Creek, and tucked into the back corner of the property. The lovely little church on the hill looked more gray than white. It needed a good painting. A board dangled loose from the bell tower and the doors hung at an awkward, canted angle, so they wouldn't shut properly. A chain looped through the handles to secure them.

Ari's great-great grandfather, Angus Christmas, had been one of the area's earliest settlers. He came west with his young bride, determined to minister to the other pioneers eking out a living in the new territory. They'd lived in a split-log cabin with a dirt floor while Angus built this beautiful little church. The bells had been shipped in with great care and expense. During the same time, her great-great grandmother buried their first-born in a plot behind.

Angus said folks needed the bells, needed to hear the call of the Lord. The little church would be a safe haven, a place of comfort against the hardships they had to endure on the frontier. He was right. Folks came from miles around to worship in the little chapel and especially to be married. Angus rang the bells for services, deaths and births…for any occasion. Those bells were an important part of Hope Creek long after Angus passed.

The Lord rewarded Angus's dedication and the bells continued to ring with each new pastor. In fact, the chiming took on a life of its own. Legend said the bells would ring when a couple, destined to marry, kissed for the first time. At least that's what Aunt Lizzie told Ari. Back then she'd believed it. When had she stopped believing?

The image of Ian loading up his car popped into her mind again. Maybe that's when it started. Ian went off to school. Her father's work took him away from home for long periods of time. Management of their interests eventually even swallowed her mother's time and Ariana found herself floundering with no purpose, searching for an anchor and resenting the loss. Aunt Lizzie and Christmas Inn had always been that anchor.

But just like the rest of her family, Ari forgot and abandoned her roots. By the time she went off to college, her family was split in different directions and she was in full rebellion mode, missing…she didn't know what. Until today, as she stood outside the white chapel.

A gardener with a wheelbarrow full of dead leaves and plants passed.

"Excuse me. Are you preparing the grounds for the next wedding? I want to be here."

The middle-aged gardener paused. "No, ma'am. No wedding,

just the usual fall cleanup." His Tennessee drawl pegged him as a long time local.

"Do you know when the next one might be?"

He shook his head. "I don't know for certain, ma'am, but I don't think one's scheduled. We haven't had a wedding here in a long time...maybe a year."

"A year?" Ari's gaze shot upwards to the board dangling from the bell tower. "Has it been that long since the bells rang?"

The man shrugged. "Longer. I've been here almost two years and I've never heard them."

Ari stared at the man as he hefted the wheelbarrow and pushed it down the walk.

Her family's legacy was love. The bells represented that love, whether it came in the form of a renewed Christmas spirit, a wedding, or a family vacation that lived in memory for years. Christmas Inn represented Christ's peace and joy. Her family had been given the responsibility of maintaining that legacy and they...Ari included...had failed.

The modern frontier might consist of disillusionment, divorce, discouragement and materialism, but those things were just as dangerous as the wild animals and starvation the early settlers faced. Angus had it right. Christmas Inn and its little chapel needed to be a safe haven, a beacon of Christ's love and peace in the frontier...past and present.

Ariana stared at the bell tower and vowed to see her ancestral home restored to its rightful place. And maybe she'd find her own in the process.

# 4

**THE UNMISTAKABLE RUMBLE OF A** Harley Davidson motorcycle roared from the parking lot below. Taylor had just finished resolving plumbing problems in rooms seven and eight. They were the last to be finished before tackling the dining area. Then he'd move on to the family home next door. Everything was on schedule and for that, Taylor gave a big sigh of relief.

Come January first, he had big plans involving a motorcycle...like the one he'd heard moments ago. He just needed to finish this job and get through Christmas.

Hurrying to the window, he spotted the bike's driver removing a helmet next to the exact make and model Taylor had his eye on. Dark blue gas tank. Leather seats. All chrome and polish. The bike looked brand new.

Taylor had put his dream of a motorcycle tour of the U.S. on hold almost ten years ago. Now he had enough savings to buy his favorite model of motorcycle. With his younger brother Bobby licensed and poised to take over the family business, Taylor was ready. It was his turn. This time, he wouldn't let anything stop him.

"Better not let Mom catch you eyeing a beauty like that." Bobby walked up behind him.

"She'd like that big bike a lot better than the rocket you zip around on." Taylor moved away from the window, wiping blue plumbing glue off his hands.

"Hey, what can I say? Speed is my thing."

"Yeah, and you have the tickets to prove it."

Bobby chuckled. "Still, don't let Mom catch you mooning over a Harley. You might shatter her illusions. She refuses to believe you're going to ride off into the sunset and abandon the family."

"Abandon?" Taylor winced. "Dad's cancer is in remission. He's well enough to help out occasionally and you know the business. I'm not—"

Bobby punched his arm lightly. "Relax. I'm just razzing you. We'll be fine. Mom doesn't like it when any of her chicks fly the coop. Remember last year when Missy got married?"

Taylor remembered the wedding well. He'd footed the bill and postponed his trip yet another year to see his sister properly wed to her best friend.

That wasn't going to happen this year. Taylor would be on that bike the day after New Year's. He wasn't even sure where he was going. He just knew he would be on his way.

"Speaking of beauties."

Taylor looked up at his brother's muttered words. Ariana Christmas stood in the doorway, her gaze searching the room. She looked gorgeous in a long, deep purple tunic that did something wonderful to her brown eyes. They seemed prettier, warmer…if that was even possible.

As soon as she saw the two of them, she flashed the dazzling white smile that made Taylor's stomach feel like he'd been punched.

"I'd love to put *her* on the back of my bike and zip around town." Bobby's low comment squelched the effects of Ariana's smile.

"Back off. She's a client." Taylor regretted his words almost before they were out of his mouth. His tone held too much bite.

Bobby glanced his way. "So? Since when are clients off limits? I don't see you turning away Ms. Kovacs's attention."

Taylor shook his head. "That's different." He nudged his chin toward Ms. Christmas who was walking their way. "She's different."

He didn't have time, with the spoiled beauty drawing ever closer, to explain to his brother that Ariana came from money, was too entitled and too used to getting her way. She probably ate kids like Bobby for breakfast.

"Good morning, Mr. Knox." She held out her hand and Taylor gripped the soft, white, perfectly shaped fingers and palm. He couldn't help but notice that her diamond rings were missing. Telltale white circles around her fingers marked where they had been.

"Taylor, please."

"All right, but only if you call me Ari."

He nodded. Maybe he should have stuck with Mr. Knox. Ari sounded too familiar, too intimate.

"Hi, I'm Robert Knox. But you can call me Bobby." His brother extended a hand, and Taylor bit back a groan. He shouldn't have told Bobby to stay away from Ari. His brother would follow his usual pattern and go out of his way to ignore Taylor's advice.

"I think I've seen you riding the 750. It's bright yellow, right?"

Bobby smiled and Taylor recognized the self-confident "I've-got-this-one" look he wore around conquered females.

"That's right. Glad you know your way around motorcycles."

Ari shook her head. "I used to. My brother was into dirt bikes when we were younger. But it's been a long time." Her voice trailed off and her face lost some of its glow. Taylor sensed a story behind her somber expression.

"Well, if you ever want to get back into the swing of things, give me a call." Bobby didn't seem to notice the change in attitude.

"Thanks, it might be fun."

*That's enough of that.* Taylor said the first thing that came to his mind. "I hear your aunt is doing well since her procedure."

"Yes." Her face took on that soft glow again. "They placed a microchip in her shoulder that monitors her fluid retention. The chip helps them modulate her medicine. It's worked great. I can't believe how much she's improved in the last month."

"Maybe having you for company has helped."

"I hope so. I only know I'm glad to see her doing so well. She's certainly better...kind of like this place. You're doing a wonderful job with the inn. I love the colors and the refurbishing of the furniture. The four-poster bed in room three looks brand new. It's perfect."

"Thanks. Our sister is in charge of decor, though. She's good at her job."

"And Taylor does the hands-on stuff. He's a magician with wood."

Taylor shifted his shoulders. For some reason, Bobby's compliment made him uncomfortable. He didn't like the expression of appreciation it brought to Ari's face. Her eyes shone and that caused a now-familiar blow to his stomach.

"There is something I'd like to discuss with you, Taylor, if you have a moment."

"Sure, let's head over to suite six. I need to drop off these tools. I've taken up temporary residence there. It's my office for now."

He gestured toward the door and she moved in that direction. As he followed, Bobby gave him a knowing wink and lowered his voice. "Don't do anything I wouldn't do."

Taylor gave him a wry look. "I'll probably do less."

Ari waited for him on the landing overlooking the conversation area below. She looked on as some of his crew installed durable, wood-style flooring for that old-fashioned look so important to the inn. He gestured to the entry.

"The new stuff should hold up incredibly well, even with all of the inn's foot traffic. I think you'll be pleased with it."

She gave a slight smile. "Everything you've chosen is perfect. You and your people are true craftsmen. Paulina made a great decision going with your company."

They slowed their steps as Taylor opened the door to his suite and dropped his tools on a table. He gestured back out the door towards the elevators. "Have you told her that?"

Taylor caught the elevator just as it was about to close and held the sliding portal open for Ari. Her compliment about Paulina surprised him. The manager's attitude toward the owner's daughter had not improved in the weeks since Ari's arrival.

Perhaps the resentment was all on Paulina's side and he'd just exposed it. He felt the need to cover his possible social gaffe.

"Paulina is very efficient and concerned with her work. She—"

"Resents me." Ari flashed him a rueful smile. "I don't blame her. I'd have felt the same if my father had sent someone like me into the midst of this controlled chaos. That's why I've tried to stay out of her way...until now."

They'd reached the bottom floor and she started down the hall toward the back of the inn. Taylor followed but trepidation crept up his spine. The last thing he needed was to be in the middle of a power struggle between the two ladies and he had the sinking feeling that's where this conversation was headed.

He halted. "Look..."

"Relax, Taylor. I've already discussed this with Paulina and my father. He gave me the go-ahead, but made it clear I'm not allowed to use any of the inn's funds or interfere with management—Paulina's—decisions. I have to do this on my own. I just need you to tell me how much so I can come up with the money."

Taylor stretched his neck and lifted his shoulders, easing away the tension. Easy. Whatever she wanted, he would price out of her range. He had a deadline to meet. With Christmas just six weeks away and Thanksgiving holiday coming soon, his crew had no time to spare. This job must be completed on time so he could be on his way in January. No way was he saddling Bobby with any leftover duties to manage after the holidays.

"All right. Let's get to it."

She smiled and that sucker punch hit him one more time. Maybe he'd made a mistake avoiding the lovely young heiress. What he should have done was spend as much time with her as possible so her self-centered ways would destroy the impact of her near-perfect looks. And they were near perfect. Her dark hair cascaded in long layers down her back. It looked so soft and silky, he had to resist the urge to reach out and stroke it.

She opened the back door leading to the patio area and they were met with a cool breeze. Her scent swept over him, something musky and sweet at the same time. Light. Not heavy or overly strong. Just...wonderful.

She pushed hard on the door to open it further and he had to rush forward to help her. She even made him forget his good manners.

*Get it together, Taylor. You're not some green kid like Bobby. You know better than to let a pretty face turn your head.*

But turn it she did and not just because of those picture-perfect looks. He was beginning to suspect Ariana Christmas wasn't the diva he'd first thought her to be. Her genuine regret for her treatment of her aunt was his first clue. His second was her self-assessment about Paulina. Ari seemed perfectly aware of her awkward position at the inn and admitted it was well deserved.

He couldn't help but admire her humble attitude...and a few other things. He looked away from the gentle sway of her hips as she moved across the wooden deck to the grounds.

*Eyes on the prize, Knox. You have a plan. Stick to it.*

"What do you need from me?" He sounded abrupt, ruder than he needed to be.

"Well, I know the Christmas decorations had to be removed from the upgrades because of expenses." She turned quickly to place her hand on his forearm and he again noted the whiter skin where her diamond rings had once set. "Now that I've seen the quality of workmanship you've done on the repairs, I completely understand. But frankly, Christmas Inn just isn't the same without decorations."

He had to agree with her there. The whole focus of the renovations—and the inn itself—was to create the feeling of an old-fashioned Christmas. It seemed rather pointless without decorations.

"The Hope Creek Senior Crafters have agreed to make a new set of decorations for me and I have most of those costs covered."

Covered? Wait. Taylor halted as they crossed the walkway

leading to the expanse of the grounds. Dan had told him she didn't have enough money to cover her car repairs. She'd traded the beat-up vehicle for towing expenses. Where did she get the money for handcrafted decorations? His gaze shot to her fingers. Had she sold her rings to cover the cost?

The pesky wind picked up again, blowing her hair across her face. Reaching up, she pulled the long strands loose and tucked them behind her ear. Now that he thought about it, unless his memory was off—and where she was concerned it wasn't likely—she'd sported some pretty hefty diamonds on those ear lobes. But now they were gone too.

As they stood, wind whipping the edges of her hair, she looked at him expectantly. "What's wrong?"

"Nothing. How far are we going? It's getting a bit breezy."

"Come on. What I want to show you is just ahead."

Taylor suspected they were headed to the small chapel at the back of the grounds. He had the sinking feeling that's what she wanted him to see. Now he knew for sure he'd have to overprice the job. He'd examined the building before and knew it needed new paint inside and out. New carpeting. Many of the pews would require refinishing or replacement. Any other time, he'd renovate that chapel as a labor of love. But he was determined to hit the road come January.

"So if you have the decorations taken care of, what do you need from my crew?"

"We need them installed, permanently. They can't just be put in the rooms. Not everyone is honest and we're liable to lose them if they're not secured. For instance, there's a lovely garland for the four-poster bed but I wouldn't dream of having anyone attach it to the wood, after you've so lovingly restored it. The wreaths need to be wired and bolted to the walls and the Christmas tree room...well the Christmas tree needs to be attached to the floor. I don't think it will be much but I need an estimate."

They came to the old white chapel and Ari bent to unlock the chain around the door. The wind kept whipping her hair in her face. She couldn't wrangle her hair and the chain so he took the key from her hands. "Let me."

The chains slid away and the door squealed as he pushed it open. Once inside, he couldn't get it to shut properly until he put his shoulder to it and jammed. The musty scent of dust assaulted him and he brushed his hands against his jeans. Ari walked down the center aisle, her fingers trailing over the points of the oak pews before she turned to face him.

Sunshine fell through the long window, bathing her in a golden glow. Her hair shone like molten silk. His heart stopped as he took in the warmth in her dark eyes and the earnest openness on her face.

Did she know how beautiful she was? Was she standing in the sunlight on purpose just to play his senses?

Gathering his defenses, he folded his arms over his chest. "Putting up the decorations won't take more than a few minutes each. We can probably take care of those in between jobs while we're waiting for paint to dry. I think you know that. So if you've brought me out here to ask for an estimate on repairs for this building, you're out of luck. We won't be able to add chapel repairs to our contract and still finish by Christmas—and we *will* finish by Christmas."

"Oh no, I don't want you to fix the building. I think some spit and elbow grease will have to do for now. I can clean the carpets, shine the pews and paint the walls myself."

"You'll paint the walls?"

"What? You don't think I can?"

"I'd be surprised if you've ever held a paint brush in your hands."

"I'll have you know my aunt gave me painting lessons and assured me that my skills are top notch."

Her comment and teasing smile tickled him in ways he didn't expect. A chuckle slipped out. "I think that's a different kind of painting altogether and anyway, your aunt is biased."

There it was again. That brilliant hundred-watt smile. "She is, isn't she? But honestly, I think I can wield a paintbrush well enough for a temporary fix. I want to have Christmas Eve service in here. I'm going to contact someone to deliver a Christmas sermon." She faced the altar for a long moment and a slight frown creased her brow. "I don't know if he can make it yet, but I will ask."

She took a deep breath. "No, I want you to look at the bells. They tell me they're not working and the bells...they're my family's legacy. They make Christmas Inn special. They have to work. They just have to!"

# 5

ONE VERY MASCULINE, WELL-FORMED EYEBROW
rose in a quirk. "Your legacy? The bells might get repaired but
that doesn't mean they're going to ring. That takes a special
couple."

His skeptical tone didn't hide the soothing notes of his voice.
It reminded her of brandy—rich, warm and potent.

"You know about the legend?"

"I grew up in Hope Creek. Everyone here knows about the
bells."

"But you don't believe." It wasn't a question. She could tell by
his tone he didn't.

"Let's just say I haven't witnessed them for myself."

"I haven't either, but my aunt swears the legend is true. She's
a bit of a romantic so I might not buy into her version, but Bertie
believes too, and she's as steady as a rock."

"But you've never heard them ring?"

There it was again. That skeptical tone. The wind had fluffed
his hair so that a lock fell over his forehead. She itched to reach
out and smooth the gold-brown curl back...not because it looked
mussed. Just because she wanted to touch it. His hazel eyes were
a deep forest green today. His navy blue hooded sweatshirt must
have had an impact because the color stood out more than other
days.

Ari bit her lip and looked away, refusing to dwell on the fact
that even though she hadn't spoken to Taylor Knox more than a
handful of times, she knew his daily attire and how it changed the
color of his eyes.

"No. I've never heard them ring for a couple in love. But I

believe they do. It has to be the answer because things have changed. Something is missing, not just from the inn, but for my whole family. Christmas here used to be so special, the bells, Christmas Eve services..."

"The caroling."

Delight rippled through Ari. Though why she should be glad she and Taylor shared a memory, she didn't know. "You attended the tree trimmings?"

"Of course. Christmas wasn't Christmas without our trip to the inn. There was always a ten-foot tree and a decoration for every child tall enough to reach."

"I loved the carolers in their Dickens costumes. Sometimes my aunt would play piano for them."

"And the cookies. They were the best."

Some of her happiness faded at the mention of cookies. "I've planned a tree-trimming party for this year. But the cookies might not be the best. We're having a bit of trouble with the cook. Paulina thinks he might be sneaking a nip or two."

Taylor nodded. "Things haven't been the same since old Ned retired."

Another wave of sweet surprise swept through Ari. "You knew that? He was my family's employee and *I* never knew his name."

He shrugged. "You didn't live here."

She shook her head. "No. But my heart stayed here...and I think I've been looking for it ever since."

A little surprised at her own admission, she turned. A smile played at Taylor's lips and his green eyes fixed on her. She swore they almost sparkled. The effect was devastating. She could have stood all day just looking at him. But he shifted, clearly uncomfortably beneath her enraptured gaze.

"The tree trimming evening wasn't complete without a trip to the gift shop."

Apparently he wanted to put the conversation back on safe ground. Was it because he felt that same rush of pleasure she'd felt? Or because she'd disturbed him with her personal, intimate thoughts? Whatever the reason, she'd honor his wishes and turn back the page.

"We always had the most spectacular things in the gift shop. My aunt and uncle traveled and she brought back wonderful treasures. I remember a snow globe with a dark winter night inside and stars on the top. Snow floated over Father Christmas walking in the forest. The globe was beautifully detailed but the most perfect part were the animals surrounding him. It reminded me of the clock."

"Ahhh, the cuckoo clock." Taylor tilted his head back and closed his eyes. "I'd stand in front of it waiting for the elves to come out of the workshop at the half-hour, hammering on their miniature toys as they marched to the other side and back into the workshop."

"But the best part was the chiming on the hour when Father Christmas came out in his long white gown with gold trim and that golden bag of toys slung over his shoulder. I swear his eyes twinkled."

"That clock is a beautiful piece of art. Once the renovations were well underway, I did repairs on it. Pieces of the wooden scrollwork had broken off. I glued them back on and gave the whole thing a new coat of oil. That's why it's covered. We won't unveil it until the construction dust disappears."

Ari shook her head, amazed at how eyes that sparkled moments ago, grew even brighter when he talked about working with the clock. Obviously, he loved his work. She wondered if the heart of an artist beat in his "working man" body. But she didn't dare ask. She'd made him uncomfortable enough. Still, she couldn't resist a little teasing.

"Why, Taylor Knox, I think you have more Christmas Inn fever than I do. You love this place."

He chuckled. "These days, Christmas Inn is just a job. But there was definitely something special about the place back in the day."

"Love, Taylor. That special thing was love. Peace and

Christmas joy. Couples ready to take on life together. Happy families sharing summer fun and making memories. Love filled every corner of this place. I think that's why my ancestors chose the Christmas theme, to remind everyone that love conquers all, year round. It has no time limit." She bowed her head. "My family was given the responsibility of maintaining that legacy. We...I lost it. But I'm going to get it back. I have to. It's who we are and what's most important."

He studied her. A play of emotions moved across his features. Wonder or maybe surprise? Did he still think of her as a pampered diva? She hoped not, but she understood if he doubted her sincerity. When a slight frown creased the space between his brows, her heart sank a little.

"I'll take a look at your chimes, but I can't guarantee it'll bring back the Christmas cheer."

Ari shook her head and resolve flooded through. "Nope. Only prayer can do that. But if you'll make the mechanics function, I'll do the talking to God."

He gave her another smile that was quickly squelched with a frown. "Don't get your hopes up. Those bells are pretty old."

With a curt nod, he turned and walked through the door leading to the tower steps.

"Be careful. Like you said those steps are old." He didn't respond to her warning. Just waved. As the door closed behind him, she pulled out her phone and began to type out the supplies she would need. Window cleaner. Carpet shampoo. A good wood polish. She'd have to ask Bertie about that or better yet, Taylor. He'd know the best to use. And paint. She couldn't forget paint. That would probably be her most expensive item on the list. She didn't want to spend a lot because she was saving the rest of her money for the bell repairs.

*Please God, don't let them be too costly.*

With her list complete, she had one last task. She dialed her brother's number. For the last five years, Ian had been on the west coast supervising their newest resort. They'd purchased an older

# 6

**THANKSGIVING CREPT UP ON ARI.**

Hope Creek's Senior Crafters had kept her busy running errands as they finished the last of the Christmas decorations. With the work she'd been doing on the chapel, time slipped away. Neither she nor Aunt Lizzie had made plans to travel for the holiday. Hope Creek's normally mild winter had taken a turn to the stormy side and Aunt Lizzie didn't need to be out and about in bad weather.

Bertie was home too. Her sister Bea was in town to visit her daughter, Lydia, the newly installed IT specialist at the inn. So the five of them joined each other for Thanksgiving dinner at Christmas Inn.

Dinner was supposed to be served at six o'clock. When it hadn't been served by 6:30, Ari hurried into the kitchen to see if she could lend a hand.

Things were a mess. The turkey was still raw. Cold potatoes and dressing waited next to burned veggies. Apparently no dessert had been planned. When Ari tried to get answers from the chef, David Lewiston, the distinct smell of alcohol drifted towards her. The man was beside himself and completely unable to make a decision.

Ari suggested that he retire to his office and rest while she and Angie, his sous chef, took over the management of the meal. He was more than happy to comply. When she checked on him later, he was crashed on the floor, passed out. Fortunately, due to the renovations, few guests were in attendance and Ari was able to smooth over their frustration while Angie salvaged dinner. The pumpkin pudding she whipped up was to die for and helped to mollify the guests' dissatisfaction.

Paulina had taken time off to visit her parents for the holiday but come Monday morning, Ari intended to have a conversation with her regarding Chef Lewiston. She hoped the problems with their employee could be resolved but she doubted it.

Ari had planned to wash the tall windows of the chapel the day after Thanksgiving, but now, staring out her aunt's living room windows, she changed her mind. Dark, billowy clouds filled the sky and a cold, whistling wind whipped the trees. It was the perfect day to spend with two of her favorite people.

Having decided to allow her sister Bea and niece Lydia some much needed mother-daughter time, Bertie had lit a fire in the huge fireplace. She now sat on the couch in front of it, flipping through a colorful craft magazine. Aunt Lizzie played a very somber Beethoven piece on her piano. As Ari turned from the window and Lizzie finished the piece, Bertie jumped up and tossed the magazine down.

"That's enough of that. Play something fun and fast."

Lizzy smiled and immediately launched into a piano version of the fifties hit *Peggy Sue.*

Bertie clapped her hands in time to the music and did a fast two-step across the floor. "Now that's more like it. Come on, Ari, let's dance."

Before Ari could answer, Bertie grabbed her hand and pulled her away from the window.

Laughing, Ari stumbled over her feet. "I don't remember how."

"It'll come back to you. When you were younger, we spent many a summer afternoon doing this while Lizzie played. Just follow me. Step, step, half step. Step, step, half step."

Bertie was a force. Ari found herself trying to match the older lady's pace and keep up. Soon they were laughing and spinning around the room. Then Lizzie launched into *Chantilly Lace.* Bertie swung Ari in a circle and stepped back. But as their fingers should have linked, Bertie pulled free and Ari stumbled back...straight into strong arms. The scent of crisp pines and snow drifted over her.

Taylor! She'd recognize that scent anywhere. They'd been bumping into each other more frequently since she'd asked his help with the decorations. A quick break in the dining room over coffee and rolls. Consultations over decorations and repairs to the bell tower. They'd met enough that she'd begun to recognize his aftershave.

She spun around to face him.

"What—what are you doing here?"

"I had some work to finish and my granny asked me to make a delivery to Miz Bertie. So here I am. Someone left the door ajar. But the real question is, are we going to let this good music go to waste?"

A warm, strong hand gripped hers. His arm went around her waist and he spun her across the floor. Ari was two-stepping and twirling with a perfect partner. Taylor had great rhythm and kept his steps small to match hers. They sailed across the floor and back again as Aunt Lizzie moved from one song right into another. Taylor spun her around and caught her. Then he crossed his arm behind her and walked beside her for a few steps before turning her back around with a spin. By the time he finished, she was stumbling over her feet, laughing and breathing so hard she had to stop.

"Uncle. I cry uncle. You win." Out of breath, she bent over.

Aunt Lizzie finished the song with a flourish and both she and Bertie began to clap.

"Where did you learn to dance like that, Taylor?" Lizzie asked.

"Well, ma'am, I am a southern gentleman." He let his Tennessee drawl spill out. "As well as the oldest brother of three sisters and the partner of choice in the practice sessions...at least until Bobby got tall enough to be a decent partner. Although, I suspect he purposely hunched down to look smaller for quite a while."

The older ladies laughed and Ari smiled with them. She loved how polite and solicitous he was. Must be his Southern manners…but more likely his own kind temperament. She also loved how smile lines creased his slightly tanned features. He had wonderful boyish looks, tamed by some rugged outdoor attributes. Skin tinted by the sun. Laugh lines. Calloused hands. Gentleman but all man.

Basically perfect.

But she knew that already. The difficult part for her was not noticing how wonderful he was.

"I'm sorry I interrupted, Ladies. I best fetch my boxes for you, Miz Bertie, and I'll get out of your hair."

"Don't be silly. You aren't in our hair. You're welcome here any time."

"Still, I'll get those boxes and get on with my work."

"I'll help you carry them up." Ari grabbed her jacket off the coat rack and hurried out the door behind him.

The wind blew cold and steady as the inn's entry doors slid wide. A few drops of chilly rain came with it.

"Looks like we're getting these boxes out of the back of my truck just in time." Taylor jumped up on the fender and handed down two wide, wreath-sized boxes. He hefted three larger ones on top of each other and jumped down. The wind threatened to sweep Ari's top box away. She grabbed it, laughing, and they both ran inside just as the rain started to fall in steady streams.

When they returned to the suite, Bertie opened the boxes and examined each of the wreaths. One was all white with red and white candy canes crossed in an "x." Red, curling ribbons filtered through the white bristles of the wreath. In another box, the long, garland for the four-poster bed lay complete with small, sparkling pieces of oranges and apples, cinnamon sticks and berries. The glistening fruit was one of Ari's favorites. But not the only one. All of the decorations were incredibly beautiful.

"If they pass your inspection, Miz Bertie, I'll get started putting them in their places. I don't want my workmen to fall behind."

A twinge of guilt swept over Ari. "Is that why you gave up

your Thanksgiving weekend, to take care of the decorations?"

He ducked his head. "Only part of the reason. I do have other duties and a timetable to keep."

Not for the first time, Ari wondered what was so important about the contract's deadline. But now wasn't the time to ask. "Do you mind if I tag along? I might be able to offer a hand and I'd feel better after causing you to give up your weekend."

"You didn't—" Taylor paused. Ari was certain he was going to tell her no but he changed his mind. "Sure. Why not?"

*Yes, indeed, why not? Don't you like me, Taylor Knox? Because I sure like you. Am I still just a nuisance to you?*

Maybe, working by his side, she'd have the opportunity to get some answers. Picking up her boxes, she skipped to catch up with his long-legged stride.

He turned to her. "By the way, my granny says thanks for the invite to the tree-trimming party."

Ari laughed. "The Knox family deserves their own private party. They've practically brought the inn back to life by themselves, from the renovations to the decorations. You all seem to have a talent gene I'm missing. I couldn't have done it without all of your help."

"If you want to fit in you need to say y'all. Not you all. And I don't know how you could be missing a talent gene. What about that painting you're doing in the chapel? I thought your aunt said you were 'all that.'"

The teasing twinkle in his eye made her heart do flip flops. Maybe he did like her after all. A pure rush of pleasure got in the way of her tongue. All she could do was smile at his teasing.

"Let's tackle that garland first. You were right. I wouldn't trust anyone else to mount it on that four-poster bed." He led the way to the suite. A box of tools and a step stool sat inside the room. Taylor stepped up on the stool and temporarily secured the garland with tape.

"What do you think? Is the swag even?"

"No, the left side is longer."

He adjusted it, then began to drill small holes in the posters to secure a wire for the garland. When he finished, Ari swept up the wood shavings and gave the posts a quick polish.

"Thanks for showing me this brand." She held up the polish. "You think it will work well for the pews in the chapel?"

"Sure. It's the best." He pulled out the white garland with the candy canes. "I presume this is going in my room."

"Are you in the North Pole suite?"

"Yep, that's me. Complete with a white bedspread and a fake polar bear rug."

Ari couldn't stop the giggle that slipped out. Taylor did that a lot...made her laugh. Just another of the many reasons she liked being around him. "I thought the rug might be a little over the top, but when I found it online for such a good price, I couldn't resist. I thought some little boy might just love it."

He lifted his tools, the stool and his boxes then gave her a wink. "Guaranteed. This little boy loved it. But...I was afraid my work boots might do some serious damage so I asked housekeeping to leave all the white stuff in the wrapper till I'm gone."

Gone. That word took all the laughter out of Ari. He led the way to his room. He'd pulled the large desk that normally sat by the wall closer to the window. Gray light spilled over the rolled plans and a stack of papers at least a half foot high.

"Forgive the mess. Final construction phases are full of inspections and paperwork."

Final. He placed the wreath above the mantel and measured each side. All the while the words "gone" and "final" tumbled through her mind. The work at the inn would be completed soon. Taylor had mentioned enough times how he was determined to finish before Christmas. She also had the sinking feeling he had something big on the agenda for his next job.

"Is this even?"

His question jolted her out of her thoughts. "No. A little lower." She chewed her lip as he moved the wreath and glanced back for her approval. She nodded and he turned back. Ari took the leap.

"Taylor, I understand you need to meet the contract on time, but I get the feeling there's another reason you're so determined to be out of here by Christmas."

Climbing off the stool, he grinned. "There is. January first, I'm retiring."

"Retiring...you're too young." Her tone sounded as shocked as she felt.

"True. I won't be retiring permanently. I'm handing the reins of the business over to Bobby. Then I'm hitting the road on a motorcycle and heading out into the wild blue."

Heading out. Leaving Hope Creek. Just when she'd found him.

"I—I see. How long will you be gone?"

"As long as it takes." The grin on his lips was bright and happy. He wanted this very badly. She wanted to want it for him. To wish him luck and to be as excited as he, but she couldn't form the words or shape her mouth into any kind of a smile. If she tried, it would probably come out as a grimace.

Instead, she feigned interest with a brisk question. "So where are you headed first?"

"I have no idea. I'm just going to see where the road takes me."

She nodded. "OK. I guess the more appropriate question is what are you looking for?"

He pondered her question and the smile faded. "I don't think I'm looking for anything. I just...I want to see what's out there." He did it again, that gesture where he lifted his neck and shifted his shoulders as if he were releasing a heavy weight.

"It's just...I've been taking care of my family since I was nineteen. I went to college just long enough to learn what I needed to get my contractor's license. Then I started running the business. I've been tied down ever since. It's time for me to be free, to find out where I fit and what I want."

*Oh, Taylor, you* are *shifting a weight off your shoulders, a weight you've carried for far too long. You deserve to not be tied down, to be free. I need to be happy for you, happy you're leaving…even if I think I'm falling in love with you.*

# 7

**TAYLOR TOOK A SIP FROM** a disposable coffee cup that had the words Christmas Inn on one side and a sparkling Christmas tree on the other. Inside was hot cocoa that didn't come out of a package. In fact, it was so creamy it melted in his mouth. It had to be the Christmas Inn recipe he remembered from his youth.

A ten-foot tree complete with strings of lights filled one corner of the lobby. Nearby, boxes and boxes of ornaments waited for little hands to hang them. A fire roared in the oversized hearth and Christmas tunes played softly in the background.

He took another sip of his hot chocolate and studied the tree imprinted on the side cup. Specialties like this were hard to find. He had no idea where it came from or how much it cost but he knew who was responsible for it.

Ari walked toward him. She'd just come from the kitchen and even though she wore a slight frown, it didn't detract from her beauty. The woman was a piece of art in motion. She'd swept her hair up into a messy but perfect bun at the back. Wispy tendrils brushed her face and her neck. Her dress was some sort of blue velvet that appeared touchable and silky at the same time. The dark blue was the color of a midnight sky, but the way it moved over her was like poetry. He needed to look away, needed not to love the way she glided toward him or the way her smile lit her brown eyes. But he couldn't stop staring. All he could do was watch as something special sparked in her eyes when she turned his way.

Him. Taylor Knox.

Yes, she was beautiful. Pampered and spoiled. That dress probably cost more than his pick-up truck. But when she looked at him like she was looking now, life blazed into full color.

"Hello."

Even her voice, so soft and sweet, seemed full of rich color, like blue rippling waves. For a moment, he couldn't readily find the power of speech.

"Hello yourself." He gestured around the inn's common room full of invited guests and townspeople. "Your party is a grand success."

She frowned slightly. "Tell me that later, after you see the cookies. We had a bit of a foul-up in the kitchen. But Paulina's got it under control."

"I wondered why I hadn't seen Paulina."

"Yes, she's on top of it. I know she and I got off to a rocky start, but she's a great manager. We're lucky to have her here."

Taylor smiled.

Ari caught the expression and smiled, too. "Yes, I've told her so, many times in recent days. I even texted my dad with a great recommendation."

He nodded. "I'm sure she'll appreciate that."

She looked around. "So does it feel like the old days?"

He lifted his cup of hot chocolate. "With some new improvements. You've done an incredible job. You're very good at this event management type stuff."

"I'm just finding that out." She gave him a bemused smile. "I'm discovering a lot of new things about myself."

She ducked her head. A wisp of hair floated near her mouth, brushing close to her lips. A cryptic expression slid over her features. Was it puzzlement? Confusion? Or just plain sadness?

"OK. No fair. No mysteries. You can't hand out a leading line like that, then clam up."

He couldn't resist. Reaching out, he tugged on that wisp of hair. His fingers brushed close to her lips...so close he felt the intake of her breath.

"What did you find out about yourself...besides the fact that you're fantastic with a two-step."

Light laughter bubbled out of her. The lilting sound rippled through his body.

Just then, Santa came out of his clock house. They both turned as he marched to the end of his perch and *O Tannenbaum* trilled across the room.

The room grew quiet while everyone watched Santa, in his white-and-gold-trimmed gown, beam down on them. When the song ended, he rolled back inside and the dark wood doors closed.

Ari smiled. "Sorry. It's seven o'clock. Time for me to go to work."

Did she really have to start the festivities or was she just using it as an excuse to avoid his question? Ariana Christmas was proving to be as unpredictable as this year's weather. She walked to the center of the room and held up her hands. "Ladies and gentlemen, boys and girls, may I have your attention?"

The room quieted but excitement ruffled through the air like the feathers of a bird on high alert.

"First, let me thank you all for joining us tonight. It's been a long time since we had a tree-trimming party at Christmas Inn, and we're so glad you could all come. Thank you."

The crowd clapped and someone whistled. Taylor suspected it was his brother Bobby, sitting nonchalantly next to Granny on the center sofa.

Ari gestured to three maids, all dressed in their finest old-style uniforms, black with white aprons. Even Jason and his fellow bellhops wore black slacks and shirts and white bow ties. Leave it to Ari to think of the little details that would make this a truly old-fashioned Christmas. The maids stood on one side of the tree, the bell boys on the other, right next to opened boxes of Christmas ornaments.

"We'll start with the youngest to the oldest. If I could have all the children ages two to six come forward and line up beside me."

With squeals of laughter, children dressed in their finest ran toward Ari. She smiled as the herd rushed forward and surrounded her. One little cutie with long blonde curls and a big red bow wrapped her arms around Ari's leg and hugged. She almost tumbled backwards before catching herself. Her delighted laughter trilled across the room, right into Taylor's heart. Bending swiftly, she scooped the little girl into her arms and started a very serious conversation. Taylor couldn't hear the words but the toddlers curls bobbed back and forth in the affirmative. Suddenly, she threw chubby arms around Ari's neck and hugged her.

Ari pressed a quick kiss to the little girl's temple and Taylor's heart stopped beating.

Something about that beautiful child in Ari's arms...the bouncing blonde curls...Ari's complete innocence and adoration. The sight touched him so much, he had to look away.

Ariana was nowhere close to innocent. Why had that thought and image popped into his mind? Maybe she was right, and he was catching too much of the Christmas Spirit...Christmas Inn style. He needed to get a grip.

"Now..." Ari carried on, completely unaware of the havoc she'd created in Taylor. "Do you all have your ornaments?"

The little decorating crew nodded almost as one. "Great. Now, see my Aunt Lizzie sitting at the piano? As soon as she starts to play, I want all of you to walk forward—slowly and carefully—and hang your decoration on the tree. OK?"

Another nod from the miniature munchkins. Lizzie launched into a rousing rendition of *O Tannenbaum* again and the children surged forward, scrambling for a place on the tree. When all their ornaments hung in slightly chaotic array on the branches, Ari called for the next age group and Lizzie played *Silver Bells*.

The decorating went on for almost an hour before Ari called the last band of teenagers to the tree. Lizzie played one more round of the Christmas tree song. The kitchen staff, dressed in traditional white coats and tall hats, came out bearing trays of cookies. Taylor recognized his favorite chocolate chip cookies from the Hope Creek Bakery.

So that was the catastrophe in the kitchen. Something more had happened with Chef David Lewiston. Taylor suspected the cookie affair would be the last straw and Lewiston would be on his way to new employment. But somehow Ari and Paulina had worked together and solved the problem. He had to admire Ari's efforts to overcome Paulina's resentment. In fact, he was finding a lot to admire about Ari...and that was not a good sign.

The last of the decorations now adorned the tree, and Ari gave a signal. Someone dimmed the common room's lights and the Christmas tree flared to life. White lights twinkled and caught the colors of the ornaments, creating rainbows of flashing lights that danced around the room. One of those rainbows flashed across Ari's face as she stood close by. A smile played across her lips and she looked up with such contentment, Taylor knew Ariana Christmas had finally found her place.

It was a good thing. It made him happy to see her happy. Maybe too much of a good thing. He needed to be not so pleased because no matter how much he enjoyed watching Ari, no matter how glad he was that she'd found her place here in Hope Creek, he was not staying. His dream was out there, waiting for him to find it. He'd put this trip off for too long. He had to find his place, God's purpose for him. As dedicated as he was and always had been about helping his family, those efforts never provided the contentment he craved. Not here anyway. But it was out there some place—he knew it. He needed to get out there and find it.

He turned his back and drank down the last of his hot chocolate. Someone walked up behind him and even before he turned around, he knew it was Ari. How? Did he smell her sweet perfume? Had he recognized her step or just sensed her presence? That thought scared him.

"Well, that went better than I expected."

Taylor nodded. "You're obviously good with kids"

She laughed and the sound eased his irritated nerves. "Yes, who knew? I've never been around children much. I spent most of my life in hotels where spoiled little children rampaged through the halls tearing up things. That's my experience with children. Not very good, I'm afraid."

She paused and gave a little shake of her head. "But I shouldn't be so critical. I was one of them."

A memory filtered through Taylor's mind, one that could help him get back on stable ground. "I seem to remember an article about a very expensive New York hotel room trashed by two young men fighting over one lovely young debutante."

The pretty glow on her features darkened slightly. Guilt swept over Taylor. He hated being the dark cloud in a bright night but it needed to be done, for both their sakes. Ari didn't need to get involved with a man with one foot out the door.

"They weren't fighting over me. It was a party and they'd been drinking. I wasn't even a part of it, but my name was the most recognizable so they put it in the report."

"Are you saying you didn't earn your reputation?"

Genuine hurt flickered across her features. She looked across the room. Taylor stomped on the rush of guilt that flooded through him.

"No. I'm not saying that. I've done things I'm not proud of. That's why I'm so happy to be here and now—" She gestured around the room. "Now I know this is what's important. I'm glad to be here."

He couldn't deny that truth. "You're right. It's good to be on the right track. The community will benefit from it. I wish you the best of luck."

He tossed his cup into the trash, preparing to leave when his brother Bobby joined them.

"Hi, Ari."

"Hey, Bobby."

"Great party. Granny wanted me to thank you again."

"Oh? Is she leaving?"

"Yeah, she's getting tired." He turned to Taylor. "She rode here with Missy and our sister promised to stay until after the party to, uh…" He cleared his throat. "Re-arrange the heavy bottom half of the tree a little more artfully. I rode my motorcycle so Granny was wondering if you'd mind driving her home."

Ari let her hand rest on Bobby's forearm. Taylor's insides

He deserved the sting of her scolding. "Yes, ma'am. You may be right. But there's no future for us."

"Why not? Because of that grand adventure you're planning? You need to stop being foolish, Taylor, and start listening to your own heart."

"I *am* listening, Granny. My heart's been searching for something for a long time. It's time I found it."

"That's not your heart leading you away. That's the Knox wanderlust. We've all got it. That's what drove our family west all those years ago."

He glanced her way for a moment before directing his gaze back to the road. "Yes, and we helped settle this land. Are you saying that wanderlust is a bad thing?"

Her tone softened. "No, not bad. But it's easy to confuse wanderlust with what your heart really needs. Make sure you don't do that."

# 8

"HI, DAD."

"Ari, I'm so glad we finally reached you. Mom and I were worried. I was able to reach Paulina once the storm started but not you."

The rain that started the night of the tree-trimming party had continued off and on for weeks, finally leading to a full-blown snowstorm complete with road closures and power outages. Cell phone service had even been disrupted, but a momentary clearing in the storm allowed reception.

"My phone's not the best." Ari was quick to reassure her dad. "So let's talk fast. They say this is just the calm before the next wave. Another snowstorm is scheduled to hit soon and it's supposed to be worse than the last one. They're already talking about stopping flights and more road closures. I'm glad you called right now. It may be your last chance for a while. Paulina and her staff have been wonderful. They had the inn's generators going so we had heat and lights even though public electricity flickered a couple of times. She's taken care of all the guest concern and situation. Paulina's really a great employee, Dad. Like I told you a while ago, she deserves a commendation."

"Funny. She said the same thing about you."

"Really?"

"Yes, she said you've kept the guests busy with activities…board games, group charades. And she told me the tree-trimming party was a grand success. She says you should have *carte blanche* to plan activities not only at Christmas Inn, but at our other resorts as well. Your mother and I are very proud of you, Ari. We knew you could do it."

She laughed. "I wish you had clued me in. I had no idea."

"I didn't know event planning would be your strength. I just knew you had a good purpose ahead of you."

Ari's thoughts automatically shot to a handsome, caramel-haired man with color-changing eyes. "Yes, I think I've found my purpose."

*And my heart's content. Too bad he's leaving first chance he gets.*

"It sounds like we have a lot to discuss when your mother and I arrive. We can't wait to see you."

"Me too. Let's just hope this storm doesn't prevent you from coming for Christmas."

Her father's chuckle rumbled over the phone. "Not likely. I grew up in Hope Creek, remember? We might get a nasty storm like this once every five or ten years, but when the snow stops falling, it starts to melt. Just stay warm until then."

"Thanks, Dad. I plan on it."

Ari clicked off and stared out her bedroom window. The snow slanted across her view, completely blocking any sight of the grounds. This storm might have caused problems for Paulina and some of the guests but for Ari, it was a Godsend. The Lord had answered her prayers. Being snowed in gave her more time with Taylor.

For all intents and purposes, the remodeling of the inn was complete. All that remained was gathering the stamps of approval from a few inspectors on some minor work. Taylor and his crew had completed their contract not only on time, but ahead of schedule. Still…he had not packed his bags and left. To date, he showed no signs of leaving and once the storm hit, he'd jumped into all the activities with abandon.

He and Ari had shared several games of checkers and a heated contest of Scrabble. Ari was ahead seven to his six games and she intended to keep her lead. Taylor seemed just as determined to beat her and applied his efforts every time they were together…which was a lot.

Ari took that as a good sign. Taylor's reluctance to leave the inn gave her hope. The opportunities to spend time together also confirmed that Taylor enjoyed her company as much as she enjoyed his. Even though he never said it out loud, she knew it was true.

He'd been the first to issue the game challenge and while they played, they talked. He shared stories of growing up in a large family as the oldest sibling. He described how he'd taken over the business so his father could concentrate on his cancer treatments. Taylor loved the work, building was a joy, but someday he wanted to focus on wood crafting. Creating perfect designs, and one-of-a-kind furniture for Knox Construction. That was his dream...and one day he wanted to build his own home.

In turn, Ari told him how different her life had been, growing up in penthouses and hotel suites. Mainly those stays were in California and New York. But her family'd also spent several years in London where she attended a school for the children of American diplomats. Even though she didn't like talking about her travels—she wanted no reminders of Taylor's impending trip—he enjoyed those stories the most. And she loved to look at him while she shared them. Those fine little lines would appear at the corners of his eyes. His gaze would flash with pleasure and it was always fixed on hers.

Perhaps that's what she liked most, the way he looked at her. Honest, open, so up front and completely without artifice. Her life for the last few years had been full of games, everyone putting up a false front to hide what was beneath. Ari didn't have to do that with Taylor. For the first time in a long time, she could be herself and surprisingly, she liked who she was.

Even if Taylor bought a motorcycle and rode out of her life, she would be forever thankful to him for allowing her to be the real her. It was a lovely gift and he needed to know how much it meant to her.

Grabbing her heavy parka with the fake fur-lined hood, she hurried downstairs. Voices drifted up from the lobby, along with the laughter of Chrissy Sheridan, the six-year-old daughter of one of the guests. She was a delight and had added tremendously to all of Ari's efforts to keep the guests entertained. Other guests were scattered around the room, playing board games or chatting. Taylor lounged near the blazing fireplace, reading a paper. He glanced up, almost as if he'd been looking for Ari, and smiled before he rose and came toward her.

"Good morning."

She gestured toward the snow swirling outside the windows that overlooked the deck. "Well, some people might not call this a good morning."

"I know. I just saw some poor traveler check in. He said the roads were simply too bad to negotiate."

"Oh, that's too bad. I'm glad we had room for him. What about you? Don't you have something you need to do?"

"Nope. I'm happy to stay off the roads."

"Not even Christmas shopping? With such a big family? I can't believe you don't have some last-minute presents to buy."

"We draw names, and since I'm only one, I buy for only one…and that gift was purchased a long time ago. I drew Bobby's name this year so I bought him an upgraded helmet and travel backpack for his motorcycle. Now that the contract is completed—well mostly, completed—I'm enjoying a much needed mini vacation."

"Oh." A vacation. So he hadn't stayed because of her. Ari tried not to let her disappointment show. To keep her face averted, she hooked her coat over the back of a chair. "Sounds like you've got everything in hand."

"Everything but our Scrabble challenge. You're one up on me and that can't happen. Are you ready for another go at it?"

Ari smiled, she couldn't help herself. His enthusiasm broke through a few layers of disappointment. "Sure. If you think you're ready to lose again."

Taylor's grin completely blew away any lingering bad feelings. That happy face lit up her world.

"Not this time. I have a plan." He winked and Ari laughed. She just couldn't stop enjoying everything about him.

"How about you fetch the game box and I'll get you a cup of hot chocolate. Extra whipped crème, right?"

*He knows how I like my hot chocolate. How can he not know how I feel? Am I still hiding my true feelings? Aren't they written all over my face?*

She watched him walk away. When he glanced back, she turned quickly and moved toward the shelf where the games were stored.

*Don't ruin the time left to you, Ari. Just enjoy the moment.*

The pep talk helped. By the time they settled in across from each other, Ari was ready to give Taylor a challenge. They played hard and fast for the next hour, laughing and teasing. When Taylor finally gained the upper hand and won, Ari clapped for him.

"Ready for another?" He was already gathering Scrabble tiles.

She shook her head. "How about we leave it at a tie? Even Steven."

He nodded slowly. "I like that idea."

*Now, Ari. Now is the time to tell him.* As he pushed the box to the side of the table, she laid her hand over his. Strong, calloused, warm...but tense. A wrinkle appeared between his eyebrows. The beginning of a frown. He stretched his neck slightly and shifted his shoulders.

Ari chuckled. "You don't need to do that."

"What?"

"Move your shoulders like you're preparing to lift a heavy weight."

"I did that?"

"You always do it when you're feeling a little stressed."

He sat back in his chair and his hand slid free from hers. A slightly stunned expression replaced the frown.

*Yes, we both know each other better than you thought.*

She slid her own hand back and clasped it in her lap. "I just want to thank you, Taylor. You've given me a precious gift and I don't think you even realize it."

The frown was back. "What kind of gift?"

She smiled. "Myself."

"I don't understand."

"I know what you and Paulina thought of me when I first came here." He started to protest but she raised a hand. "Don't worry. I don't blame you. I'm surprised you didn't both throw me out of that meeting and dust off your hands. I might have. At least the old me would have."

She swallowed. "You never judged me or made me feel bad. You just let me...find myself."

"I didn't do anything special."

"I know. You were just yourself. But that's the point. You were kind and forgiving and I think that gave me the courage to be kind to myself. I felt free to try new things, to step out and do what I felt was right. If you hadn't been so accepting and encouraging, I might not have discovered how much I love helping others and bringing folks together."

"You're giving me too much credit. You're the one who did all the work."

"Maybe that's true. But I wouldn't have dared to try if you hadn't been so accepting. So, you helped me find my future and I thank you for that."

He shook his head. "But I didn't fix your bells. I know how much that meant to you. I tried. I did everything possible. The wiring has been replaced. The new timer I ordered is perfectly functional. There's just no mechanical reason those bells still won't work."

"Maybe the reason hasn't anything to do mechanics. Maybe it was always about love. We forgot that. But I'm going to spend the next few months bringing love back into this old place. I'll talk to my father about more renovations to the chapel and I'm going to run some specials and ads. I'm bringing weddings back to the inn. Maybe then the bells will return."

He gave a little shake of his head. "You have a lot more faith than I do. We live in a jaded age. Weddings don't necessarily mean love these days. People get married for a lot of different reasons and some of them have nothing to do with love."

Ari agreed. "And a lot of people fall in love but don't get married."

She dared not meet Taylor's gaze and the quiet moment turned into two…three long minutes.

When he didn't speak and the silence became awkward, she ran her tongue over dried lips and pasted a bright smile. "Booking weddings is the only way I know how to start. So weddings it is."

"I'm sorry to interrupt." Paulina's quiet voice was actually a welcome intrusion. "Chef David didn't show up for work today. He had planned to finish out the week but his family staged an intervention yesterday. He agreed to go to rehab and they went to visit the facility in the hills. Now they're stranded. I told them not to worry. Angie is doing a good job of covering, but she's way behind. Lunch will be late and I don't even know what we'll do about dinner."

Ari grasped her hand. "Don't worry. We'll figure it out."

"Thanks. I'm getting a little frazzled."

"Go, calm down. Tell Angie to take the time she needs. We'll make it work."

Ari looked around. Outside, the pelting snow had eased to gentle flakes. She hurried to the window with Taylor trailing behind. The wind had stopped almost completely and the sun poked through a hole in the dark clouds. An inviting blanket of sparkling snow covered the grounds.

"I've got an idea."

Taylor winked. "I figured. Go for it."

Turning to face the crowd, she held up her hands. "Hey everyone, how about a little time outside before the next wave hits? Let's have a snowman contest. Aunt Lizzie and Bertie will be the judges."

Enthusiastic applause broke out and Ari divided them into teams. "All right. We'll meet on the grounds beyond the deck in fifteen minutes. Everyone go to your rooms and gather your supplies."

She faced Taylor. "How about you?"

"Another competition? You know it. I'll grab my coat."

He hurried toward the elevator. Ari punched in her aunt's phone number. Lizzie and Bertie agreed to bundle up and meet them outside to choose the best snowman.

Ari hurried out. While she waited, she drew lines in the snow, boundaries for the territories. Then she waited for others to join her.

When the noisy, excited group stood outside, she was thankful for her idea. The pent-up crowd needed this physical release. Taking a deep breath, she laid out the rules. "No taking snow from anywhere except in your section. No stealing of ideas and you have thirty minutes to finish. On your marks. Get set. Go."

She caught Taylor off guard. "Hey, no fair."

Ignoring him, she packed a ball and began to roll. Her partners, Karynn and Savannah—sisters, celebrating a birthday at the inn—jumped in. They were as energetic and competitive as Ari.

The girls finished the bottom section of their snowman, a rather lopsided base for the top two balls but there was no time to redo it. They started on the second ball and since they were running out of snow, it took all three of them to roll it to the farthest edge of their section. Unfortunately, when they placed it on top, it slid off the lopsided bottom. They squealed as it slipped to the ground.

Ari glanced over. Taylor's team had already completed the body of their snowman and was adding black-rock buttons to the front.

"We're falling behind. You two gather arms and legs and I'll round this guy out."

Her partners dashed off in search of rocks. Ari gathered handfuls of snow and patted them into the lopsided spots of their snowman. Karynn and Savannah returned with sticks and rocks just as Lizzie shouted. "Time's up."

With a groan and a laugh, Ari stepped back from their creation, leveled her gaze on her honorary aunt. "That's why we're going to stop being so hard on him. Besides, you don't want me stuck with someone who doesn't want me as much as I want him, right?"

"Of course not."

Lizzie's soft voice echoed across the room. "Dee Knox, Taylor's mother, delivered the chapel decorations. She says the day after the storm, Taylor bought his bike. He's been riding all over the county practicing for the road."

Bertie lifted the empty box. "She also said he's not himself. It's like a dark cloud has settled over him. She says Taylor has always been easy going, happy and positive, even when he had to take on the family business. It was a lot of responsibility and he took it on without blinking an eye."

An image of Taylor stretching his neck and shifting his shoulder's to lift the heavy burden flashed through Ari's mind.

Bertie shook her head. "Dee says he's quiet and moody now. Not like himself at all."

"See? My impulsiveness caused all kinds of trouble again. Taylor doesn't deserve everyone talking about him and speculating. He needs to do what he feels is right and we need to let him. So...no more talk. Let's move on and enjoy the wonderful gift of us all being together again." She met their gazes. "I love you both. And I love that you love me so much, but let's put all this aside."

Her silver-haired aunt crossed the room and threw her slender arms around Ari. "Have I told you lately how proud I am of you?"

Ari shook her head. "Impulsive gestures and all?"

Lizzie's eyes twinkled. "Especially the impulsive gestures. I think they're rather amazing."

Laughter spilled out of Ari. "I'm sure Taylor has a different opinion."

One of her aunt's silver brows rose. "I thought we were done discussing him."

Ari laughed again. "Right. We are."

"I can't wait to hear what Ian has in store for us this evening. I'm sure it's going to be wonderful."

"I can tell you he's nervous. I heard him practicing earlier this afternoon and he told me he was shaking. But he's always had a gift. Whatever he shares will be a blessing."

Bertie returned from carrying the empty box to the vestibule. "That's right. It's going to be a very special night—and I hear voices outside the doors. I think it's time to let our guests inside."

"Good idea. Why don't you open them, Bertie. I'll light the candles."

Happy voices rose as people filled the chapel. Ian came to the podium as Ari lit the two free-standing candelabras on each side of the altar. He spread his papers out and cleared his throat in what Ari recognized as a nervous manner. She patted his arm for reassurance, then blew out her match and headed to her family's pew at the front.

Bobby Knox and his sister, Missy, helped Granny Knox to a seat. Ari smiled, even as her gaze automatically darted through the Knox crowd for Taylor. Sure enough, he was seated next to another young lady, chatting. He didn't even look Ari's way. But she didn't let that bother her. She couldn't be disappointed. She was simply happy that he didn't allow their encounter to keep him away from the service.

Ian signaled Aunt Lizzie, who took her seat behind the upright piano. She led them through several Christmas songs, and then a few worship songs before returning to the family pew. Ian cleared his throat again.

"I want to thank you all for joining my family tonight. I can't tell you how happy we are to be together here at Christmas Inn. It means a lot for all of us. It's been a long time since I've been in front of crowd like this. For some reason, I got the notion that I had to choose between two paths." He smiled and shook his head. "I don't know where I got that idea. Our Lord's powers are infinite, and if He gave me a heart for two things or fifty, He'll find a way to make it work. My job is just to follow orders. So here I am. I'm rusty so I'll keep it simple, but be warned...I'll be back."

The crowd laughed, and Ari could see Ian relaxing.

"For now, I want to share a family tradition. Every Christmas Eve, one of our family reads a beautiful passage, which reminds us of the true meaning of the season. So if you will, please turn to Luke 2:8-20."

Ian read in a clear, beautiful voice, the wondrous passage of the angel announcing the birth of the Christ child to the shepherds. The passage never failed to bring tears to Ari's eyes and it was even more special this Christmas, with her family gathered around her at Christmas Inn.

When Ian finished, he led them in another prayer and invited them all to share some refreshments in the grand room of the inn before returning home to their own festivities with their families.

Ari's mother hugged her. "That was beautiful, simply beautiful. Thank you, sweetheart."

"Thank Ian, if you can get to him." A crowd had gathered around her brother, thanking and encouraging him.

Her mother smiled. "I'll wait my turn."

Others stopped to welcome Ari back and thank her. By the time the crowd had thinned and Ari turned to look, the Knox family had gone.

What did she expect? For Taylor to hug her and thank her for making him the center of Hope Creek's gossip? She laughed at her own foolishness and turned back to her family who were bundling into warm coats and seemed ready to head to the inn. She grasped Bertie's arm and wrapped her arm around Aunt Lizzie's waist. "Thanks for all your help. I can finish up here. Why don't you two join the party? I'll be there as soon as I make sure all these candle are out."

"All right. Just don't take too long. I have a feeling we didn't prepare enough refreshments. We didn't expect quite so many people."

Ari smiled at her aunt's pleasant reminder. "Yes, it was good.

Do me a favor, please, and switch off the lights on your way out."

She blew out the candles along each side of the chapel, one by one, until just the candelabras at the altar remained. They flickered, casting a golden glow over the altar. She ran her finger along the edge of the white wood, thanking God for the ancestors who had built this beautiful place of worship. The smell of the candles, the lingering essence of pine and the sweet silence of the sanctuary swept over her. She closed her eyes in silent praise.

Her eyes flew open at a noise from the back of the chapel. Taylor emerged from the shadows and walked down the center aisle with steady purpose. Moonlight spilled over him through the tall sanctuary windows, casting a silvery glow over his hair.

Dressed in a blue suit and tie, he looked so handsome, so confident as he walked toward her...and the altar. The sight of him lit an impossible fire inside her. An impossible dream. More than likely, Taylor and she would never have an altar aisle between them. But right now, with the silver light kissing his face, he was hers. Joy filled her.

He stopped just below the steps and looked up. She was staring. She knew it...knew she needed to stop, but it took all of her effort to look away. Trying to gather her thoughts, she said the first thing that came to her mind.

"I'm so glad you waited. I wanted to apologize. I'm so sorry I caused so much trouble by kissing you. I acted on impulse and, as usual, didn't think about the results of my actions."

He shook his head. "In all the time I've known you, you've never *not* had something to say."

She ducked her head. "I know I talk too much. I just can't stand the silence. I rush in to cover the awkwardness."

He smiled. "You've done a lot of things on a whim—lots of things you regret."

She nodded.

He lifted her chin until her gaze met his. "But this shouldn't be one of them, Ari. You don't control the bells. They don't answer to you or even to natural law. Apparently, they answer to a Higher Power."

The sincerity, the sweetness of his words sent a thrill through her. She hoped it wasn't a false thrill. Ari slowly shook her head. "Please don't say something you'll regret later, Taylor."

"I already did that. I'm sorry I said all those things about love."

"No, you were right. Just because we connected and have a few things in common…"

"We have everything in common, Ari. Love of family." He gestured around them. "This old place and all it means. Goals for our futures and the desire to follow the path created for us by the Lord. Everything." He nodded, sealing the word with conviction.

"I thought what I needed was out there someplace…waiting for me. All the while, everything I needed was right here."

Ari's lips parted but no words came out.

"Well, that's a first. You're at a loss for words."

She shook her head. "I'm not at a loss. I…I just don't… I left my heart here, at Christmas Inn. I had the opportunity to find out for myself where I belonged and what I needed to do. I don't want to be the cause of you giving up that opportunity. Don't give up your dream for me, Taylor."

He clasped her hands. "Who said I'd be giving up anything? Correct me if I'm wrong, but don't event planners need to travel to their events?"

He pulled her closer. "Ari, every time I got on my bike and took off for a ride, all I could think about was how I needed you to be there with me. I wanted to know what you'd say about the quaint sixties motor hotel I passed, or how you would have loved the mountain waterfall."

He wrapped her arms around his waist and tucked her in just right. "I wanted to know how this would feel. But most of all I wanted to try another kiss. The last one sort of got messed up." He leaned down, his lips inches from hers.

"Ariana Christmas, I don't want to go anywhere without you. *You* are what I've been waiting for all my life. Will you kiss me again?"

For the first time in Ari's memory, the words wouldn't come. So she simply wrapped her arms around his neck and did as he asked.

This time when the bells tolled, Taylor pulled away just long enough to give Ari a special, knowing smile. Then he kissed her again...and the bells rang on.

# ~ About Tanya ~

**TANYA STOWE** is an author of Christian Fiction with an unexpected edge. She fills her stories with the unusual…gifts of the spirit and miracles, mysteries and exotic travel, even an angel or two. No matter where Tanya takes you…on a journey to the Old West or to contemporary adventures in foreign lands…be prepared for the extraordinary.

**tanyastowe.com**
**facebook.com/TanyaStoweReadersPage/**

# ~ More Titles by Tanya Stowe ~

**Coming Soon**
*Fatal Memories*

**Tender Series**
*Tender Touch*
*Tender Trust*

**Heart's Haven Collections**
*Leap of Faith*
*Haunted Hearts*
*Wounded Grace*
*That Doggone Baby*
*A Cowboy Christmas_* (Co-authored with Delia Latham)

**Christmas Stories**
*White Christmas*
*The Evergreen Wreath*
*Lea's* Gift (Co-authored with Delia Latham)

**Suspense**
*Never-Ending Night*
*Sedona Sunset*
*Santa Fe Sunrise*
*Mojave Rescue*

## Love at Christmas Inn Collection 1
*Christmas Bells are Ringing (Tanya Stowe)*
*Bells at Midnight (Marianne Evans)*
*With Bells On (Mary Manners)*
*Bells on Her Toes (Delia Latham)*

# Love at Christmas Inn

## Bells at Midnight

# MARIANNE EVANS

# Bells at Midnight

## Marianne Evans

*There is a time for everything, and a season*
*for every activity under the heavens.*
*~Ecclesiastes 3:1 (NIV)~*

# 1

**WOMEN WITH DIMPLES HAD ALWAYS** been Graham
Forrester's weakness.

He pushed through the expansive, double-door entrance of
Christmas Inn and stomped blackened slush from the surface of
his boots, littering a wide plastic mat that featured a colorful
Christmas tree and the words, 'It's the Most Wonderful Time of
the Year.'

He gave an involuntary snort. "Seriously? No. Way."

Sure, his muttered condemnations stemmed from a jaded
attitude more than anything else. After all, who wouldn't be jaded
after finding themselves stranded at the side of the road due to a
broken down car, in the back-of-beyond, in who-knows-where
Tennessee, at t-minus three weeks to Christmas? For now, all
Graham wanted to do was land in bed, hunker in for the night, and
start fresh in the morning by making a hasty exit.

And this Christmas Inn place the tow truck guy had
recommended and driven him to? Honestly? The place was so full
of Christmas cheer it made his teeth ache. Wonderful, indeed. But,
all that noise aside, the lovely woman who occupied an office spot
behind the reception area provided him with a welcome and
warming distraction.

After all, there was just something about dimples…

"Excuse me?" Graham addressed the woman while he dropped

his computer bag and oversized duffle on the floor at his feet. Dimples tossed him an inquiring look, and a smile. On the inside, he froze, and held, because, on top of those dimples, oh—what a smile.

"Hi. Can I help you?"

He regrouped on the fly. "Yes, please. I don't have a reservation, but I need a room for the night if there's one available."

"Sure. Let's get you settled in." She wheeled back in her chair and spun. "Paulina!"

Graham focused on her legs as she maneuvered her seat. So, Dimples was petite. Petite, but sweet looking. Innocent and wispy. Looking at her, Graham pictured all things airy, pixyish. Warm moved rapidly toward *very* warm. For the first time in hours, he even cracked a smile and continued to enjoy the view as his hotel-helper returned to work.

"Good evening, sir, I'm Paulina Kovacs, manager of Christmas Inn. How can I help you?"

Ambushed from his right by the arrival of a woman, dressed in full-on business attire—at way past business hours, Lord bless her—with dark hair twisted into a roll at her neck. Paulina pushed the frames of her black-rimmed glasses to a higher perch on her nose and offered a welcoming smile.

"My car broke down about a mile outside town and the gentleman who gave me a tow told me you might have a room available."

"Ah, yes. That'd be Tom Sanders. He's a good man, and a top rate mechanic. You'll be up and running in no time. Welcome to the inn, and don't you worry about a thing. We'll set matters right in the morning. I have a wonderful room available on the second floor that overlooks the courtyard. Unlike some resort-style B&Bs, it even has a private bath."

Graham stifled a shudder. A private bath. She spoke the words as though they were an amenity rather than a necessity. He covered fast with a trademark, camera-ready smile. He'd had a lot of practice at that lately—faking his way through things to avoid the growing mess of his life. Life worked better when you could move right along and dodge the bullets—sort of like a high-stakes paintball tournament...

"I appreciate your hospitality. The room sounds great."

"Follow me." Paulina gestured toward a curving stairwell while Graham retrieved his bags. "Typically, this is our honeymoon suite, but I doubt any honeymooners will be straggling across the doorstep in this weather."

"Highly unlikely," he muttered, looking around as she led the way. "Ah...don't you need my credit card information, or..."

"Oh, no problem. It's late, and I'm sure you're tired. We can deal with that in the morning. Just check in with me then. Lydia, I'll be right back. Thanks for manning the fort."

"No problem."

So, Dimples had a name. Lydia. He rolled it around in his head a few times, and his smile went from manufactured to real. Ascending the stairs, he kept an eye on her, watching as she clicked away at her keyboard, leaning forward to check her monitor.

"Lydia Cutler. My Internet specialist. As you'll see, we've got some dust settling as we renovate the Inn. Lydia there is dragging me, kicking and screaming, into the age of technology. Lovely, isn't she?"

Busted. "Oh...yeah. Sure." Overtired to begin with, Graham nearly took a tumble when Paulina's wily observation called him out and jarred him to proper focus. "She's lovely, of course."

Paulina chuckled as she paused in front of the first door they came to, marked by a brass number four. "Here we are. Christmas Inn has been family owned for generations. It's kind of a fixture here in Hope Creek."

Hope Creek. Of course that was the name of the town where he had landed. Graham ached to give a derisive snicker, or at least roll his eyes. Polite behavior had him nodding in gracious understanding. After all, it wasn't the manager's fault he was so burned out and cynical these days. Nope. The fault for that rested entirely on his shoulders, and his New Year's resolution was to perform an about face.

But how? The answer to that question continued to give him trouble.

"...from early 1900, and the courtyard is a gem. Rimmed by evergreens and all lit up with Christmas lights. Straight ahead is Jingle Bell Creek, and to your left is North Pole Bridge."

He had drifted while Paulina played tour guide. Had she seriously just said Jingle Bell Creek and North Pole Bridge? Shaking it off, determined to nip his rude behavior, Graham joined her at the big bay window where she had drawn back a sheer to reveal the view below. Not much could be seen in the night except for a flood-lit courtyard where metal benches circled a small open area now covered by a layer of snow. The white stuff continued to build and drift as the wind picked up and whistled against the glass pane. Trees and bushes formed a perimeter. Walkways had been recently shoveled, it seemed, but rapidly filled with a fresh layer of white. The trees, though thoroughly coated, still glowed with diffused multi-colored light.

Graham looked over his shoulder, returning his attention to the interior of the room, which was something akin to crashing the theatrical set of A Christmas Carol. Damask wallpaper featured shades of red, green and gold. Thick fringed tassels held back elaborate swags of heavy brocade. Swoops of faux evergreen decorated the top of a mahogany four-poster and a subtle undercurrent of apple, pine and cinnamon piqued his senses. Then there were the elaborate, seemingly hand-painted ornaments that danced on varying length ribbons from the inner sill of the window, sparkling and spinning as the heat vents came to life. Warm air did battle against the cold and snow that danced thick from an ink-black sky. Renderings of St. Nicholas were positioned throughout, upon end tables, tucked into a far corner...

"If there's anything you need, just dial zero on the phone there by your bed." Christmas Inn's warm but studious manager crossed the room and opened the door. "I'll leave you to get a good night's sleep."

"Thank you, Paulina. Your kindness is just what I needed." And the truth was, he meant it.

"Happy to oblige. G'night."

Once the door closed and he was alone at last, Graham forced his muscles to ease. Working to unwind mentally, he wandered his suite. The quiet that settled helped. In spite of the travel-crushing snow storm, he was grudgingly charmed by the over-the-top décor. If only he wasn't so put off by the world at large right now. Dissatisfaction, on a number of levels, pushed at him from all sides, negating any kind of exit, or respite.

He needed a new life. He needed a change. He needed to shift course and rediscover himself, his passion. If he didn't, he was going to end up wasting the life he'd been given. Sighing, he connected and charged his cell phone then did the same for his laptop, opting to log on to his e-mail account and check recent traffic. Anything to keep from dwelling. The most recent offering came from his big sister, Becca. He'd see her in a few days for the annual Forrester family Christmas celebration. He smiled at the thought, until he took in the subject line of her e-mail. *Any Publicity is Good Publicity. Right?*

Graham frowned. What? He clicked, and began to read.

*Hey, G,* –Becca had always referred to him as 'G'—*you might want to check out social media feeds at your station and Knoxville Express magazine. The broadcast of that cook-off segment you judged yesterday seems to have made a few virtual waves. BTW? That pompous, arrogant jerk you ousted on yesterday's segment totally deserved it. Not even a question. Don't let what he said afterward bug you. K? Love you and see you soon! Becca*

Frown deepening, Graham chased the links Becca had included. Via Twitter, he was led straight to YouTube and a video of his weekly visit to Knoxville's KRTN-TV where he worked the entertainment beat. For years now he'd provided insights and information about local events around Knoxville as well as restaurant visits and reviews.

His monitor came alive with the image of a mocked-up kitchen stationed on the ground floor of a massive, three-story mall. In the background, holiday shoppers bustled. In honor of the upcoming holidays, this segment featured a cook-off between three local chefs. The episode had been shot a few days ago, and Graham had acted as one of the judges along with a local radio personality and the star running back of the Tennessee Titans.

Graham tuned out the banter and back-and-forth discussion of the final food evaluations that would lead to the crowning of an overall champion. Instead, when the time came, he hyper-focused on the dismissal of the first of three combatants—a young and self-aggrandizing chef named Frederic Mendell.

Lips curled into a sneer, Frederic addressed the judging panel after being eliminated from the competition. "Of course, I thank you for the opportunity. I don't agree with the verdict, but I understand the laws of subjectivity." His slicing gaze made it clear he falsified humility in favor of being affronted. "I've orchestrated nine-course meals for the governor of our state. The reviews of my bistro represent a social media explosion. So, at the end of the day, I can honestly say it's better to be the chef who *can* rather than a wanna-be chef who judges and critiques rather than attempting success by being one with food."

Frederic didn't call Graham out by name, but the exiled chef didn't need to. Everyone who watched Graham's restaurant reviews on TV, or read his foodie travel articles in *Knoxville Express* understood the implication. Tact and grace had kept Graham from spewing the hot retort that bubbled on his tongue. On camera, Graham and his colleagues worked together to shrug it off, but a poisoned dart had struck home, injecting a heavy dose of self-doubt—and disappointment.

Shaking free, Graham slid open dresser drawers, stashed what few items had followed him to Hope Creek. He stripped off his button-down shirt and tossed it on the bed as he headed to the bathroom, ready to brush his teeth and get to sleep.

All the same, thoughts of Frederic Mendell followed close, continuing to stir Graham's anger—and uncertainty. By over ten-to-one, the comments Graham had just tracked on the social media site decried the bitter outburst, giving Graham nods of support. The encouragement was great, sure, but still he felt needled as poison leaked beneath his skin. He had worked hard in the culinary arts, training in classic French cuisine at the Atlanta Culinary Institute. Now, he was nothing more than a talking head, a meaningless television and magazine food critic on the outside of the food world he loved, looking inside through an impenetrable sheet of plate glass.

He had gifts—but he wasn't using them. Shelving his talent, he grew to realize, was the equivalent of holding God in contempt. Maybe Frederic's rude and jarring shove to the ego was just what Graham needed in order to move forward along a new, albeit riskier path.

He groaned, dropping his head back. More turmoil. What a perfect end to a perfect day. Once he toppled into bed, exhausted, drained and disappointed, Graham's last thought before succumbing to exhaustion was of a lovely woman with twinkling amber eyes, a dynamite smile, and the most kissable pair of dimples imaginable...

The image sent him into a deep, restful slumber.

# 2

**LYDIA WAS A FAN. SHE** had seen Graham Forrester a number of times on TV. Copies of the travel magazine *Knoxville Express* were delivered to the inn for guests to enjoy while lounging in a fireside easy chair, so she often read his articles about food preparation and tips, also absorbing his latest news and reviews on restaurants and restaurant openings around the area.

Having now seen the man in the flesh, she decided the head-shot that accompanied each article failed to do the man justice.

Lydia nibbled at the end of a pen and stretched back from her office desk at Christmas Inn. Those compelling dark eyes packed a powerful punch, and that thick tumble of dark brown hair made her fingers itch with the urge to explore. Broad shoulders and a tall, lean build capped a really appealing package. Graham was charismatic in a warm, charming way that seemed to flow straight from his eyes, and his smile. She had kept it cool last night, feeling sorry that he had been stranded in a snowstorm. Poor guy had seemed so strained, lost in more than just a physical sense.

Thoughts of the man thoroughly distracted her from streaming lines of much less interesting computer code. She didn't need the pen, of course—pen and paper were so last millennium—but there was a sense of assurance in fiddling and twiddling with the time-honored object as she updated algorithms and tried to figure out ways around power surges and intermittent outages caused by the snow storm.  Both elements combined to wreak havoc on her freshly installed IT network.

Bored by the creation of infrastructure, Lydia launched her web design program and got to work putting Christmas Inn on the techno-grid.

"Good morning."

She knew Graham's voice before she even saw his face, thanks evermore to television media. "Good morning. I hope you had a good night's sleep."

"I did, thanks, Lydia."

He called her by name. Blushing, swept through by tingly ripples of awareness, Lydia turned away from her computer and met him at the reception desk. "Ready to check in?"

He cast a forlorn glance out the bay window that framed a sweeping stretch of the front yard. Towering pines dotted the landscape, cut through by a long, curving drive. "Yes, I am. I called the repair station a little while ago, and they're basically shut down. They have no parts in stock to repair my car, and even if they did, their chief mechanic is stranded by the storm."

Lydia could have called on Paulina, who generally worked reception, but opted to take care of Graham herself. He needed some cheering up and she wanted to make that task her own.

"My next call was to a car rental place," he continued.

"Dixon's Motor Pool?"

"Yeah, that's the one. No luck. They're closed by the storm, and their answering service referred me to an emergency contact who said their cars were snapped up like crazy as the storm intensified. They have nothing in stock."

"I'm sorry. Looks like you'll be stranded here for a day or two, so why not let me show you around?" She took custody of Graham's credit card and registered him as a guest. "I may be biased, but Christmas Inn is best appreciated during a fresh snowfall."

"Which continues to come down. Heavily. You're masochistic, right? In the throes of a secret longing to be buried alive in an ocean of white ice?"

She beamed him a smile. "See? You understand me. Let's finish with check in and then go for a reviving, mind-refreshing walk."

Graham stared. "So strange."

"What's that?"

"To find such a free-spirit working in the world of IT."

"What can I say? It takes all kinds."

Following a saucy head toss, she ran his credit card, swiped the approval slip from the printer and turned to hand it over for his signature. When she faced him once more, she noticed the intent way he studied his surroundings, in particular a shelf that rested several feet above Lydia's head.

"That's a gorgeous nativity set," he remarked.

Lydia's motions stilled and she viewed the piece along with him. The antique, crafted of distressed wood, featured delicate, porcelain figurines and rested in prominence above the reception desk. The piece had long been a favorite of Lydia's.

"The Christmas family has owned and operated this inn for generations. The figurines there? They were hand painted back in 1928 by Eloisa Christmas. She operated the front desk for almost twenty years and wanted Christ's birth to be the welcoming point to what was then her home. Now that it's an inn, we carry on that belief and share it with our guests."

"Which is just as it should be. Hand crafted. That's amazing."

"The stable was sawed, sanded and nailed by Eloisa's husband, Homer. The work of his hands has stood the test of time, like anything of value." Graham's interest remained, so Lydia continued. "For them, and for those that work here, Christmas isn't just a heart-warming holiday about gifts, or a gimmick to get folks through the door of our resort. We keep Christ in the holiday, and at the heart of what this place is all about."

Following her spirited exposition, Lydia half expected an indulgent, tolerant reaction, or perhaps a simple, yet dismissive nod designed to end the conversation. Instead, Graham kept his focus on the crèche.

"There's nothing wrong with that. I admire the commitment. Respect it."

Wow. Fascinated, Lydia watched while he dipped his head and scrawled his name along the signature line of the receipt. Overhead light from the crystal chandelier shone against waves of deep brown hair. She wanted to smooth back a slice that slid against his forehead.

"Would you like to take a walk with me?" The idea struck Lydia and broke free before she could filter the impulse. Graham lifted his head and looked at her askance. "For real. Since you're stuck here, let's make the most of it." His focus softened. Intensified. Tingles rippled beneath Lydia's skin, leaving her warm and lax while she waited on his reply.

"Know what? I don't mind if I do."

Graham returned to his room and Lydia danced back to her desk, giddy as she placed a temporary wrap on a few work details. She tucked into a puffy down coat, a pair of thick gloves and some boots. A quarter of an hour later she strolled the perimeter of the grounds at his side. Snow dusted the entire universe with white, and silence created its own unique sense of God's peace. Communion, refreshment. That's why she loved this place so much.

"I have a confession to make." Lydia looked up at him.

"What's that?"

"I've always admired your work." No sense denying it, or hiding from facts. "I recognized you from TV when you showed up last night, but you seemed so tired, and I didn't want to hold you up, or gush, or—"

"Pardon me while I cringe."

She slugged his arm in a playful tease, but levity died fast when she took a longer look into his eyes. He was visibly troubled. "Hey. What's that all about?"

A blink and smile later, the mood returned to center as Graham seemed to shrug off the reaction. "Nothing."

"Liar. I saw the shift."

"The shift?"

"Yep. The one in your eyes, and your smile. You went from genuine to Hollywood. From the real you to the poised and polished Graham Forrester I always see on screen." Lydia shrugged, lifting her face to the flakes, to the icy kiss of winter.

"No need to build a buffer. Just consider this to be a conversation with a stranger. No misconceptions, no bias. It's a form of freedom. Try it."

Silence fell as sure as the carpet of snow, drawing her focus to Graham once more. She could tell at a glance he vacillated between the ideas of being open, and known, and remaining safely guarded by a projected image.

"I'm that transparent?"

"No. I'm that intuitive." She snickered, linking her arm through his. "C'mon. Nothing spells great therapy and mental relief like walks and talks."

"Funny. You seem less like that stranger you mention and more like some kind of pixie angel who's currently coated by a layer of white." In emphasis Graham's real smile bloomed as he brushed his hands against strands of her hair, her shoulders and arms. Snow released, blowing into the wind like white glitter dust.

"So, then, tell the angel everything." She coaxed playfully, hoping to earn some trust and draw him out. She liked Graham. A lot. The recognition sent a flow of heat through her system. The rush of delicious warmth contrasted richly against a gust of wind that rippled through her hair and tossed loose wisps across her face.

Graham continued to study her in an intent, searching way that was so potent and tender Lydia had to remember to breathe properly. Distraction was called for, pronto, so she opted to play the tour-guide card. "This is the bridge your room overlooks. North Pole Bridge. We named it such because it resides at the north end of the property." She pointed to their right. "Over that way, just out of view, is South Pole Bridge."

A line of trees and an iced over riverbed stretched before them. Lydia tugged him toward the bridge which spanned a narrow waterway and directed their steps to its center arc. Lights strung along the rails and support columns of the metal structure cast multi-colored prisms across the snow, along the shimmering ice below, and the wide, sturdy planks where they now stood.

Refocused, Lydia returned to their conversation. "So, I believe you were about to confess something to the snow angel?"

Graham smiled, but the effort didn't reach deep. Instead, a sense of tribulation scripted subtle frown lines against his brow, along the length of his full, long mouth. He turned his attention to the frozen world around them.

"I'm at loose ends, and I need to work past it."

"How so?" She got the feeling he didn't confess things often, or to just anyone, so she felt honored, and compelled to tread with the utmost care.

"I wish I could be more specific." Graham's huff of frustration sent a plume of vapor into the air. "Know what I want? I want to start over again. I want to be fresh out of college, the whole world ahead of me. No complications or expectations or dashed dreams."

"You liked your younger days."

"I did. I studied food and I interned under a head chef named Geoff Cortand at a French bistro called *Jacques.* When I graduated, I became his sous chef and had the time of my life. I worked my tail off, and I didn't have a penny to spare, but Geoff was incredible. I learned from the best and felt like I was straight on with God's plan. That period of my life created a love affair with food that...died."

"How did it die?"

"Lack of sustenance. Lack of proper nourishment. After a few years of living paycheck to paycheck, I started to get itchy and ambitious. I couldn't make a living where I was, and Geoff wasn't ready to retire, or turn the reins of his restaurant over to anyone else. I shopped around a little, but I loved that bistro, and the friends I made, the vibe. I didn't have seed money to launch my own place.

"At that point, a producer at KRTN happened to be having dinner at the restaurant. We started talking, and he told me the station might launch a cooking segment on the weekly program *Knoxville Living.* I wrote it off as a lark, but a couple months later, he returned to *Jacques* and asked me to do an audition. I was hired a week later, and the money they offered was like an answer to prayer. From there, I figured I'd scrimp and save, and finally be able to live my dream."

"A place of your own."

Graham nodded, swiping his hands along the bridge rail to banish snow cover from lights of yellow, red, green, blue…

"Pretty soon, the TV work consumed me, especially when *Knoxville Express* stepped up with an additional offer to cover restaurant openings and reviews. As success has grown, so has discontent. I've become nothing more than an image, trading off on my background in culinary studies and what the media likes to call an 'easy' personality." He ground out a growl. "The trap of comfort and security closed over me so slowly and unexpectedly that I had no way to know I was drowning until it was too late."

Lydia had no easy answers, no epiphany to share. Instead of offering platitudes, she rested her hand against his and waited him out for a moment. Graham's answering squeeze to her fingertips was reassuring.

"I'm still in the culinary world," he continued. "But not in the way I imagined. So, I guess, for the foreseeable future I'll spend my life exploring food and the idea of making it accessible to everyone. If I can't create my own career as a chef, at least I can find great cooks, great restaurants, and bring them to life. I can help promote them and bring them to a wider view. It's a good life, and I know it. I'm blessed, and I know it."

"But still, you're unsettled."

"I am. And I suppose that's what happens when you run a divergent, yet parallel path to the life you dreamed of."

Silence beat by in time to the downpour of dusty, stilling snow. Communion, she thought. Blessed, precious communion. "Look at it this way. Maybe the struggle you're facing is the reason God landed you here as you sort things through. Maybe He's using the inconvenience of car trouble and a snowstorm to slow you down and give you time to focus and plan without distractions or pressure. In the meantime, there's nothing wrong with what you're doing, Graham. Your work brings life to restaurants that might otherwise fold, and—"

"Maybe."

"Oh, that cut-in tells me you're far from convinced."

He skipped a sheepish glance in her direction. "No, you're right, but…let's just say I expected…I wanted…more from my life. I'm unfulfilled, and I'm trying to figure out if it's God talking to me or if what I'm really hearing is the devil of dissatisfaction." He shrugged; the rise and fall of his shoulders hiked the lines of a long, wool coat. "I'll stop right there, because I refuse to whine. Deal?"

"Deal." She added a smile and handshake to the agreement. They still had a day or two left, and Lydia knew how to be persistent and persuasive.

"Your turn, Dimples."

"Dimples?" Startled by the nickname, Lydia automatically touched gloved fingers to her cheeks.

Graham's laugh rang out long and sweet. "I love them."

"You're about the only one."

"I'm sure that's not true."

Caught off her typically sassy guard, Lydia ducked her head and began to walk, completing their hike across the bridge and leading them into an impressive drift of snow. Man, was it *ever* going to stop? Casting a swift look at Graham, she had to admit she almost hoped not…

"Tell me about yourself, Lydia."

"Hmm…let me see. Well, I'm an Aquarius. I love long walks along the beach, and hope for world peace, and an end to hunger, and I—"

Graham's laughter bellowed. "Thank you, beauty queen finalist. Now, how about the real deal?"

She giggled, loving the way he caught on to her humor and sparred so easily. "OK, hang on, master chef. You're about to be bored to tears."

"Bring it on. I'm all braced. Except for the snow and ice." Graham held her arm, offering stability as they traversed a small slope.

"Ha, ha, funny man." They rounded toward the inn. "There's not much to say. I'm a recent graduate of the University of Tennessee with a Bachelor of Science in Information Technology."

"I didn't notice a ring or anything—are you married? Involved?"

"No, and no. I'm too busy transplanting my life to get involved."

"Transplanting your life? Lydia, that's far from boring."

She blushed and tucked her arm through his. "I took a leap of faith a month ago and quit my job in Nashville."

"That's brave. Why'd you do it? Were you unhappy?"

"No, nothing like that, exactly." Lydia drifted into the past, into a world of big city life, corporate cultures lived at high-speed with high-stress, especially when it came to IT issues. "I loved the work, but I hated the over-frenzied culture. My mom and her best friend Lizzie have undertaken a huge project to restore Christmas Inn. Lizzie is like family to me. I wanted to help."

"Commendable." They plowed forward through the snow. "Will an IT position at Christmas Inn sustain you over the long term?"

"Probably not, but I've got some money saved. When the network installation and web design are finished, I'll find a job elsewhere. Maybe here in Hope Creek, maybe a bit further out, in Knoxville or somewhere in that area. I might freelance. Who knows? "

"IT is an in-demand field, to be sure, but you're OK with the uncertainty?"

Lydia met his gaze straight on, irked a bit by being questioned. "Yes, I am. I'll be OK. I plan to work hand-in-hand with my family, and with God, to see where this venture leads. I think it'll be exciting, and refreshing, not to mention a great deal more aligned with who I am and who I want to be. I didn't like running a corporate rat race."

"I'm not asking because I doubt you, Lydia. Just the opposite. I'm amazed. I admire your faith, and your confidence. I could probably learn a lot from you about reaching out in trust. I've never experienced that level of courage."

Lydia's heart went soft and warm. "Again—maybe that's why you're here. Maybe God's all over your disquiet. Maybe He's getting ready to deliver a miracle."

His answering smile reached through to her soul. "If only life were that simple and easy."

"It can be, Graham. It really can be."

# 3

**LYDIA'S MOM HAD ARRIVED AT** the inn, and she was in a tizzy. A royal, knock-your-socks-off, three-alarm-fire tizzy. No snow storm would keep Beatrice Cutler on the sidelines of her meticulous Victorian a few blocks away if she sniffed any sense of trouble on the brew for her sister, Roberta. Bea Cutler was a buttinski at times, but always with the best and most loving intentions.

A blessing and a curse to be sure.

When they walked in, Roberta was in mid-rant. "Yes, Bea, financial restructuring forced us to scale back food service to just a few meals a week, other than the breakfast we offer, but with the storm being what it is, we can't be expected to provide full-on meal service."

"I know, Bertie, especially when David Lewiston's skills in the kitchen were, shall we say, sadly lacking. Not to mention the…well, issues…he had with intoxication on the job."

Roberta harrumphed. Her eyes narrowed and her cheeks flushed in a rare escalation of budding temper. "Intoxication. That's being more than kind. Plus, he stormed out of the inn in a toddler's huff when a guest dared to complain about the quality of their meal. He couldn't run a kitchen. He always riled up the cooks and wait staff. I think, in all honesty, he believed the position was beneath him."

"And that's why we need to figure this out. Food service is part of what's offered at Christmas Inn. At minimum, breakfast is part of the rate that's charged for renting a room." A petite, silver-haired fireball, Mom stalked through the office behind reception. Worry cut lines above her brows.

"Beatrice, calm down. Our guests were fed. Not in typical

fashion, I'll grant you, but all the same—" As ever, Aunt Bertie assumed the role of reason. And she referred to her sister as Beatrice rather than Bea. That meant Bertie's ire was on the rise and her patience was on the wane.

"Today's breakfast was nothing much more than oatmeal, boiled eggs and toast. I know we're low on supplies, and for the most part folks have understood, but we need to feed our guests or we could be held liable."

Lydia stepped into the fray with a gentle laugh, deciding to join the conversation and do what she could to alleviate any further heartache. "Mom, I hardly think our guests will litigate over struggles that occur as the result of a history-making snowstorm."

"It's not about litigation, Lydia, it's about a moral responsibility." Mom turned, freezing momentarily, eyes going a touch wide once she spied Graham. "We need to help, and that's why I'm here. I'm sure Bertie and Lizzie feel a sense of responsibility for the happiness and wellbeing of their guests. I want to step in, but how? What can we do?"

Mom twisted her fingers while she looked around the lobby and focused on the open area of the adjoining dining room— empty for now but staged—as though a miraculous solution might suddenly materialize and fill each empty spot.

In the meantime, Lydia took notice of the way Graham eyed the swinging doors that separated the elegant, old-world style dining room from the kitchen proper. Were those wheels she saw chugging and clicking and rolling just above his head?

"Maybe I can help." His gaze tagged Lydia. "Show me what you've got."

"Show you what I've got?"

Lydia's stare, her bemused question, stirred a low chuckle that rumbled. "Meaning what have you got in the way of kitchen utensils and supplies?"

"Excuse me, you are?"

Lydia jumped when her mother pushed her way back into the

conversation.

"He's a guest of Christmas Inn, Bea." Bertie gave her friend a warning nudge. "Graham Forrester. You might recognize him from TV. He's a chef, and a food critic. A good one at that."

Graham shot Bertie an adoring look. "You're a sweetheart."

"I'm Beatrice Cutler. Lydia's mother."

A handshake ensued and Graham focused a charming smile on Lydia's mom. "It's a pleasure to meet you."

"You, too." Mom made a humming sound, worry lines easing into speculation and open interest.

Lydia stifled a groan. *Mom, don't even consider playing matchmaker. Not for one single second.*

"Give me the tour and put me to work." Graham clapped his hands together.

Lydia gaped at him. "Cooking. You're considering a food service. Graham, you're not even halfway serious."

"You're right. I'm not. I'm all the way serious."

Just like that, she made the connection to a God-sent solution for the inn's present food issue. Christmas Inn had been gifted by the presence of a world-class chef, trained in French cooking. He was offering his help and expertise.

Had they hit the jackpot or what?

Ignoring her mom, ignoring Bertie and everything else but crisis containment, Lydia grabbed his hand and swept him across the threshold of the small but spotless and well-established commercial kitchen.

Gratitude spurred her on, but all the same, fear of taking on this challenge beat like a drum through her chest. Soon enough, excitement crowded out fear. "I know it's not anything like you'd find in the kind of gourmet kitchen you're probably used to, but it serves its purpose."

"It has an oven. A refrigerator. A sink. I see some pots and pans."

"Smart aleck."

"Dimples? Trust me, we're in business."

The cooking gears in Graham's head went to work, seamless and smooth. His culinary instincts kicked into high gear the minute Lydia yanked him through the swinging doors that divided the kitchen from the dining area.

First, he rooted through the freezer. There was a big bag of frozen lobster, unopened and featuring a name-brand logo. Not great, since it wasn't fresh, but not bad, either. In the fridge he discovered a healthy stash of butter and cheeses. They had some sharp cheddar. Perfect. Puzzle pieces started to form into a whole, because in the pantry he came upon bags of bowtie pasta, some nutmeg, some flour and breadcrumbs.

Oh, yeah. He could work with this.

"How do you feel about lobster mac and cheese?" Not waiting on her reply, already cooking in his mind, Graham added black pepper and kosher salt to his lineup of seasonings. "I'm not keen on using frozen lobster. I'm a snob, so I prefer fresh, but this'll work."

He muttered and paced and eyed some large pots, a sauté pan that hung from a nearby peg wall.

"You're not even here right now, are you?" Lydia's voice penetrated his fog of cooking euphoria.

"Huh? What?" He looked her way and found she stood nearby, hip braced against the long, stainless prep counter. She tracked his movements, brow arched, lips quirked…what a great grin. And those eyes…

She definitely had his full attention now.

"You're in a zone of your own. Kind of cool to see, actually. It's the real you, and I can already see you're going to be my knight in shining armor."

"Well, if feeding the hungry masses qualifies me for the position, you bet. Can I? Will you let me?"

He was sure his anticipation, his eagerness to take the helm, transferred from voice to eyes to body language.

"Let you? Graham, this kitchen is all yours. Think you can pull it off?"

"I refuse to dignify that with an answer." By design, the reply reeked of cheeky fun and mock hauteur. Seconds later, he panicked. "Uh-oh…milk. Do you have milk?" He darted to the fridge in a hurry. Plenty—thank goodness. "I'll need some vegetable oil, too."

Lydia pulled down an industrial sized container from a metal storage unit in the corner. "Voila! Anything else?"

Graham shifted into full-on chef mode. "Here's what we need to do next. Let's get a schedule set up and any hands on deck that you think can help prep and serve. We'll split the guests into two meal shifts. Group one will eat at five o'clock. Group two will eat at six thirty. That'll give us time to prep things appropriately and get it served fast. I need to know head-count as well so we know what kind of quantities we're dealing with."

"I'll pull up the registry and poll guests. Most of them are lingering around the grounds anyway, so that should be easy."

"Good." Graham drummed his fingers against the prep counter. "What can we serve with it? Do you have any kind of salad fixings? Vegetables?"

"Yep, we always keep veggies on hand, and I can help with that if you want me to."

"I want you right here with me, my sous chef."

"Sous chef. I think I like the sound of that."

And there came the dimples, right on cue and precisely positioned at the crest of her smile. Graham was half-tempted to ditch dinner plans and just stare at her, or place a light kiss to each upturned corner… Instead, he tapped the tip of her nose with his finger. "I think I do, too. Let's apron up and do this thing."

From a series of pegs drilled into the far wall, Lydia retrieved a couple of aprons and handed one to Graham. "I'll be back. Let me get that schedule in place and get you a head count."

"Perfect."

Light of foot, Lydia fled the kitchen and Graham kicked matters off by washing his hands, familiarizing himself with available cooking tools, organizing spices and pans. Out of habit, he snapped the hand towel over his shoulder so it'd be ready to use later, then put himself to work.

He was so engrossed in food prep, he barely registered Lydia's return until she joined him at the counter and tied an apron at her waist. Carrying two heads of iceberg lettuce she went to work chopping with admirable finesse.

Graham looked away from heating a pre-seasoned sauté pan to give her an approving look. "Nice technique."

"Thank you, chef."

He smirked at her officious, over-done response and gave her shoulder a playful nudge when she paused for a second. He added the lobster to his pan and heated it through, barely crisping the edges. To salted, boiling water, he added the pasta then wiped steam-moistened hands on the towel at his shoulder.

"So, tell me about your mom. She's a powerful character."

"And you're a diplomatist. She means well, one hundred percent, but yeah, she's not the type to withhold her opinion, or her heart."

"I admire that."

"Me, too."

"My mom is Beatrice, but everyone calls her Bea. She's the older sister to my Aunt Roberta. Everyone calls her Bertie. They're both fixtures here at Christmas Inn. Paulina you've met. Lizzie Franklin used to manage the inn, until her health went downhill. She's mending, but having Paulina on our staff makes things a lot easier for her. Paulina, along with Lizzie's niece, Ariana, pretty much run the show, but Bertie and my mom help out in any way they can because they adore Lizzie. Mom's authoritative attitudes are a blessing and a curse."

Graham jiggled the sauté pan to keep the food in motion while he watched Lydia. "Why do I get the feeling that statement runs deeper than just the doings here at Christmas Inn?"

"She's after me."

"For?"

"For the purposes of finding Mr. Right, settling down in a beautiful house in the burbs, and presenting her with numerous pitter pattering grandbabies."

"Oh. Well. If *that's* all…"

Shared laughter mingled with the rich aroma of nutmeg—Graham's secret ingredient in this particular recipe—which he mixed into the melted butter and sizzling lobster. He retrieved a large metal mixing bowl from a high shelf above the stove and set it in front of Lydia so she could start filling it with her chopped greens.

"So that's why I felt the weight of her regard." When Lydia cringed at his conclusion, Graham squeezed her shoulder in a gesture meant to be both affectionate and understanding.

"Pretty much. You're a guy, a great looking, successful guy, similar in age to me, and trust me, the first thing she looked at was your ring finger—"

"Empty, since I'm single."

"And, oh, how I'm certain her heart rejoices. In her mind we're already married."

Lydia sighed, but Graham whistled through his teeth, blood thrumming for reasons both personal and professional. So, interest. Romantic interest. In Lydia. Hey, it could happen, easily, and that truth provided for a most unexpected turn of events—on top of this already unexpected exercise in culinary rescue.

Mastering a kitchen, he thought. With a beautiful woman as his helper and guide. What a rush. He waltzed from spot to spot, prepping his dish, watching the clock as the day inched closer to service number one.

"She's confused about me." Lydia hiked her shoulder, dicing an assortment of veggies, piling them into the mixing bowl. "I resigned from my IT position at Greater Product Infrastructure—GPI, Inc. for short."

"Oh?"

"Yeah. I was needed here, by my family—noble enough, to her mind, but she's made it clear she wonders why I'd abandon my security blanket and brave a few steps on my own without the promise of long-term stability."

"Lydia!" Bertie burst through the swinging doors, papers in hand, face flushed, steps quick as she interrupted the conversation. "Lizzie separated the guests into two shifts, like you asked, and here's the head count. Looks like we'll end up feeding about thirty people total."

Lydia glanced at their temporary head chef. "Does that sound OK? Do we have enough food?"

"I think we're about to multiply the loaves and make a miracle happen. Yeah. I'm comfortable with that number. Two shifts of fifteen is doable."

Bertie charged to Graham's side and lifted to tip-toe so she could peck his cheek quick without getting in the way. "Your stay is on the house. Seriously. This is incredible of you. Thank you!"

"No problem. It's a pleasure, so no worries."

"Then I'll get out of your way. You guys keep cooking. Paulina is on board to help in any way she can, plus Ari is on her way in, trading her designer shoes for sneakers so she can serve, too, and so will Bea and I."

Lydia grinned, heaping some shredded cheese on top of the salad fixings. "I'm sure Ari will charm away every negative vibe our guests might have."

"Absolutely—and with her on the team, I think we're all set. I have to tell you, the guests have been so appreciative. I think you're right, Graham, this is a miracle just waiting to happen."

Graham glanced Lydia's way. "So, refresh my memory. Who's Ariana again?"

"Ariana Christmas. Future owner and operator of Christmas Inn, once the dust settles and our revitalized standing in the world of resort lodging is complete. Her father is a hotel tycoon, and Christmas Inn is a big part of his family's legacy. She's taking some of the weight off Lizzie's shoulders and has come through like a champ."

"And Ariana and Lizzie are related, right?"

"You catch on quick. Yep, Ariana is Lizzie's niece." Lydia grinned as she sliced and diced some celery and onion. "And when you meet her, don't let Ari's super model style fool you. She's a debutant with a heart of gold."

So, he was staffed up, food preps were coming together, and the influx of positivity pushed him on. Busy as he was, though, Graham kept watching Lydia—and he couldn't imagine a more beautiful way to spend his time.

# 4

**EXAGGERATED FEMALE INTEREST SPILLING OVER,**
Ariana Christmas stood next to Lydia, peeking through a slivered
opening of the doorway and into the kitchen where Graham
worked on dinner. "*Who* is *he?*"

"Graham Forrester," Lydia whispered. Hissed, actually. Last
thing she wanted was to have their volunteer chef overhear two
women gushing about him. "He's our temporary head chef."

Ari's perfectly shaped brow inched upward. Her lips curved.
She even added an approving hum to the mix. "Nice. I want one."

Lydia giggled at her friend's harmless antics. Nothing stopped
Ari in her tracks like the sight of a handsome man, but nowadays
she was all look, and no touch. With good reason.

"Hey, step off already and leave some for the rest of us. After
all, you already have your very own construction contractor to
love and admire."

In an instant, at the mention of Taylor Knox, Ari went from
sassy and edgy to soft as cashmere. "Yeah, I do, don't I?"

It did Lydia's heart good to know Ari had become happily
involved with Taylor, whose construction company had
performed the physical restorations at Christmas Inn. Lydia was
shorter than Ari by a handful of inches, but that didn't stop her
from slipping an arm around Ari's waist to deliver a tender
squeeze. "You lucky thing."

"He's the greatest. Ever." Stepping away from the doors, Ari
perched her hands on her hips. In a blink she went from dreamy
to all business. "So, we've got dishes, glassware and utensils.
We've got pitchers for water and we'll be able to offer coffee—
regular and decaf—but Aunt Lizzie tells me we're short on pop
selections, so we'll have to be careful about what we offer in the

way of beverages."

"Yep, Graham noticed that, too, but we've got a hungry, and very grateful group of folks about to descend on us, so I'm not too worried. They understand we're working with minimal supplies."

Ari slipped a hair band from around her wrist and tucked waves of long brown hair into a neat ponytail. "And they're happy to be fed."

"Fed by a really great chef," Lydia murmured. She couldn't keep her lips from curving into a smile, which probably came across every bit as dreamy as Ari's a moment ago.

"Well, aren't you sweet? Let me help you make him proud," Ariana snickered. She fluttered her lashes and pressed a hand to her chest, picking up on Lydia's interest as if tuned in by radar. The tease.

Lydia groaned. "Oh, get over yourself."

\*\*\*\*

"Hey, Lydia, taste this!"

Lydia turned from dishing salad onto small white plates as Graham's words enticed. First round dinner service drew closer and closer and enthusiasm danced through his eyes in sparkles and flashes. He extended a tasting fork, presenting a small heap of his lobster mac creation for her to sample.

A droplet of cheese slid away from the middle tine, a temptation of its own. From the opposite side of the counter, she stretched forward to blow on the steaming morsel, then accepted his offering. Their eyes met and held. An involuntary sigh bloomed from her chest as warm, gooey cheese, flavorful pasta and spicy bits of lobster melted against her tongue.

"Oh, my goodness—that's *heavenly*," she whispered.

Graham's smile hit her like a ray of sunlight. "Let's hope our guests agree."

"If they don't then just make me a really huge leftovers bag."

A frenzied bout of plating took place as guests filed into the dining room. Lydia helped, loading large round platters for their impromptu service staff. During a break in the action, while weaving through the dining room, Lydia spied Graham leaning against the frame of the swinging doors that led to the kitchen. Lips curved, gaze moving across the inn's dinner patrons, he absorbed the proceedings and Lydia sensed his satisfaction, the contentment that pushed outward from his soul. She caught his eye and gave him a celebratory wink.

Not a lot of time existed for introspection, though—service one neared conclusion, with service two coming at them momentarily. Judging by the satisfied comments she received, Lydia knew they had hit a homerun. Thanks to Graham. Thanks to his generous offering of time, talent and heart.

Hours later, Graham snagged Lydia's hands and pulled her into the now empty dining room. He angled toward one of the ladder-back chairs that surrounded a cleared and re-staged table.

"This was so much fun. I mean, I don't think I've had this much fun in years. Literally. Years." He helped her to sit.

"I could tell you enjoyed yourself."

"That was just about the best adrenaline rush ever."

Lydia laughed, smoothing a subtle ripple from the stretch of white linen that crossed the tabletop. "Even during that change over from the first service to the second?"

Graham brushed that off with a relaxed smile and the swipe of his hand. "Even then. Yeah, things got a little dicey, and the orders stacked up for a minute or two, but all things considered I can't believe how well it went."

He left their spot to pour them each a glass of iced water from a pitcher still resting on a service tray. His proximity to the kitchen door resurrected a memory Lydia longed to share from the evening. "I like that you took the time to watch."

"Watch? What do you mean?"

She sipped, watched him do the same, and then fell into his deep dark gaze. "You stood in the doorway and you watched. You took it all in during the dinner shifts tonight."

"Yeah, guilty. I love watching people enjoy the food I've

created. Makes all the hard work worthwhile."

"Spoken like a true chef. I'm a relative outsider, and I don't know you well, but you came to life in the kitchen. You miss being a chef, don't you? The actual process of creating, and cooking, and serving."

Graham didn't acknowledge her with a look or instant response. Rather, he gathered a deep breath and nodded, almost reluctantly it seemed. "With every breath. Lately, I'm becoming more and more aware of that fact."

"Then you should return to the kitchen." Lydia leaned forward in earnest. "Take it from a person watching from the outside, who isn't emotionally invested in the choices you've had to make. You're amazing."

Graham looked at her long and hard and Lydia's bones dissolved into a heated yearning that took her completely by surprise in its power and impact.

"Feel like taking a walk?"

At his unexpected suggestion, she shook free of her thoughts. "Walk? Where?"

He slipped his fingertips beneath the spot where her hand rested on the table and held tight, helping her to a stand. "Outside. Where else?"

"Outside. In the snow."

"Yeah. You chicken?"

"Not at all." She tugged on the front of his button-down shirt, acting oh-so-tough when in reality being propped against the warmth of his body left her senses tingling. "I just thought the city boy might be a little put off by the white stuff."

"Not at all," he mimicked in a tone ripe with cocky challenge. "In fact, I'm kind of growing to like it."

Lydia's teasing glower softened into a grin. "You don't say."

\*\*\*\*

Silence enveloped Graham at once when they exited the inn. After the chaos of executing a 'seat-of-your-pants' dinner service—

times two—the deepening carpet of snow provided a welcome peace. But that carpet of calm nearly crested his boots when he trekked with Lydia toward the rear courtyard. He linked his gloved hand with hers, half to offer companionship, half to share a steadying ga as they moved along. "Earlier tonight, you started to tell me about your job in IT."

"My former job, yeah."

"Tell me about it. I'm intrigued."

"Because?"

"Because I admire that level of faith…and trust." Squelching a rise of frustration, and wishful thinking, Graham released his hold on her hand. Was he even worthy of grasping such a beautiful, free-flowing spirit when his own life was so boxed, so set to a pre-ordained pattern? He battled the sigh that rose. "I've failed miserably on that count, so maybe I can learn a thing or two."

Oh, sure, he framed his words in a cloud of humor, but there was truth in humor.

"I worked for a company called Greater Product Infrastructure, or GPI, and I loved the work. For the most part, the people were great, too, but—" She sucked in the cold air, blew it out in a plume of curling, waving white while she looked ahead, as though formulating her words and feelings. –"It's like that moment when you get cut off in traffic by a jerk who's in a hurry to get wherever it is he's going, and he barely leaves enough room for air between his bumper and the paint on the front end of your car. From where I sat, the corporate world was all about maneuvers just like that. I figured my chosen field had to offer a whole lot more fulfillment and enjoyment than being part of a culture that negates people."

Quiet descended while Graham took in her words and felt them take swift root.

She shoved down the hood of her parka, shooting him a sheepish look. "Guess that sounds a little high and mighty. Sorry to go off like that."

"Don't apologize. I'm impressed. What you say gives me a lot to think about. Lately my professional zeal is decreasing in direct correlation to a rise in frustration, and a sense that I'm not doing what I'm meant to do."

Conversation quieted once again while their booted footsteps created a melody of crunching snow. Flakes continued to sift and swirl, but more often than not, it was growing wind gusts that tossed snow to earth from nearby tree branches and skimmed a sea of white waves across the undulating surface of the ground.

"Lydia, I think making a move like you did is incredibly brave."

She linked her arm through his, gave a short laugh. "Well, thank you, but my family takes a somewhat different view. Mom most especially."

"Let them. Let her. Making a change like that is bold. Confident. I wish—" Graham stopped there, stumbling over the pattern of his own life, the dreams and wishes that had carried him far…but not quite far enough. "You know how I told you earlier that I wanted something different? That I wanted a life built around creation? Tonight brought me back to that truth. Food is like a canvas to me. I love the process of mixing things together— the spices, the cheeses, the herbs and meats and veggies. It's creative magic. I was convicted of that recently when a competitor was dismissed on a cook-off television show I helped host. In a very arrogant manner he gave me his opinion about what I do, and he did so in public, on TV. I'm sure he achieved the utmost satisfaction from shaming me that way after he was eliminated."

"I happened to watch that episode."

Of course she had. Why wasn't Graham more surprised by that fact?

Lydia's breath sent puffy white curls into the nighttime air. "I wanted to see who claimed the big prize. Bottom line? That guy was nothing more than a sanctimonious heel. Truly. On top of that, everyone watching knew as much the instant he opened his big, bragging mouth."

"I get that, Lydia. All the same, those indictments hit home and left me at a crossroads. Even without the splash across YouTube and all the comments left at the television station's webpage I've come to realize changes might be necessary."

"I sensed there was more to your distraction last night than the idea of being stranded."

"Perceptive."

Even in the mild, snow-cast light, Graham could have sworn he saw a rise of color in her cheeks. "Like I said, I've followed you on TV, and"—she chuckled—"I try to pass along what tips I can to Aunt, Bertie. She's chipped in with a few kitchen duties since our chef, David Lewiston, quit. After seeing what you did tonight, I think ramping up food offerings and improving our kitchen should become a top priority as we consider ways to keep improving Christmas Inn."

Lydia used just a few short words, and offered no more than the promise of an idea. All the same, she'd laid out a tempting form of bait. Should he even pursue it, or was she speaking in general terms? Tough to judge, though she waited on him in a building silence. Should he ask her to elaborate? Nah. He'd let it drop. Tonight's foray into the world of cooking left him itching to overreach, to push for something that might never come to be. Besides, it seemed Christmas Inn was just hitting stride again. Even if management considered hiring a head chef, management wouldn't be able to afford him.

Right?

Disquiet attempted a bloody coup, so Graham extinguished, then side-stepped, the spark that had so briefly burst to life. "Tonight affirmed that what I do is basically meaningless. I'm not making use of the education I received, the joy I find in cooking. Sure, that contestant had an axe to grind, but I have to be honest. He didn't say anything that wasn't true. He didn't lampoon anything about me that I didn't deserve. I'm plastic. I'm manufactured. Up until now, that's been acceptable. Not anymore. What I tumbled into tonight—creating food with nothing more than bare essentials and my own technique—is a challenge that thrills me and makes me happy, but I've never stepped off the cliff and let that pathway, that passion, lead me away from the safe zone. I've never had that kind of guts. Not like you."

In a way, Graham answered Lydia's questions about increased food offerings at Christmas Inn. Still, the deeper elements of that idea remained suspended between them, and for now, that was fine. They were just talking, throwing out thoughts and dreams with no true knowledge of what might happen next. All Graham knew for sure was that he wanted to operate a restaurant kitchen, and he wanted to keep seeing Lydia. He longed for their connection to somehow remain, despite differing lives.

But being realistic, how could such a thing possibly happen?

"So, all of that drama happened the day you left town to go home for Christmas?" She slanted a glance his way, interest like a bright flame in her eyes.

"Timing is everything, isn't it? I was on my way to Ashville, North Carolina for Christmas with my folks and my big sister, Becca."

"I'm so sorry, Graham. Right or wrong, whether it leads you to an epiphany or not, what happened on that show was wrong."

"Thanks. I'm determined to fulfill my purpose in life, but that requires risk, and a lot of thought. I don't want to *settle*." She tucked against his side as easy as a dream. "I love cooking. I've come face-to-face with that fact all over again. The life I live right now? Being a face and a mouthpiece rather than creating great food? That's not how I want to spend my life."

"And if you could have anything you wished?"

Anything he wished. Graham closed his eyes and allowed that movie to play out, a movie full of scent, texture, taste and the clatter of cooking, serving, eating. "That's easy. I'd be back in the kitchen. After what happened tonight, here, with you, I can say that loud and clear."

"Then do it, Graham. *Do it*."

She stopped, blocked his way until their gazes met, and held.

Her prodding was so simple in theory, so perfect on paper, but breaking out of and exiting the cocoon of security and all of his life's known quantifiers—both good and bad—wasn't as easy as *'Do it.'*

"I wish I hadn't sold out, Lydia. I wish I hadn't created such a superficial life."

"Your life isn't superficial. You followed opportunity and embraced it for as long as it suited you. There's no crime in that. No fault. You've lived your life as you saw fit. What I'm hearing now is that you want to change direction. There's nothing to stop you from that change, Graham. If cooking is what you want, then do it."

So honest. So fearless. "I used to have that kind of unquestioned belief and determination."

"What happened?"

"Life. Affirmation. A quest for security. None of them bad things, but combined together, choices are made and pathways are taken that leave you wandering away from your dreams and plans before you even know what hit. That's why I give you so much credit for taking custody of your life."

"It's not easy."

"Nope. But necessary." Necessary, just like that cozy layer of security that had wrapped itself around him in a needed, but at times confining hold. All at once he wanted to leave the bleak, the restlessness, behind. He took Lydia's arms in a gentle grip and turned her until they were face-to-face. "You're awfully easy on me."

"Not easy. Just honest."

There she was again, tender and sweet, soft as a caress and equally as tempting. Graham lost his breath, and stared into her eyes, captured. Lost, yet found. "Do you know what I want to do? I want to freeze frame this moment. This feeling. I want to put my life on hold just long enough to drink this in and actually start to believe again."

"Believe in what again?" Her voice trembled with a telling,

emotional vibration. Need. A need he tasted and felt as surely as she did.

"I want to believe in miracles again. I want to believe in beauty and love and life lining up with proper focus and feeling good again. That hasn't been the case for me in a long time."

He cupped her face between his hands and drew her gently, inexorably closer...closer still...until lips brushed, wispy as the touch of falling snow. A kiss began, built and swirled like the dance of silent white all around them. The warmth of his skin melted flakes into pinpoints of dewy moisture.

Suddenly the pealing of church bells cut through towering pines, through the ink black of night. The kiss they shared moved in slow and gentle exploration, in time to the twelve strikes of the nearby church bells that heralded the hour.

Midnight. The turning of one day to the next. A fresh start. A clean slate.

All at once, Lydia broke free of the spell they had created and gasped. "Graham...the chapel...the bells...they... No!"

"No, what?"

"Those bells only ring for special occasions, for...weddings, for funerals, for celebratory gatherings. For love. Mysteriously, whenever love is found, no matter what the time of day, the bells resound."

Her voice trailed off and Graham's skin prickled like a live wire. Love? Mysterious bell chimes? What was going on here. His alarm rose. "Should we check it out?"

"No...Graham, trust me, there's nobody there."

"But what if it's an intruder, or..."

Though still trembling and functioning on high-alert, Lydia shook her head. "I...I'm sure it's just a...a fluke. Anyone who means harm would hardly trouble themselves by sounding the bells."

Still, he noticed the way Lydia stared at the distant silhouette of the cross-tipped church spire just barely visible through the trees. Graham continued to absorb her shivers, which stemmed not from the cold, or any kind of physical threat, but from something deeper and infinitely more mysterious...

Love.

And he wondered—what kind of message was God trying to send tonight? To both of them?

# 5

**THE FOLLOWING MORNING, GRAHAM'S PHONE** came to life. He lunged for the device and pulled it from the charger, hoping the auto repair shop was calling with an update about parts delivery. Instead, caller ID revealed a name from his contact list that hadn't seen much use over the past few months. Geoff Cortland.

"Shame on me," Graham muttered, "for negligence."

He engaged the call at once and was treated without preamble to the booming voice he knew and loved so well, despite logistical distance.

"Graham! Happy holidays, my friend! How are you?"

Geoff wasn't a believer like Graham, and he relegated Christmas salutations to the generic. Still, Graham loved the man, and longed for a day when that fact just might change.

"Hey, Geoff! I'm good. Stranded for now, but I'm good."

"Stranded? Where? What happened?"

Graham caught him up and they shared some updates before his culinary mentor got around to the point of his call.

"I wanted you to be one of the first to know. I'm retiring."

"What? Retiring?" Graham strolled the length of the fireplace in his suite, glossed a hand absently against swags of faux evergreen. Mini-ornaments and tiny lights glimmered and danced at his touch. "You can't be serious. You're way too young to retire."

Geoff laughed, hearty and strong. "Life is short, Graham. I'm going to travel, sample cuisine from all over the world, maybe even publish some books before I'm nothing but a memory. There's a lot more to food than just the restaurant, and I want to explore that truth." Stunned speechless, Graham went stock still.

He stood eye-to-eye with a Father Christmas statue stationed at the center of the mantle. Garbed in swaths of burgundy velvet and white fur, the figure possessed the strangest, most piercing blue eyes…

He blinked and snapped to in a hurry to rejoin the conversation. "You're happy? You're sure about this?"

"I certainly am. It's all good." Rich layers of enthusiasm imbued the words. "Kathleen and I are headed to Paris just after the first of the year."

"Wow—that soon? What about Jacques? What will happen to the bistro?"

It was Geoff's turn to hold silence for a beat or two. "I have temporary measures in place, you know, like when I take any other vacation. Long term though? Well, that's why I'm calling. I want to give you the right of first refusal. Jacques can be yours if you're interested. Actually, I'd love to see you as owner-operator, Graham. No one mixed passion and skill for both the food and the business like you. It's time. Give up the reviews and the TV stints and get back in the trenches, my friend. You're a no-brainer to succeed me. You'd be incredible."

Graham squeezed his cell phone in a death grip, considering the ramifications of Geoff's offer. "I…I'm…" Wow, what a great time for words to fail. He cleared his throat, forced himself to breathe. "I'm flattered, first and foremost. I'm honored you'd even consider handing the reins over to me."

"Why wouldn't I? Jacques is part of who you are as a chef. Part of your history, and your coming of age in the food world. Your taking over here makes perfect sense to me."

"And I want to jump at the chance. Every instinct I have is burning to say 'yes' right here, and right now. I'd love to have my own place, as you know."

"And as you've earned. Make it happen, Graham. Let's talk it over and see what comes next. You have too much skill to leave your passion, and your drive, to reviews and food analysis. Both are great tools—they'll enhance you as an owner and as a head chef, but they'll never provide the whole picture. There's nothing like the hands-on process of creating great food. You can do it. I have no doubt or I'd never be able to make this call. I'm letting you know now so you can think it over. Let's get together at some point the week before Christmas at Jacques. Can you make it to Atlanta by then?"

"Ah...sure. Of course." For an opportunity like this? No question. The call to arms that came from someone he cared for and trusted as much as Geoff was like answered prayer. He closed his eyes, tried to center, and was instantly haunted by a wide, easy smile, by brown eyes full of sweet innocence and a pair of kissable dimples that kept his mind bouncing with one complex and contradictory complication to that grand plan.

*Lydia.*

****

Lydia looked away from her computer monitor when Paulina's purposeful stride caught her attention. Tablet in hand, Paulina moved past the easy chairs positioned near a wide mantle adorned with elves and lavish piles of sparkly cotton snow. She gave Lydia a nod of greeting.

Preparing to join the inn's manager, Lydia completed a script update that would enable the website to accept and process on-line reservations. She clicked enter one last time then allowed herself a satisfied grin. "With that, Christmas Inn, I welcome you to the age of technology."

Lydia tapped a few more keys to close out programs so she could focus on what was to come, a debriefing of last night's events. The inn's management team began to assemble in a conference room that adjoined the offices situated behind the resort's reception area. At the appointed hour of ten, chair spaces filled along a large, oval table. Once everyone was accounted for, Paulina began the weekly meeting with a recap of latest business statistics along with projected timelines and costs for on-going improvement plans.

"In conclusion, I wanted to touch on the extraordinary events of last night." Seated at the head of the time-worn but sturdy oak table, Paulina continued. "From start to finish, we were amazing. Our emergency dinner service was a textbook example of how to effectively work together, with everyone pitching in, to create a great outcome. Our guests are still talking about that wonderful, fly-by-the-seat –of-your-pants meal Graham Forrester delivered."

Paulina eyed each of the meeting participants. Ariana sat next to her. Next was Lizzie, then Bertie, along with a handful of housekeeping staff who had braved the storm's remnant winds and cresting drifts. Snow tapered, coming down more like sparkle dust rather than the ardent, more powerful downfall of the past few days.

Rising from her seat at the head of the conference table, Paulina paced. "Toward that end, I have an idea to propose, an idea that came to life after watching, and participating in, the dinner service."

"Which is?" Lizzie posed her question then sipped from a dainty, flowered tea cup of porcelain—a hand-painted antique handed down from her grandmother. The aroma of chamomile spiced by lemon drifted Lydia's way, causing her to long for a cup. A matriarch in her sixties, Lizzie sported short silver hair and a rounded frame that spoke of a life spent cushioning and comforting others.

"I'm in complete agreement, Paulina." Ari stood and addressed the inn's lead advisors. "We need a chef. As we complete and polish our present restorations, I think it's unilaterally agreed that we should amplify our resort-style offerings to win over new guests—tourists—and even re-court the locals. Returning a full-service restaurant to Christmas Inn rather than the three days a week currently in place would mark yet another important step forward. That said, I think Graham Forrester's talents fit the requirements perfectly."

"That sounds wonderful, Ari, but could we afford him?" Lizzie set her cup down with a subtle clatter. The sound drew Lydia's attention, forced her to blink and consider the offer under debate. The initiative was bold, one she had nearly broached with Graham the night before. Hiring Graham was a terrific idea, no question—an answer to prayers both professional and personal as far as Lydia was concerned.

But there was no way a man like Graham—successful, well-paid, media visible and charismatic—would agree to a fairly non-descript job as chef at Christmas Inn. The facility was just starting to find its footing again after years of unintentional neglect, after seasons of wear and tear that had, for a number of reasons, gone unchecked.

"He has an engaging style, both as a chef and as a person. I'm impressed." Lydia chimed in, and spoke from the heart.

"True. And he's a far cry from our last chef." Lizzie made a face. "David Lewiston was a diva with no chops to back up his flamboyant, arrogant attitude."

"My point exactly." Paulina nodded emphatically. "I want your approval to make Graham an offer. Today, if possible. He may turn me down flat, but I've received approval from the Christmas family for an impressive package."

Ari spoke next. "I'm behind this proposal completely, and made that clear to the board of my father's firm. Besides, we'll never know if we don't ask, right?" She shrugged broadly, and Lydia realized anew how powerful a businesswoman Ariana had become. She assumed the care of Christmas Inn in ways that made Lydia proud.

Paulina launched into the details of a proposed salary package that made Lydia blanch a bit from a cost perspective. It was definitely a highest-and-best offer, but there would be no needless back and forth. All or nothing. The gamble versus the payoff.

And just last night Graham had told her, right before that magical midnight kiss, that he felt so electrified, and happy. He had used the word happy. That had to count for something, right? Fulfillment versus material success? Maybe this offer was just what he needed to spark that creative drive and quest.

She nibbled on her lower lip, staring blankly at the glossy wooden tabletop, dimly aware of her surroundings, the meeting at hand. How had Graham's presence come to affect her so deeply, and so quickly? What kind of fast-moving train had taken custody of her heart and sent it hurtling forward? She drifted into a memory of their kiss, of chapel bells drifting through the air, chiming the hour of midnight, of Graham's lips soft and expert against hers, eliciting a thrumming warmth, a dizzying fall…

Was his arrival in Hope Creek, both personally and professionally, built on some mysterious form of destiny?

"Lydia?"

Ari's slightly raised voice broke through. Lydia shook to alert and cleared her throat. Guilt zapped her nerve endings. "I'm so sorry—I drifted. What were you saying?"

"We wanted to know your thoughts about the offer."

She couldn't remember a thing about the discussion, so again, she simply spoke from the heart. "I don't have much to add in the way of business-plan analysis. I leave that to Paulina, and you. All I know is gut instinct tells me he'd be worth every penny."

At the conclusion of the meeting, Lydia slouched, feigned study of her scribble-filled note pad. She kept to herself while Ariana gathered her itinerary and a small stash of folders then followed the model-perfect Christmas heiress from the conference room to the general office of Christmas Inn.

At last, Ari heaved a sigh and cast Lydia a look rife with exasperation. "Talk to me. You were miles away from the meeting today. Care to share any deets with me?"

"No, not really." Especially since her nerves endings sang with raw, edgy heat and her emotions were muddled. Seriously. What was going on here? What was she thinking? Graham? Romance? Long-term commitment?

After no more than three days of knowing each other?

"It's OK, Lydia. I don't need a roadmap. Your face and your actions tell me everything I need to know."

Ariana snickered, gliding across the threshold of the main

office. She clicked the door closed without further comment or even a backward glance. At that moment, right when Lydia was ready to shut out the world and resume her IT tasks, she caught sight of Graham. He trotted down the curving stairwell, smile spreading when their gazes connected. She couldn't look away— furthermore, she didn't even want to try—even when a rogue thought pushed against attraction.

Was this man an answer to prayer...or looming heartbreak?

**** 

Graham crossed through the lobby and headed straight to reception where Paulina chatted with a guest. When his turn came, he stepped forward and propped his elbows on the front desk, leaning forward so he could see Lydia better. As usual, she crafted techno-speak into her computer, most likely crafting mega-doses of web magic. Following a mind-clearing blink, he exchanged pleasantries with Paulina then cut straight to the point. "I was thinking, if you're interested in the help, I'd be happy to return to the kitchen for you, maybe see if we have enough supplies on hand to put together a light lunch service in a couple of hours."

Paulina's business-like demeanor evaporated when she let out a delighted coo, but it was Lydia's reaction Graham tracked most closely. Her focus slid away from the dual screens she had been studying and her gaze swung his way. When she pushed back from her desk, Graham took in the supple, teasing arch of her brow, the grin that quirked her lips. His sense of vindication skyrocketed. He had won her interest, and that was more than enough to make his pulse pound.

"Mr. Forrester." Lydia sashayed to the front desk. "Are you a glutton for punishment?"

"Hey, c'mon. Be fair. Last night was fun, not punishment. How about it, sous chef? Can I count on you to spare me a few hours?"

Lydia pursed those delectable lips, narrowed her eyes in speculation. "I suppose I could be enticed."

He curved his lips into a deliberately wolfish grin. "I was hoping."

All sassy interplay aside, Graham wanted to tell her about the offer from Geoff. Sharing his old friend's proposition with Lydia would make it feel more real. Perhaps working through emotions, and details would help him figure out what should come next in his life. Just like last night.

During that world-rocking kiss…

"Mr. Forrester, I'd like to speak with you at some point this afternoon, if that's all right." That request from Paulina turned Graham's thoughts around in a hurry.

"Oh—is everything OK?"

Paulina wiggled her hands back and forth in dismissal. "Couldn't be better, and no worrying. People are getting their feet back under them following the storm. I'd just like to discuss a few things with you before you leave."

"Fair enough. I'm pretty sure I'll be here until tomorrow. Because of the nasty weather and messed up delivery schedules, the replacement car part hasn't been delivered to the repair shop yet."

"And I appreciate your time. For now, though, don't think a thing of it. Work out the food details with Lydia here and if you're going to be at work in the kitchen, I'll just come find you. Thanks again for all you're doing, Graham. You're an absolute natural in the kitchen, and a real good man to boot."

"I appreciate the compliments but I enjoyed helping out. All inconvenience and storm-drama aside, I'm lucky I landed here."

That spicy, leading end-note he delivered straight to Lydia, embracing the now familiar wave of awareness that worked through the air…and his heart.

# 6

**THE INSTANT GRAHAM TOLD HER** about the purchase offer from his former boss and mentor, a sinking sensation smothered Lydia. Her stomach took a nosedive and crash-landed on the floor somewhere near her feet.

"What a great opportunity." She worked hard not to choke on her words.

Standing at his side in the kitchen where they used the prep counter to build lunch plates, Lydia buttered sesame rolls and set them in the toaster oven. She busied herself, wanting desperately to infuse her encouragement with as much joy as possible. The opportunity Graham described *was* great. He was being awarded a chance to re-spread his wings as a chef. How could she not rejoice?

All the same, she couldn't meet his eyes. She didn't want to absorb the further blow of the enthusiasm, the joy she knew she'd find in their depths. Given this turn of events, there was no chance whatsoever Ariana's offer would be accepted. No way could Graham refuse a chance to run his own restaurant.

"It's an established bistro, and Atlanta is about as vibrant and inviting a city as can be imagined. Every foodie like me dreams of coming into an opportunity like this." Graham talked while he sliced ham. Finished, he reached around Lydia to grab a brick of mild cheddar which he unwrapped and prepared to slice as well.

Wordless, mood flat, Lydia nabbed the mayo and mustard from the fridge, grateful for the blast of cold air that took the hot sting from her cheeks and eyes—if only for a few seconds.

"Could you please grab me some lettuce as well?"

"Sure. There's not much."

"No problem. We'll be spare with it and make do."

His attitude was so 'up'—so rejuvenated. Lydia returned to building sandwiches, still avoiding his eyes, but she kept the mask of her features as bright as possible. And, oh, was it tough. She wanted to be happy for him. She *was* happy for him—but still, she wanted to wither.

"Hey, you OK?"

"Yeah, sure. I'm fine." Lydia winced. So much for being a poker face, but then, subterfuge had never been her strong suit.

Graham frowned. "You don't seem fine." His knife cuts went still. "Is something going on? With Paulina or something? Is that why she—"

"No, no. I don't really get involved with business decisions here at the inn—"

"Business decisions?"

Lydia winced, yet again. She had spoken without forethought, or a filter. "No, no. Not business. Not, well…I mean, if Paulina wants to talk to you, and makes it seem official, it just makes me wonder if it has something to do with the inn. Kind of my default reaction with regard to the running of this place. Over the last several months she and Ari have had a lot to deal with—Lizzie's illness and recovery, the restoration, the process of reasserting Christmas Inn's position as a preeminent resort."

She knew she babbled, but added a smile to the words then went on to distract them both with details pertaining to the luncheon service to come. In tandem they polished off the meal service and prepared to serve twenty guests a deli-style lunch. All the while, Lydia struggled and stewed. Paulina. Graham. *The offer*. Paulina had no idea what was about to happen with regard to the upcoming meeting and her plan to make Graham the head chef at Christmas Inn. Furthermore, Lydia could do nothing to prepare her.

He was leaving. A hot sting built in Lydia's eyes once more, but she blinked the tears away—hard—resolved to squelch this ridiculous infatuation, attraction or whatever else it might be called. After all, these unexpected, tumultuous emotions were centered on a man she barely even knew.

Hours later, matters turned worse when Christmas Inn received a visit from Tom Sanders, chief mechanic at the town repair shop. He strode to the front desk where Paulina waited as usual. Tom whistled while he dusted snow from the surface of his puffy goose down jacket. "Morning, Miss Paulina. I'm looking for Graham Forrester. Dropped him off here a few nights back. I believe he's still registered as a guest."

Lydia's ears perked and tingled. Web updates stalled when her fingers went still on the keyboard and she focused on the conversation.

"Hello, Tom. Yes, indeed. Do you have good news about his car?"

"I do at that. Received the part at my house this morning. Stopping here was easy enough since it's right on the way to the shop. I just wanted to tell him personally that his car'll be back in shape no later than tomorrow morning. Snow caused some delivery delays, o'course."

"To be expected. Lord, bless us. Have you ever seen a blizzard like this?"

"No, ma'am, and neither have my folks and grand folks. Nasty stuff."

"Want me to page him, or—"

"No, ma'am, don't bother him, but I'd be grateful if you passed along the update."

Lydia's muscles went stiff. Good news…that was a point for debate as far as she was concerned. She felt a sudden and evil itch to somehow break into Sanders Repair later today, swipe the replacement part and dump it in the nearest trash bin. Anything to keep Graham in town a little while longer. Just long enough for the simple joy and beauty of Hope Creek to take root in his heart and soothe away some of those rough edges he had been battling.

Just long enough to give their feelings a chance to be explored.

She tried to refocus on work, but failed abysmally. She couldn't concentrate, didn't even want to give present IT issues a second thought. All she wanted to know for sure was what would come next—for Graham, and for her.

\*\*\*\*

Suddenly, Graham's world had turned upside down.

All it took was the presentation of maybe a half-dozen or so pieces of paper, tucked into a neatly labeled manila folder placed innocuously upon the desk before him. Seated across from him, behind that desk in the office at Christmas Inn, Paulina watched him, waiting in a silence that built to awkward with each resounding tick of the nearby wall clock.

"I'm sure this is a surprise to you, Graham. To be honest, this whole offer, this scenario of bringing our kitchen back to life, comes as a surprise to me as well." Her gentle laughter rang and she gestured wide, encompassing the folder, the offer letter and contract spread between them. "I'm no less than confident, though. You'd be a fantastic addition to our staff, and you'd probably still be able to maintain your work with the newspaper, if you'd like. The television segments you're doing now are more problematic due to logistics, and timing, so that would probably come to an end if you accepted the position, but—"

"Ms. Kovacs—Paulina—this package is incredibly generous. I'm honored by this show of…of…faith, and confidence in my work. That means a lot to me."

She leaned back, brows lifting. "Stop right there, OK? Do me a favor and don't even go into the 'but' that I hear coming at me like the bill for snow removal that's headed my way in, oh, maybe another hour or two."

True enough. Beyond the window that framed the outside area behind Paulina, Graham spied a large, yellow utility truck, cab lights flashing like strobes while the vehicle crunched and scraped a path through the split service street leading to the inn. While he watched the truck execute a smooth turn into the driveway and continue to blast its way through a daunting level of snow removal, Graham sighed.

What was he supposed to do?

This offer in no way competed with laying claim to his own bistro in a top market like Atlanta. But Geoff's offer in no way competed with a call to his heart, and his spirit, to slow down, to savor life.

To love.

It was like he was being offered two different lives, and he needed to choose the one that would fit him best.

If only he knew which life that would be...

"Timing, they say, is everything."

Paulina's chair squeaked when she leaned forward and propped her forearms against the desk. "What do you mean?"

"I received a call last night from a man I worked for when I first graduated culinary school. He offered me ownership of the bistro he owns, the one I basically grew up in as a chef."

Silence fell between them once more. Paulina's shoulders sagged, but still she smiled, albeit with a measure of easy-to-read sadness and resignation. "You deserve it, Graham. Congratulations."

If only he could accept the salutation with a clean and eager heart...

He stood, jammed his clenched fists into the pockets of his slacks while he paced.

"When my car broke down, when I crossed the threshold of Christmas Inn, I knew my life needed redirection and a renewed focus. Clarity, I guess, on where I want to be in five years...or even ten." He returned to the window, drawn to the rhythmic blink and swirl of the snow plow safety lights. The bulbs flashed in perfect tandem to the pulse of his heart, his longings. Lydia. Jacques. Life. Love. Fulfillment.

*Love.* Was he inching closer and closer to surrendering his heart? This quickly? This completely? Nothing else could explain his temptation to chuck everything he had ever wanted, everything he had ever known and expected to achieve in order to reach instead for a life spent side-by-side with Lydia.

When silence grew long, Paulina gently prodded. "And now?"

"Now it's been brought to my attention that maybe God sent me here for a purpose. To come to some important decisions and confront a crossroads in my life." Graham spun from the window, grateful for Paulina's patience as he talked things through and absorbed this new, strange reality of the soul. "I had more fun last night, making dinner for your guests, than I've had in years." He returned to the chair in front of the desk and sank into its comfort. "Lydia's the one who showed me that truth and took the time and care to explain it to me. I think she's right. Trouble is, the professional answers I most wanted to receive are being answered in the affirmative."

"But you seem hesitant."

"I am."

"Because?"

"Because while those answers appear to be affirmative and rewarding, I'm just not sure anymore. My heart is showing me a different and equally fulfilling path I might take."

Paulina's smile mixed understanding and tenderness to perfection. "Since assuming my duties as manager of Christmas Inn, I've learned to go by my heart. What does your heart say?"

"My heart sees the beauty of Hope Creek, the joy of being part of a close-knit community. My heart is telling me the answers I most wanted to receive might not be the ones that'll lead to what's best. I never expected this." Graham squeezed the bridge of his nose, leaning heavily against the back of his chair. He had never expected to encounter someone as sweet and beguiling as Lydia, either. That fact remained unspoken, but Paulina would understand the implication—he had no doubts about her powers of perception. "May I have a couple of days to think this over? Obviously I'll be leaving in the morning. I need a little time to make some decisions and put my professional life in order."

"Of course, and that's nothing less than I'd expect."

"I can't say yes, but I'm not rejecting your offer either. Not yet. I have to figure out a way to reconcile myself, know what I mean?"

"I absolutely do, Graham, and no matter what, I'll respect your answer, as well as your determination to do what's right. Thank you for giving Christmas Inn your consideration."

They concluded the business meeting with a formal handshake and a warm farewell, but Graham's stomach tilted and rolled.

What was he supposed to do next?

# *7*

**GRAHAM RESUMED HIS PRE-STORM HOLIDAY** plan by paying a quick visit home, to his childhood home in Ashville. The pair of days he spent in North Carolina were punctuated by a whirlwind of welcomes, hugs, family reunions, gifts to wrap, then place beneath the already installed Christmas tree. Glittery, colorful packages piled into shimmering rainbows of love beneath a live evergreen tree that dominated a corner of the great room in his parent's Tudor-style home. The tree was radiant with sparkle lights, with generous drapes of garland, bows and ornaments that spun, shimmering with every breath of air, every push of movement and vibration of laughter.

On the professional side he had called Geoff and set up a meeting. While lounging by a crackling fire and fingering ornaments—his favorite being a small, woolen sheep with 'Graham' engraved on its collar and the scripted words, 'Baby's First Christmas' he sounded out his sister, Becca, with regard to both the YouTube episode and the two professional offers that left his emotions embroiled and his stomach tied in knots.

"My advice?" She slid her hand through the crook of his arm and leaned her head against his shoulder, her features cast in the glow of the multi-colored lights. "Meet with Geoff, hear what he has to say, then pray. Go still. Go with what your heart tells you."

So much like Paulina's words from just days ago.

On the personal side, Graham attended church at his childhood parish, Fallwood Christian, fortified by the strength of his family. He sang hymns of praise and God's faithfulness that rang with particular power this year. He offered up prayers not just for himself but for the friends he had come to care for back in Hope Creek, at Christmas Inn. Although he had arrived there snowbound, inconvenienced and frustrated, with the exception of his childhood home in Ashville, no other place had ever felt so much like genuine welcome, like home.

Regardless, the chance to own Jacques called to him as well. Graham couldn't wait to see Geoff again to discuss details and the process that would come about should he take on the heady and challenging venture of making the time-honored restaurant his own.

The thought accompanied him while he dashed through the chaotic maze of Atlanta International at the height of the Christmas season. Soon after landing, he slid into the backseat of a yellow cab and settled in for the trip downtown. Geoff had sent him no paperwork to review. No formalities were in place, but he knew that's what today's meeting would uncover. Much like Paulina, Geoff had indicated he'd have official details in proper order today, all set for review. He'd hand over specifics during the noontime meal they were about to share at Jacques.

The cab sped north along I-75 and Graham pulled a manila folder from the inside pouch of his computer bag. The tab was marked by Paulina's neat script. A single staple kept a Christmas Inn business card securely attached to the front.

Graham settled against the leather seat, ignoring the flashing motion of cars, the billboards and increasingly tight-packed buildings. He rubbed his lower lip, studying the legalese from Christmas Inn for what had to be the dozenth time since receipt.

Two roads. Two options. Two life-changing avenues of equal worth just waiting to be explored.

*"Maybe the struggle you're facing is the reason God landed you here as you sort things through. Maybe He's using the inconvenience of car trouble and a snowstorm to slow you down and give you time to focus and plan without distractions or pressure."*

The memory of Lydia's words played through Graham's soul. She was a smart woman, full of keen insight. However, in this instance, she was wrong on both counts. No distractions? No pressures? Her advent into his life was the very definition of an unexpected and thoroughly intriguing distraction. Graham was trapped between the ideas of taking custody of Jacques versus the opportunity to live a quieter, simpler life running the kitchen at Christmas Inn. Could he find happiness there? Near Lydia? As part of her life—forever?

Pressures inched upward by the moment, because he was torn in half, drawn by the idea of two very different lives: the life he had dreamed of and imagined from the very start, and a life that was completely unexpected. He hadn't been looking for love, yet God had sent his life straight into the path of a remarkable woman—a woman who had been gifted to him on a snow-covered odyssey that he never in a million years would have taken of his own free will. From the moment of that first midnight kiss, when supposedly inoperative church bells had tolled, everything had turned. Not just from one day to the next, but from one pathway to another. An entire shift of his universe, his ambitions.

Grinding out a groan, Graham slapped the folder closed and rested his head against the back of the seat, taking in the funky aroma of the cab while around him the cityscape of Atlanta rose and crowded and jostled with activity. Skyscrapers filled space rather than rolling land, a hushed snow and a peaceful sense of quiet. Horns honked, engines revved and brakes squeaked. The shrill cadence of police sirens punctuated the air and people scurried, most of them blinded by their focus on techno devices, or urgent conversations and that mysteriously driving pulse that seemed to fuel the city.

Returning felt familiar. In a way, it felt good, too. But being back in Atlanta didn't feel quite like home. Not like…

Christmas Inn.

He slammed the mental door on that conclusion and perked when his driver swerved the cab neatly into place in front of a canopy that welcomed patrons to Jacques. His lips curved. The place looked great. Timeless. A brownstone façade lifted three stories high with the restaurant claiming the first two floors. The third housed a stylishly appointed loft-style living space for Geoff and his wife Kathleen.

Inside the restaurant, Graham moved past the hostess stand and through the main dining area. He followed the aroma of simmering vegetables, meats, and the drifting scent of fresh baked bread. In the kitchen proper, he found his friend jiggling a sauté pan that flamed and sizzled. Geoff focused on his task but barked directions to his staff as dinner preps swung into full gear.

Geoff caught sight of Graham's arrival through a pair of swinging doors and chortled. "Graham-tastic! Put on a jacket and help me."

Graham snickered and rolled his eyes at the ages-old nickname, enjoying every second of being pushed back into his role as sous chef. He swiped a white jacket from the wall peg to his left and snapped it into place, stationing himself across the stainless counter from his friend.

"What is this? An induction by fire?" Graham teased the other man, even as he accepted a batch of arugula and a knife from Geoff. He went to work dicing.

"Get used to it, there's lots more of it to come in your future. There's a mixing bowl on the lower shelf of that counter, right by your knees—"

Graham cast his mentor a wink. "I remember the setup, Geoff."

"I'm counting on that. Guess I'm just in the zone right now. The spinach over there needs to have the stems removed then it can be added to the bowl of greens."

"On it."

For an hour, they simply prepped, speaking only when work demanded it. They established a familiar rhythm that sent beautifully plated dishes to guests in the dining room. Salmon, petite filets, ahi tuna—the aromas swirled and enticed and called to the deepest reach of Graham's spirit. *Lord,* he prayed in silence, *thank You. This feels so good...*

Once the main thrust of the dinner service began to subside, they claimed a window-side table adorned by crisp, white linen cloths, matching napkins, deep blue china, sterling place settings and shimmering glassware. The city bustled by, touched by the magic of colorful Christmas decorations that adorned nearby shopfronts.

Kathleen joined them, tucking a chair next to Geoff's. They shared seared ahi tuna over a bed of wild rice accompanied by a house salad. Following a few friendly updates, she extended a stack of documents for Graham's review. *Déjà vu,* Graham thought. *Déjà vu.* An attorney would review the finer details of both offers later in the week, but it didn't take long for him to absorb the big picture. Yes, the surrender of Jacques to his care would result in a big hit to his savings. Yes, he'd have to set up formal financing. Yes, the work would be grueling, but the financials were impressive. Laying claim to an established well-respected restaurant would mean an excellent, and instant, rate of return.

Owning Jacques would be a smart investment—and a smart professional move. Why, then, did his heart feel empty?

"This…this is overwhelming. Geoff, I know I've said it before but…I'm honored. Seeing the offer laid out in black and white makes everything real. What you've outlined, what we've talked about, is an answer to the questions, the prayers I've been sending out for months now."

"So why do you sound like you're trying to convince yourself?"

"Because you know me well. Because, in a way, that's exactly what I'm trying to do. And I shouldn't need to convince myself. Not about something like this. Running my own place? Calling the shots? Being the one in control? Exploring food again, hands-on? That's all I've ever wanted."

Geoff eyed him cautiously in the pregnant pause that followed. "I'm waiting."

Graham wadded the crisp linen napkin spread across his lap, clenching the fabric in his fist, attempting to release what tension he could. "Now it feels like ego."

"Ego?"

"Yeah. Ego. Part of why this opportunity appeals to me so much is that it would prove the jerk who shot me down on air and maligned my whole way of life was wrong. This opportunity would show the world I'm a chef, first and foremost."

"You're talking about that guy from the cook-off."

"Yeah."

Geoff scoffed and muttered a mild curse. "Talk about ego. That guy had ego, and arrogance, unmeasurable by human standards. Seriously. What a pompous—"

He laughed, appreciating the loyalty and support of his friend. "All of that is very true, but he got to me. His smack-down made me think about my life, and that's not a bad thing. You said it yourself when we talked last week. It's time for me to break away from being a mouthpiece, a media presence, and earn my chops again."

As though in answer to that very statement, Geoff opened his arms wide. The gesture enveloped the filling tables, the chink of dinnerware, the constant rolling vibration and hum of conversations and laughter.

Kathleen leaned forward, visibly encouraging Graham as well. "So do it!"

"I know, it's all right here, but I found all of that, and more, in Hope Creek, at a resort that's on its way to being amazing. In ways both personal and professional, the time I spent stranded there changed me. What I experienced at Christmas Inn brought me back to who I truly want to be, and what I enjoy the most—not just as a chef, but as a man, as a person with life and a purpose beyond the kitchen."

Silence held sway. Geoff and Kathleen exchanged a long look before Geoff asked the million dollar question. "Are you saying I better start looking elsewhere for a new owner-operator?"

All Graham could see in his mind's eye and in his heart was Lydia. "Yes. I am. But I'm grateful to you both. More grateful than I can ever say."

# 8

**SNOW RETURNED TO HOPE CREEK.** Not to the extremes of 'The Great Storm' from a couple weeks ago, of course. All the same, the new fall of crystal flakes transported Lydia to that moment in time when she and Graham shared a mystical kiss beneath a snow-ridden sky. Today's Christmas Eve snow was more like a soft, sporadic sifting accompanied by stillness—then sudden gusts of wind.

One such jolt sent wet snow pinging and tinging against the stained-glass windows as she entered what she thought of now as 'the chapel of the midnight bells.' She had always loved the cross-tipped, white clapboard structure, but now it held even richer significance. Floorboards sang and creaked beneath her feet, giving voice to the history, the lives this chapel had touched and nurtured.

Inn guests and Hope Creek locals filed in for the Christmas family's traditional prayer service. Family, friends and inn employees filled the aged, wooden pews. Lydia peeled off her coat and chose a spot toward the front. She extended a padded kneeler and sank into prayers so deep, so encompassing and filling the session transported her far from the prayers and praise just a few minutes from beginning.

Just as she finished and lifted her head, a gentle hand came to rest on her shoulder. "May I join you?"

*Graham?* Her eyes went wide and she froze, staring ahead at the small but ornate altar, unable to turn toward him right away, to allow herself to believe or to hope. But suddenly the freeze thawed and a tremble set in. She looked up, into the eyes that haunted her every dream. "Of course. Please."

He claimed the spot next to her. In his eyes lived such love, such reciprocal hope, and something even deeper, even more intriguing. Peace-filled contentment.

"I've missed you," he whispered. He slid close, wrapping an arm around her shoulders, and rested his forehead against hers.

Lydia's heart pounded, accelerating into a rocket pace. "I've missed you, too. So very much."

Only a handful of days had passed since Graham's leaving, but his absence had hit her hard. During that time, she had buried herself in work, trying to distance herself from the idea of being struck by love's lightning flash. What a dangerous and foolhardy idea. But the force of her conviction to leave Graham behind only left her sullen, uncharacteristically quiet and introverted. Lydia realized all these facts, so did her family and friends, yet she couldn't seem to budge. Thoughts of him, empty longings and wishes, spun through her head, leaving her mind in a fog.

Lydia's mom claimed the pew behind them. Lydia's attention fell on her for an instant as her mother's brows lifted high and a spark of hopeful interest lit her eyes. Lydia squelched an affectionate, tolerant laugh. Evidently mom's optimism with regard to Lydia and romance sprang eternal. Bless her heart.

"Can I speak with you outside for a moment, before service starts?"

Graham's request preempted all the distractions, all the comings and goings of the building crowd. Lydia nodded and they stood in unison. She grabbed her coat and slipped it on. Graham captured her hand in an easy swing as he escorted her down the main aisle of the chapel and led the way past double wood doors flung open to welcome the evening's worshipers.

Like a stroke of the Spirit, a curving brush of wind-song moved through the trees and curled around them as they stepped outside. Snowfall had ceased for the moment, but sparkling white powder danced through the air. A few of the sprinkles landed on Lydia's cheeks. When her hair tossed, Graham stroked back the curls and smiled into her eyes.

"You came back," she murmured, at a loss for further

elaboration.

"Unfortunately, only for today. I'm headed back to Ashville first thing in the morning for Christmas with my family. I'm leaving at stupid-o'clock in the morning to be with them, but I had to see you first."

Lydia nodded, trying to understand, her throat tight. "Why's that?"

"Because...well, for one thing, I wanted you to be the first to see this."

From an inside chest pocket of his down jacket, Graham removed a folded sheaf of papers stapled neatly in the upper left corner. He handed the pages to Lydia so she could examine the offering.

Her breath caught when she read the top lines of the Christmas Inn employment offer. "Graham?" She flipped to the back, afraid to even dream that she'd find his signature, but sure enough, the contract was executed on his side, emblazoned by strong, bold brushstrokes toward the future.

Lydia couldn't restrain a happy exclamation. She launched into his arms and Graham laughed, spinning her in a delicious, dizzying circle. "I'm taking it on, Lydia. I believe in Christmas Inn. I believe in you." After a breath-stealing pause, he concluded. "I believe in us. In what we already are, and what we can come to be. I hope you do, too."

A happy shout later, Lydia squeezed him tight all over again. "I do, Graham. Believe me, I do!"

He paused, held her hands in his. Deliberate and visibly nervous, he took a breath. "Will you come back with me? To Ashville? For Christmas? I want you to meet my parents, my sister and family."

The trembles hit again, and they had nothing whatever to do with chilly weather. Her soul came alive. "I'd love to, Graham. I'd be honored to share the day with them...and with you."

Graham bent close, capturing her lips in a kiss as masterful and confident as it was warm and silky soft. Lydia's pleasured sigh broke the stillness an instant before a strong push of wind wrapped around them like loving arms.

High above, in the shelter of a weathered but sturdy steeple, bells began to chime, softly at first, then building before they faded to silence once more.

Graham broke free of their kiss and Lydia joined him in listening to the melody and looking up...way up...at the steeple.

"Gotta be the wind. The wind is doing that, right?"

Graham's words prompted Lydia to smile, and stroke his cheek. She kissed him once more, with all her heart and with all the joy that consumed her. "Maybe. But let's make sure we never forget."

"Forget what?"

"That God is in the wind..."

# ~ *About Marianne* ~

**MARIANNE EVANS** is an award-winning author of Christian romance and fiction. Her hope is to spread the faith-affirming message of God's love through the stories He prompts her to create.

Readers laude her works as: "Riveting," "Realistic and true to heart," "Compelling." Her Christian fiction debut, *Devotion*, earned the prestigious Bookseller's Best Award as well as the Heart of Excellence Award. Hearts Communion earned a win for Best Romance from the Christian Small Publishers Association. She is also a two-time recipient of the Selah Award for her books *Then & Now* and *Finding Home* as well as a three-time recipient of the International Digital Award for her books *By Appointment Only*, *Maria's Angel* and *Operation Breathless*.

Marianne is a lifelong resident of Michigan and an active member of Romance Writers of America, most notably the Greater Detroit Chapter where she served two terms as President. Marianne loves to hear from readers, so connect with her at:

MarianneEvans.com
seriouslywrite.blogspot.com/
twitter.com/MarEvansAuthor
facebook.com/marianneevansauthor/

# ~ More Titles by Marianne Evans ~

## Coming Soon
*The Stronghold (Fishermen of Antioch, Book 2)*
*The Journey (Fishermen of Antioch, Book 3)*
*A Long Way to Run*
*Point Zero*

## Christian Fiction Titles
*Forgiveness*
*Devotion*

## Fishermen of Antioch Series
The Return (Fishermen of Antioch, Book 1)

## Sisters in Spirit Series
*Sisters in Spirit, The Complete Anthology*
*Aileen's Song*
*Siobhan's Beat*
*Kassidy's Crescendo*
*Maeve's Symphony*

## Sal's Place Series
*Search & Rescue*
*Beautiful Music*
*By Appointment Only*
*Windfall*

**Woodland Church Series**
*Woodland Hearts, The Complete Anthology*
*Hearts Crossing*
*Hearts Surrender*
*Hearts Communion*
*Hearts Key*
*A Face in the Clouds*
**Christmas Titles**
*Finding Home*
*Snowflake Kisses*
*Christmas at Tiffany's*
*Bella Natale!*
*Love at Christmas Inn, Collection I*
*Love at Christmas Inn, Collection II*

**Heart's Haven Collection**
*Operation Breathless*
*Maria's Angel*
*Jodie's Song*
*Nobody's Baby But Mine*

**Pure Amore Titles**
*Date Night*
*Then & Now*
*The Fairytale*

# Love at Christmas Inn

# With Bells On

# MARY MANNERS

# With Bells On

## Mary Manners

Published by Haven Group

Published in the United States of America

Contact information:
Haven Group: havengroupauthors@gmail.com
Mary Manners: sunriserun63@aol.com

*"Therefore, if you are offering your gift at the altar and there remember that your brother has something against you, leave your gift there in front of the altar. First go and be reconciled to your brother; then come and offer your gift."*
~Matthew 5:23-24, NIV~

# 1

**EMMY LANCASTER SETTLED BACK IN** the leather seat of the posh limousine her aunt Dahlia had sent to fetch her from McGhee-Tyson airport. The fuss hardly seemed necessary—a simple rental car or even a taxi would have sufficed for the short ride into Hope Creek. But Aunt Dahlia wouldn't hear of such a thing, insisting on only the best for her favorite niece. So Emmy embraced the kindness.

The next several weeks would present a flurry of activity and challenges. Emmy would take on the lead entertainer role in Aunt Dahlia's holiday show, slated to benefit a new pediatric wing at the local hospital. The week-long stretch of rehearsals, followed by a series of a dozen shows, would lead straight into Christmas.

Holiday tunes that filtered through the limo cemented the fact that Christmas was well on its way. Currently, Bing Crosby's warm bass-baritone yearned for a cheerful blanket of white. Emmy hoped for snow, too. In Hope Creek, it seemed almost mandatory at Christmas time.

"Are you there, Emmy?" Aunt Dahlia's signature, upbeat southern twang came through the cell phone pressed to Emmy's ear. "Are you listening?"

"Yes, I'm here." Emmy fought the urge to hum along with

Bing. She could hardly help herself. Like Aunt Dahlia, singing had proved to be her passion from the moment she realized she could use her vocal chords to string notes together. "What were you saying?"

"My driver, Louis, will take you to Christmas Inn, where I've booked a room for you on the second floor—room eight, I believe."

"Right. Room eight." Emmy filed away the information.

"You should be off the road and settled in soon."

"Yes. Traffic's not too bad tonight, and we've traveled the roads in record time, thank goodness. I think we're almost there." Emmy peered out the window as snowflakes drifted through the air to kiss the polished car. Along the parkway, Christmas lights twinkled across a black-velvet canvas of sky. Their merry dance of illumination bolstered Emmy's mood as well as her ability to fight off the ache that had pitched a tent along the small of her back. The flight from California, with its layovers and unexpected delays, had proven grueling and had stolen Emmy's energy while putting her behind schedule a solid six hours. "I'm sorry I missed rehearsal this afternoon."

"It couldn't be helped, but we'll get an early start in the morning and go until we can't dance another step or sing another note."

"Now, auntie…you know I never grow weary of singing. The dancing, though, is another story altogether." In reality, Emmy sometimes felt as if she had two left feet. She'd worked tirelessly through a decade of ballet and jazz classes to counteract the curse. "I'll do my best, though."

"You always do, my dear. I'm not a bit worried about your part in the show. But Harvey, on the other hand…" Aunt Dahlia's voice trailed off. "Well, let's just say that the theater is closed to the public—no shows on Mondays and Tuesdays this week—so we'll have plenty of time to put things in order."

"I'll wear my dancing shoes and bring along a supply of potato chips and juice." Salt was good for strained vocal chords, a trick

Emmy had learned early-on from Aunt Dahlia. "I'll be ready. I've heard Harvey is a fine dancer, and I was able to tell through the demo clip you sent that our voices blend nicely. A bit of practice together should make the harmony shine. You mentioned that he's been working hard on the show's choreography, so I'll simply follow his lead and—"

"Emmy, dear...about Harvey..." Aunt Dahlia cleared her throat and, after a lengthy pause, continued in an uncharacteristic monotone. "There's been a slight change in plans due to—"

"Oh, Aunt Dahlia..." Emmy interrupted as the limo crested a slight hill and Christmas Inn came into view along a backdrop of ethereal, moonlit mountains. "Oh, oh, *oh*...it's gorgeous!"

"What's gorgeous, honey?"

"The inn...oh, the inn!" Emmy leaned forward, craning her head to peer through the windshield as the wipers worked to clear flecks of snow. "It's breathtaking...so much more majestic with holiday cheer than I remember."

Grand turrets rose three stories high, flanking an expanse of brick and glass that shimmered against the night sky like magical starlight. A candelabra glowed from each window, as if guiding her home. The grounds along the entranceway seemed to dance beneath a whisper of shimmering snow. She'd always loved spending time here when she was in high school and later college, before she left for the West Coast. Exploring the undulating gardens for signs of the changing seasons had been an activity she'd treasured.

More often than not Jayson had been at her side. The memory gnawed at her. Where was he now?

"Yes," Aunt Dahlia's voice drew Emmy back. "The Christmas family has kicked renovation plans into high gear, working to restore the family inn to its legendary state of grandeur. I knew you would be enchanted by the progress, Emmy, that's why I chose to book a room there for you. That, and—"

"We're pulling into the drive now, Auntie." Emmy's gaze flitted from the stately turrets to the sweeping, circular drive as she drank in captivating details of illumination. Suddenly surging with Christmas cheer, she felt the urge to belt out the refrains of *Jingle Bell Rock* and *Silver Bells* all rolled into one. "Oh, oh, *oh!*"

"Yes, the inn is lovely," Aunt Dahlia affirmed once again. "But, Emmy, dear, focus for just one moment. I have something to tell you about tomorrow…about the show."

"Whatever it is, Auntie…whatever you need, I'm there for you. Yes." Emmy gathered her purse, bobbling the cellphone as she slipped the strap over one shoulder. She recovered quickly and continued. "I know how important the hospital project is to you, as well as seeing to the children's needs. Just share the details with me in the morning. I'll be there with bells on, ready to kick up my heels and belt out a tune or two."

"I know you will, dear, and I appreciate your generosity, but give me just a moment before you flit away again. This is important—"

Not to be deterred, Emmy reached for the overnight bag she'd dropped on the floorboard and prepared for a quick exit. "You mentioned earlier that Louis is going to pick me up tomorrow morning in the limo, right?"

"Yes. At eight o'clock sharp. But about the rehearsal—"

"Eight o'clock sharp." Breathless with excitement, Emmy was unable to draw her gaze from the rooftop where a pair of ethereal angels welcomed visitors with trumpets formed of mesmerizing, golden lights. "Yes, right. Louis, eight o'clock…long rehearsal." Snow crunched beneath the vehicle's tires as it slowed at the entranceway to the inn. Emmy released her seatbelt and tugged at the door latch. She knew Louis would see to her luggage. "I have to go, Aunt Dahlia. I can't wait to see the inside of this place again. It's incredible, amazing… simply gorgeous."

"If you must…go explore, then, while you still have a bit of energy left." Aunt Dahlia sighed, seeming resigned to the fact that Emmy refused to be lassoed into further conversation. "Get a good night's sleep, dear. You'll need it."

"Thanks, Auntie, for booking the room. I just know that I'm

going to love it here, to the moon and back."

"Yes, we'll see."

"I promise I will get some sleep as soon as I've checked things out a bit. I wonder if the inside is as grand as I remember. And the chapel, with its wondrous bells…"

*Ah, the chapel…the bells…how long since they'd rung to signify love…?*

Emmy had shared her first kiss on the chapel steps with Jayson Taylor, and they'd heard those bells toll at the affection. And though legend nodded toward the belief that the bells rang only when true love was found, they'd laughed and chalked it up to a breeze through the steeple…nothing more. That was eons ago, when she was young and naïve. She'd believed teenage love could last forever, and had thought Jayson did, as well. Emmy brushed away the memory and the hurt that filtered in. She would not allow such thoughts to dampen her joyful mood.

"I've heard the kitchen is undergoing some renovations," Aunt Dahlia informed her. "But if you ask, I am sure Ari Christmas or her chef will see that you get something to eat. You'll need your strength in the days ahead."

"I'll check on that." In fact, Emmy's stomach voiced a not-so-delicate growl. She'd taken her last meal before noon.

"Of course you will. Happy exploring, my dear. I'll see you in the morning. " Aunt Dahlia chuckled softly, and then added a cryptic, final statement. "You'll want to talk with me more then, I'm sure."

# 2

JAYSON TAYLOR TOSSED THE EXTRA length of a two-by-four aside and brushed sawdust from his hands, then retrieved a fistful of nails from the tool belt slung low across his hips. With each swing of the hammer, he muttered a mantra.

"What…why…how do I get myself into these fixes?"

"You're gonna lose a thumb that way, boss." Manny Lawson glanced up from the opposite side of the set platform they were constructing for Dahlia Brewster's upcoming charity Christmas show. The term Manny used, *boss*, was more of a tongue-in-cheek, playful jab than anything else, because he and Jayson had been friends since their college days. "Your agreement with Miss Dahlia is a done deal. Let it go."

"I'm an idiot."

"If you say so."

"And a glutton for punishment."

"OK." Manny's eyebrows disappeared beneath a frame of shaggy black hair, but his wide brown eyes held a hint of concern. "So your point is…?"

"I'll never—"

"Never say never, boss."

"Is there an echo in here?" Jayson drove the final nail with more force than necessary, sinking the two-inch length of metal with a single blow.

"No." Manny rose to stretch kinks from his back. "Sorry, boss, but—"

"Hit the pause button on the play-by-play analysis, Manny." Jayson grimaced. "I know what a fix I'm in. I'm just…venting a little."

"Sure, boss. Like a teakettle about to blow."

"Thanks for that visual." Jayson drew a deep breath as he rubbed his throbbing temples. He had hired Manny onto the Dahlia Brewster Family Theater crew two seasons ago, and figured it was one of the best decisions he'd ever made. But sometimes Manny allowed his tongue to wag ahead of his brain. This appeared to be one of those times. "I get the picture. I'll tone it down a bit. Just—"

"Say no more." Manny mimed a locking motion across his lips, tossed the imaginary key over one shoulder. "I'm done with the color commentary—for now. We've got work to do, and not a whole lot of time."

"You've got that right. The cast will be arriving soon...at least part of the cast." He tried not to think about Emmy, or the fact that they'd be working side-by-side for the better part of the next several weeks. He wasn't sure how *that* was going to go over. The last time he'd seen her—walking away from him with her chin lifted to the air and tears streaming down her cheeks—had been more than seven years ago.

*Women...there's just no understanding them. Especially when it comes to Emmy.*

"So, what do you think, boss?" Manny asked as he yanked a wadded bandana from his back pocket and used it to wiped beads of sweat from his forehead. "What's next on the construction agenda?"

"Why don't you suit up before the others arrive, and start sandblasting the section of that old set that we're going to merge with this one? Hopefully we'll have everything ready to paint by morning." Jayson tested the blaster, and Max, the mastiff mix he'd rescued from the animal shelter nine years ago, let out a low whine as the machine roared. The animal crouched low to the floor and buried his head in his paws.

"I don't think your sidekick is on board with the plan," Manny noted.

"Sorry, boy." Jayson gave the mutt a pat and then offered him the biscuit he'd thought to stuff into one pocket before he left for the theater. Usually Max hung out in the fenced back yard of the rental house they'd called home for the past two years, chasing squirrels and lazing beneath a massive weeping willow. But Jayson had recently purchased a parcel of property in Hope Creek where he'd build a permanent home. He planned to break ground as soon as the holidays closed and the weather moderated, so he'd decided not to renew the year-long lease on the rental house and instead signed a monthly rental for the cottage at Christmas Inn. He loved the inn with its picturesque charm, but no fence surrounded the cottage grounds. Max couldn't be left inside all day, or even alone outside to roam with guests. "I know I've dragged you into this mess, and that you're tired, too."

If Jayson lived to be a hundred, he'd never understand just *why* and exactly *how* he'd let Dahlia Brewster talk him into co-starring in this year's charity Christmas show. Sure, Harvey Wallace had been slated with the honors before he broke his ankle while mapping out the choreography. And sure, Jayson had experience as a keynote speaker at a few charity events in Hope Creek and surrounding areas, and he'd also once co-starred with Emmy Lancaster in the annual musical when they were seniors at Hope Creek High...and dating. But that had been years ago, long before Emmy chased her big screen dreams clear to California while Jayson's design and construction days took root. Now, Jayson was much more comfortable working *behind* the scenes instead of *in* them.

He tossed a water bottle to Manny, then drew a long swig from his own.

"I don't know why you're so chipper this morning, Lawson." He swiped a hand across his mouth. "You know this deal with Dahlia will mean a much larger workload for you over the next several weeks. You'll have to handle the bulk of the set construction for the Christmas show yourself, and as you've so emphatically noted, there's hardly time to waste."

"You've been a great teacher. I can manage it, Jay." Manny nodded over the rim of the bottle, his dark eyes partially obscured by the safety glasses he'd donned in preparation for a bout of sandblasting. "No worries about me. You've got enough on your plate with songs to learn and dance moves to conquer. I know it's going to be a tough couple of weeks, but you're doing the right thing helping Miss Dahlia."

"You're right." Dahlia Brewster had been more than a friend to Jayson and his parents for as long as he could remember, and she'd always treated Jayson like a favorite son. When a car accident the summer following his graduation from college claimed his dad's life and left his mom severely injured, Dahlia hired Jayson as the head of set design and construction in her theater, affording him the opportunity to stay close to home. He would never forget the kindness that made it possible for him to stay near his mom's side as she regained her health. "I need to stop my bellyaching. I'll get through it."

Manny lowered his voice and leaned in conspiratorially. "Does she know?"

"Does *who* know *what*?"

"Emilee Lancaster, you big doofus. Does she know Harvey's out of the picture and that she'll be headlining Dahlia's charity show with you instead?"

The mention of Emmy's name evoked a mixture of memories like a flavorful gumbo with a few sour bites. He'd shared his heart with her, and for a while things had been good…better than good. He and Emmy had been downright magical together. At least he thought they were. But she must have thought differently, because she'd gotten this wild hair to go chasing a dream of bright lights and big cities. Who was Jayson to stand in her way when she announced she was leaving for Hollywood, convinced she'd make it big in movies just like her Aunt Dahlia had in the music industry?

He'd loved her, and knew it would do neither of them any good to try to hold on too tight, so he'd watched her go with a heavy heart and a parting vow. "If you ever need me, Emmy, I'll be here for you, with bells on."

Seven long years later, and she hadn't returned. She obviously didn't need—or want—him. It was time to face facts, put those bells away, and move on.

Or was it? Could it be that Emmy's decision to return this Christmas meant something more than simply helping with the show? Could there be another plan in the works, a bigger plan than Jayson might imagine?

He forced away the thought and came back down to earth as he considered Manny's question.

"Yes. I mean, I think so. Dahlia was supposed to tell her last night." He shook his head as fingers of uneasiness stroked his spine. "At least, I hope Emmy knows. If she doesn't, well...the Big Man Upstairs better help us all through the upcoming weeks of rehearsals and shows."

"That bad, huh?"

"We didn't exactly part on good terms. Maybe it was her fault, maybe it was mine."

"Or maybe you both carry a bit of regret?"

"I don't think she sees it that way." Jayson shrugged, and dread continued to tug at him. "I haven't spoken to her in ages, so there's no telling. I'm not even sure Dahlia told her I'm working on the set design for the show, let alone costarring."

"That said, can you handle Miss Lancaster?" Manny lowered his voice and leaned in. "I hear she can be a little...difficult."

"Don't believe everything you hear, Lawson." Jayson tossed the hammer aside, not sure why he felt the need to defend Emmy. After all, *she'd* left Hope Creek and abandoned their relationship, not him. But his mood proved foul, and he couldn't seem to shake the veil of gloom.

With little more than a cat nap the night before, he'd arrived at the theater early, before the sun shook off the evening stars, pulling double duty to get at least the largest part of work on the set underway before the cast arrived for rehearsal. The construction crew was in a time crunch, and Jayson's completion schedule hadn't accounted for memorizing scripts and dance numbers.

And then there was Emmy, and this change of plans thrown into the mix. He couldn't help thinking the entire venture might be a recipe for disaster.

But that didn't mean he could stand by and let anyone badmouth Emmy. "And you know better than to repeat gossip just because it crosses your path."

"Whoa. Alright, man. I get your drift." Manny took up the sandblaster, and for a moment all other sound was drowned out by the screech of air hitting wood and Max's accompanying whine. Poor guy, he'd rather be back at the cottage, chasing bluebirds or napping on the porch. But Jayson hadn't felt comfortable leaving him alone for so many hours while he pulled double duty here at the theater, and he knew the inn's guests wouldn't appreciate crossing paths with the mastiff. Max looked much like a hulking beast, and until people got to know his gentle demeanor, they were more often than not leery of his massive size.

"My drift?" Jayson waited for a break in the blasting. "And what drift is that?"

"I heard about you and Emilee Lancaster." Manny punctuated the statement with a saucy wink.

"What, exactly, did you hear?"

"Oh, no...I'm not repeating gossip, boss, per your orders." Manny grinned as if he'd just snatched the last triple-chocolate brownie from its plate. "But you're not over the lovely lady yet, are you?"

"Oh, I'm way over her." Jayson nodded, his teeth clenched tight as a vice because his heart remained in such conflict with the verbiage. Even so, he added, "That particular ship sailed a long time ago."

"Well, I think said ship just returned to port." Manny glanced to his left as he lowered the blaster to the ground and lifted his goggles for a better view. "Because here comes Miss Emilee Lancaster now."

# 3

JAYSON GLANCED UP TO SEE Emmy striding down the carpeted aisle toward the stage front. She was all legs and waves of sun-kissed blonde hair—longer and lighter than he remembered—as she unknotted the scarf around her neck and shrugged off a snow-white winter jacket. Time had been good to her, and Jayson stood mesmerized as she closed the distance between them.

"Better draw in that tongue and close your mouth, boss, before you choke on sawdust and paint chips."

Manny's comment brought Jayson back. He rubbed his palms along the front of his jeans, brushing off the sawdust. Emmy's foot barely touched the bottom step stage right when a string of barks rang out from behind the curtain, startling them all.

"Max, is that you?" Emmy didn't miss a single beat.

"No, Max!" Jayson cautioned as a clatter ensued, the result of a stack of cut two-by-fours toppling over when the forward and back wave of a massive tail displaced them. The mastiff romped into view, accompanied by the methodic thump of his ginormous paws galloping over polished wood.

The dog barreled toward Emmy, and she held her position as if playing chicken with a freight train. Her onyx eyes danced with delight. "Oh, it *is* you, sweet thing!"

"Max, no. Down!" Jayson ordered frantically, but his warning went unheeded as the oversized canine pushed past him. He lurched into motion, rushing to catch up. "Emmy, watch out!"

"Nonsense. Max won't hurt me." Emmy dropped her purse and backpack and fell to her knees with her arms held wide. She braced herself for impact, and recovered quickly to give Max's belly a good scratch. Though the dog dwarfed her, she showed not even an ounce of fear. On the contrary, laughter bubbled up as she gazed lovingly into the mutt's eyes. "Oh, sweet Max. Can I have a hug?"

Immediately, the mastiff placed his front paws atop each of Emmy's shoulders and pressed his massive jowl to her cheek in an impossibly gentle show of affection. His tail thumped wildly, strong enough to rattle the floor.

"Oh, you remember after all these years," Emmy murmured. She leaned in close to wrap her arms around the dog who quaked with unbridled excitement. Her fingertips failed to meet, so broad was his girth. "Yes, I remember you too, you big, loveable sweetheart."

Jayson shook his head as the scene unfolded, while Manny belly-laughed at his side. Just as he remembered, Emmy proved full of moxie.

"You've got your work cut out for you, boss," Manny murmured when he finally caught a breath. "She's a firecracker, for sure. I hope you're ready to sail this storm."

Jayson ignored the comment. There'd be plenty more from Manny before this show was over. He shook sawdust from his hair and stepped forward as if in a dream. Watching Emmy with Max, he felt as if time rewound to the afternoon they'd first found the dog together. Jayson had just gotten his driver's license and offered to drive Emmy home from a morning practice for the spring musical at Hope Creek High. On the way to her house, they'd passed by the animal shelter. After catching a glimpse of Max curled up near the fence of a dog run, looking as if he'd lost his only friend, Emmy'd implored Jayson to park. She'd crouched at the fence, invoking a gentle tone as she talked a blue-streak to the abandoned mutt. She'd take him home, she said, but her mother was allergic to dogs.

So, they'd left without the dog, but Emmy had tears in her eyes.

For days, she talked about Max until finally, Jayson got the go-ahead from his own folks to adopt the dog. He'd surprised Emmy by inviting her on a date, and bringing Max along to chaperone. When Emmy saw Max perched in the backseat, his head brushing the ceiling as he panted with excitement, she'd cried happy tears. It was the beginning of Jayson and Emmy's dating journey.

Who knew she would take off for the West Coast just a few short years later?

Because Jayson wanted so badly to reach out and draw her into a hug—wished she'd show the same excitement to see him that she had for Max—he jammed his hands firmly into his pockets before trusting himself to speak. The words came slowly and with a measure of hesitation. "Hey, Emmy."

She tilted her head back to gaze up at him and those dark, expressive eyes framed by long lashes nearly stole his breath. Was she glad to see him, after all?

"Hi, Jayson." A hint of a smile curved plump, glossed lips. "So this is where you hang out now. Aunt Dahlia mentioned you help construct the sets. It's good to see you. It's been a long time...too long."

"Yes, it has." He swallowed hard as he tried to force memories back into the compartment of his brain where they'd spent the past several years gathering dust, then echoed her sentiment. "Way too long."

Emmy peeled Max's paws from her shoulders and gave his head a gentle pat before rising. Her tall, slender figure brought her forehead to Jayson's chin, and he remembered how he used to like to lean in and kiss the creamy expanse of skin. The urge beckoned now, and he fought against it. He hadn't expected to feel this way...as if they hadn't spent so much as a day apart. The feelings for her remained strong, and now they rose to the surface like flotsam after a storm.

"The set looks like it's coming along." She did a slow sweep of the stage. "I like it. You were always good at visualizing set design, and then making those visions come to life."

"Thanks, but there's still so much to do." Jayson motioned to the backdrop at the rear of the stage. "We'll add a rail to that balcony. I know you're afraid of heights, so maybe it'll help you feel more secure."

"Thanks." Emmy's smile said she was touched to know he remembered. "That's really nice."

"And we still have a lot of sandblasting to do, then repainting and details..." He let the thought trail off. "Manny will handle things."

"Of course." Emmy nodded a greeting to Manny, who stood at Jayson's side. "I'm sure you make a great team. Aunt Dahlia said you're the best. So, where are the dressing rooms? I'll get ready for rehearsal, and let you both get back to work."

"The dressing rooms are that way." Jayson mouthed directions as warning bells rang through his head. Emmy didn't know yet— did she? What if—?

"Thanks. I thought I'd get an early start, since I missed rehearsal yesterday." She turned toward the seating and Jayson figured she was sizing up the audience space, imagining how the show might play out. "My flight was delayed. It was nightmarish and exhausting. I didn't think I'd ever get here."

"I heard." He could barely force the words. "You must be tired."

"A little." She gave a slight nod, and the way the light hit her chin showed off the dimple at its center...the same dip of skin Jayson used to press his lips to. Did Emmy remember those kisses? "I stayed up way too late last night exploring Christmas Inn. I'm staying there."

"You're bunking at Christmas Inn?"

"Yes. Why?"

"Never mind." Jayson shook his head, dismissing the question. Obviously, she had no idea he was using the cottage there. But she'd find out...eventually. And then—

"I headed this way early because I thought Harvey might be here, working on the choreography." Emmy searched the stage and the aisle ways, obviously hoping for a glimpse of him. "I was thinking he and I might get a jump on things, work out a few kinks before Aunt Dahlia and the others arrive."

That cemented it. Might as well let the proverbial cat—and the grand finale of fireworks that were sure to follow—out of the bag. Jayson cleared his throat and murmured, "Harvey's not here."

"Oh?" Emmy gathered her purse and slung a thin strap over one shapely shoulder. "Soon, then?"

"No. Not soon. He's not—Harvey's not—coming in today. Or tomorrow." Jayson captured her gaze and held tight, gauging her reaction as he added, "As a matter of fact, Harvey's not coming in at all."

The light left Emmy's eyes, turning them to nuggets of coal. Her voice, bright and airy a moment ago, went flat. "What do you mean, Harvey's not coming in?"

"Harvey Wallace is indefinitely incapacitated. I'll be your partner in the Christmas show." Jayson held her gaze like a vice. "We're in this together, Emmy, for better or worse...for the long haul."

****

"What?" Emmy's throat clenched and her voice refused to cooperate. She swallowed hard, working to staunch the flush of heat that washed over her. "What do you mean, *you're* my partner? You design and build sets, Jayson. That's a far cry from dancing and singing."

"I know what I do, and I also know what I'm capable of." Jayson's chin rose in a subtle challenge, and his eyes flashed hot, like the flames of a freshly-stoked fire. For a moment, Emmy was taken back to the moment she told him she was leaving Hope Creek, so many moons ago. He'd had the same look in his eyes then...as if the earth had shifted beneath him. "So does Dahlia, and she trusts me...believes in me."

"What, exactly are you insinuating?" Emmy knew how Jayson must have felt that afternoon, because she felt it now, the shifting, and there was nothing to hold onto. The realization hurt her heart. After all this time, the breakup—hurting Jayson—still hurt her. "I don't understand."

"Dahlia asked me to pick up the slack here when Harvey broke his ankle. Didn't she tell you?"

"No."

"I tried to, Emmy dear." As if stepping from a dream, Dahlia entered stage left and crossed to join them. Her signature fragrance filled the air with hints of lavender and lemon. "Last night on the phone, remember? I told you we had something important to discuss. You assured me—and I quote...'Whatever it is, whatever you need, yes.'"

"But I didn't mean..." Emmy backpedaled. Had she said that? She couldn't recall with certainty now. Everything from the evening before seemed muddled. She had been exhausted, yet the inn had called to her like an enchanted whisper, bidding her to explore. So she'd put off sleep to roam a bit. And now here stood Jayson, staring at her with those mesmerizing midnight blue eyes, as if she'd grown a second head. Why, oh why, did he have to look so handsome with his wavy dark hair and an air of confidence that seemed to seep from his skin. And, speaking of skin, how did he manage to look as if he'd just stepped from a summer beach while she stood pale as a snowman...or would that be a snowwoman? Except for the flush of heat that crawled up her neck. That, she felt sure, appeared anything but pale. "I was enthralled by the inn, Aunt Dahlia, and not paying much attention to our conversation."

"Regardless, my dear..." Dahlia crossed her arms over an ample bosom, lifted her chin, and arrowed the lip-pursed look that Emmy had learned long ago left no room for discussion. "Are you going back on your word, Emilee Marie Lancaster?"

"No. Never." Hurt blended with disbelief and a touch of anger. Emmy gnawed her lower lip as she drew one long breath and slowly released it until she felt her pulse rate settle. Resigned to the inevitable, she might as well roll up her sleeves and go with it. After all, how bad could it possibly be? She and Jayson had costarred in their high school musical senior year, and the pairing had been magical. But that had been ages ago, before their epic breakup. "Unlike some people around here, I keep my word."

"Unlike some people...?" Jayson grimaced. "What, is that supposed to mean?"

"You know what it means, Jayson." Emilee gathered her backpack from the floor and hoisted it onto her shoulder along with her purse. She hadn't been the only one with star-laden dreams dancing through her head. Jayson had spent plenty of time muttering on about his, and leaving little room for her. "It would take an idiot to *not* know what it means."

"Then I must be an idiot."

"If the shoe fits…" Emmy patted her thigh and whistled as she started toward the dressing rooms. "Come on, Max. We've got choreography to learn and ballads to practice, with no time to waste. Even though I've been duped, the show must go on. The kids and the hospital are counting on us. So, you can either stay out here with lug head and his posse—" She jabbed a thumb toward Jayson. "Or you can head back to the dressing room and chill with me while I digest all of this and warm up."

The dog tilted his head to the side and looked up at Jayson with soulful eyes. The high-pitched whine that followed seemed to implore, "How can I help myself?"

A long moment passed while Emilee thought the air around her might splinter. She wasn't sure whether to laugh or cry. For a moment she felt wildly, insanely mad with it all. The look on Jayson's face said his feelings mirrored hers.

Max's whine lowered to a throaty growl, as if to say, "Get on with it already."

"So that's how it's going to be, huh?" Jayson acquiesced with a stiff nod and a sharp wave of one hand to dismiss the dog. "Go on, then. Camp with the prima donna, you traitorous mutt."

# 4

**PRIMA DONNA...**

The words echoed through Emmy's mind as she fought through dance moves for the opening song of the Christmas show's second act. Who did Jayson think he was, referring to her in such a manner? Why, she ought to march right over there and—

"Emilee Marie!" Aunt Dahlia's tone made nails along a chalkboard seem mild. "Where is your head today—or should I say, where is your timing?"

"I'm sorry." Emmy caught herself before she plowed into Jayson who stood behind her. She'd allowed her thoughts—make that *Jayson*—to distract her, and now all eyes were upon her. Even Max, curled up at one side of the stage, seemed to censure her lack of coordination.

She huffed out a breath and struggled for bearings. They'd been at it for hours, and, though the others in the cast seemed on target, she couldn't tap into the groove. "I just can't seem to get this number."

"Here, let me help you." Jayson reached for her hand. There was no animosity in his voice, and he seemed to have completely forgotten their earlier conversation.

But she hadn't. *Prima donna...*

"I can manage on my own." She squared her shoulders and crossed her arms, stubborn taking hold.

"Of course you can." He winked. How could he be so calm when her insides tangled like spaghetti noodles? "It's not hard. Just go like this..."

Before she could object, he spun and then dipped her with an ease that seemed almost surreal. His breath warmed her neck and she got caught up in the scent and feel of him, floating in a dream that brought her back to their dating days.

She missed a step, stumbled over his feet, and then she was falling again.

"Wait." She pressed a palm to Jayson's chest and felt a firm terrain of muscles that

strained beneath his T-shirt. His hand rested gently along the small of her back, as if it belonged there. "I'll fall."

"I'd never let you fall, Emmy." He gazed at her with a look that said he meant every

word. "You almost had it. Just follow my lead. I'll get you there. We'll get there together."

"No." She broke contact and backed away. This—being so close to Jayson—was just too much. Her thoughts churned like a tumultuous storm, her rhythm frayed. She hadn't expected to feel this…such a strong attraction after so much time apart. What was there to make of it? "I need to catch my breath."

*Maybe Jayson's right…perhaps I'm being a bit of a prima donna, allowing my thoughts to sabotage this rehearsal.*

"I think we all need to catch our breath." Jayson jammed his hands into the front pockets of his jeans. The denim caressed his long, muscular limbs like a specially-tailored glove.

"Can we take five, please?" Emmy dabbed beads of perspiration from her forehead. The stage lights heated her through like an oven set to broil. "I'll take a quick look at the dance tape once more, and maybe these steps will finally cement in my brain."

"Sure. Take ten…hours, that is." Aunt Dahlia nodded from center stage, her teased blonde hair still perfectly coifed but her face flushed into a mask of concern. "We've done enough today, and I don't think you're fully recovered from jet lag, Emilee. We'll all take a break and get back at it tomorrow morning."

"Thanks, Auntie." Emmy felt Jayson's gaze burning a hole through her back. Of course, his dance moves had been seamless, as if he'd practiced for months. But she knew that wasn't the case, so how did he manage to look like Fred Astaire when she was

Left-Feet-Louie? "I am a bit pooped."

"Rest will work wonders, dear, and we still have a few days to prepare before the show opens to the public."

"As long as that winter storm the meteorologists are predicting doesn't decide to settle over us," Jayson chimed in. "Last I heard it's spiraling up from the gulf, picking up steam, and is forecasted to dump a good deal of the white stuff over the mountains—and Hope Creek—this coming weekend."

"Well, we're just not going to worry our pretty little heads about that until it happens—if it even happens." Aunt Dahlia headed toward the dressing room area. "You go on, then and enjoy your evening. I have to do a little Christmas shopping in Knoxville, so Jayson will take you to the inn, Emmy."

"What?" The idea of being sequestered in a car with Jayson—even for a short drive—thrust Emmy into full-blown panic mode. "No thanks, Aunt Dahlia. I'm sure Jayson doesn't want to be bothered with driving me."

"Of course he does." Aunt Dahlia turned back slightly to offer a saucy wink. "And Max will chaperone, so you'll be fine."

Emmy looked to Jayson, hoping he'd speak up against Aunt Dahlia's manipulation, but he merely stood there, grinning as if they'd planned this all along.

Had they?

Mindful of the cast watching this scene unfold, Emmy cleared her throat and carefully chose her words.

"But a drive to the inn might be out of his way." If Emmy remembered correctly, Jayson lived the opposite direction. But that had been years ago, so maybe he'd moved. She wasn't at all sure anymore. How much had changed since she left for California—and how much had remained the same? "I don't want to inconvenience him."

"Oh, no worries there, dear." Aunt Dahlia waggled ruby-tipped fingers adorned by rings with gemstones that glittered beneath the lights. "Isn't it a lovely coincidence that Jayson's staying at the inn too?"

\*\*\*\*

"I'm not going to bite you." Jayson glanced over the next morning to watch Emmy in the passenger seat, pressed against the door of his SUV in her attempt to put as much distance between them as possible. The heater had done a pretty good job of warming the cab before she'd gotten in, but now he wasn't sure if the arctic chill was due entirely to the dropping temperature outside—or to Emmy herself.

He'd gone by her room on the second floor of the inn to pick her up for rehearsal. They'd agreed on this last night as he drove her home—although Jayson had to admit Emmy had been more than a bit reluctant—to save Louis the ride out. But Emmy seemed to be having second thoughts now. She gripped a go-cup of coffee he'd prepared for her from the inn's breakfast nook, but remained silent.

Jayson made another attempt to ease the tension that gripped like a vice. "I promise. You're safe with me, Emmy."

"I know." She sipped, sighed, and relaxed back in the seat a bit. Just like a band of rubber that had met its limits, the tension snapped and things seemed to right themselves. Emmy offered a wistful smile. "It sure is pretty here this time of year…homey. I had forgotten how much I enjoyed the holidays in Hope Creek."

Traffic proved light along the parkway as the morning rush-hour wound to a close. Animatronic holiday displays meant to welcome travelers with their brilliant, merry lights, danced and waved as the SUV made its way along the road. Max perched in the backseat, panting as he pressed his snout to the passenger window and sniffed through the sliver of an opening Jayson had left along the top. The scent of pine mingled with hazelnut as air whispered into the cab.

"I love it, too." Jayson turned on the wipers as snowflakes spat at the windshield. The sky looked ominous, and he wondered how long until the storm hit. From the look of the thick, wooly-gray clouds marching in from the west, it wouldn't be long.

"Remember when we went sledding along Tinker's Bluff?"

"I do." Suddenly, Emmy's smile widened and a bit of laughter tumbled out. "We were on the way down our second run, and a black bear wandered out of the brush and stood there along the trail, just watching us...sizing us up."

"Right. It was only a cub, but I knew the mama bear was somewhere close. I figured she'd come hauling from the woods, and chase after us."

"Chase after *me*," Emmy said. "So you rolled from the sled and frightened the cub away by shouting at it and waving your hands. Max romped alongside you, barking."

"Oh... that's right. I had forgotten that part..." He had been thinking only of Emmy, and how he planned to give her a promise ring before they returned to college for the new semester. He wanted her to know the depth of his commitment to her. But Emmy hadn't returned to college. Instead she'd gone two-thousand miles in the opposite direction. "I must have looked like a lunatic."

"On the contrary, you looked like a warrior protecting his family. I was screaming my head off, hoping the mama bear didn't decide to make her entrance just then."

"We never saw her, did we?"

"Nope. You didn't see anything but stars for a while after that, because you slipped on a rock as you ran back my way, and hit your head on a tree stump. It took six stitches to close the wound, right here..." Soft laughter was replaced by a sigh as she leaned toward him and brushed one finger along his right eyebrow. "I still can feel the scar, although it's no longer visible."

Her touch, so tender along his skin, stole Jayson's voice. He might not remember every detail of that day, but he did remember that talent scouts had snatched Emmy up only a few weeks later, after viewing an audition tape she'd submitted. She'd abandoned her college coursework and left Hope Creek, determined to make her way in the neon glow of Hollywood lights.

He'd never had the chance to give her the promise ring. During the weeks that followed her departure, he'd considered tossing the white-gold band with its two intertwined hearts into the river, along with his dreams for their future. Instead, he'd tucked the ring, still in its black velvet box, deep along the back corner of his sock drawer. Maybe one day he'd find use for it again. Maybe...

Jayson struggled to maintain control of the SUV, and forced his attention to the road.

"I told you once—more than once—Emmy, if you ever need me I'll be there with bells on." He gripped the steering wheel. "I meant it. Still do."

"I don't think I ever thanked you for saving my life, Jayson. So, thank you." She pressed a soft kiss to his brow and then settled back as if she hadn't just rattled his insides. "And thanks for the coffee. It really hit the spot. I didn't sleep very well last night so I'm a little sluggish this morning."

"I didn't either." He'd tossed and turned in his bed at the inn's cottage until way past midnight. The fact that he could see a light burning from Emmy's room through his window didn't help matters. "We're both out of sorts."

"Yes." She slanted him a wary look. "This just isn't what I signed up for. I didn't expect..."

"What didn't you expect, Emmy?" Jayson loosened his grip on the wheel to shift slightly her way. Hair spilled across her forehead, framing her eyes. Her scent, a blend of citrus with a soft hint of soap, performed a relentless call to his senses. "You, me...this?"

"Exactly."

"But we're here, so we should make the most of it."

"That's just it—I can't believe I *am* here."

"I'm glad you are, even if you're not sure about it." The theater came into view, and Jayson knew the rehearsal ahead would leave little time for conversation. He had so much to say, so many questions to ask. Holiday tunes on the radio filtered through the cab as he collected his thoughts and then forged ahead. "I've missed you, Emmy. Did you have any success in your work along the coast?"

"A reasonable amount." She turned her attention from Jayson to the view outside the passenger window. "I've stayed busy with stuff."

"Stuff?" Jayson wished he could turn back the clock to the times they talked for hours into a sunset. In those days conversation had come as easily as walking, and Emmy's laughter had warmed him to the core. Could they ever capture such a sense of easiness again, or would she leave Hope Creek before he had the chance to say what was truly on his mind? "What sort of stuff?"

"Commercials, mainly," Emmy elaborated. "I've done three or four now, along with a few fashion shows for a local department store. I was hoping for more, but…"

"Right. I saw the spot you did for toothpaste. I've always loved your smile, Em. Especially when you're smiling at me." He slowed for a stoplight. The theater perched just beyond the intersection, while the lot wrapped around the next corner. "When do you have to head back to work?"

He couldn't bring himself to ask the question that really nagged at him…*When do you plan to leave again?*

"I don't have any auditions on my calendar, but I'm waiting on a call from my agent." She shrugged. "The film industry is more unforgiving than I thought it would be. The ratio of auditions to jobs is about fifty to one. Pounding the pavement gets tiring, to say the least. And then I've been picking up odd jobs wherever I can, to make rent. But I do OK."

The way she emphasized that last word with a stiff nod made Jayson wonder whether she was trying to convince him—or herself.

"There's always room at the theater. Dahlia's working on a new show for next season. She doesn't have a lead yet."

"She told me."

"You could come home, Emmy."

From the backseat, Max whined as if offering his opinion on

the subject. *"Yes, come home, Emmy,"* he seemed to say.

"This isn't my home anymore." But Emmy swiveled in the seat, relaxing enough to turn and give the dog's head a good petting.

"Hope Creek will always be your home. You just haven't figured that out yet." The light turned green, and Jayson tapped the gas pedal. "And it's a fact that no one would fill the theater lead better than you."

"Thanks, Jayson, but any decision about my future has to be mine—alone."

"Of course it does."

"And it's no secret that Aunt Dahlia's doing her best to get us back together—the show, the inn, and now this—driving back and forth to work."

"I like driving with you, Emmy."

As if continuing to eavesdrop on their conversation, Max barked his hearty agreement from the backseat. Jayson swore the mastiff was part human. He was glad to have him as a wing man.

"And would that be such a bad thing…you, me?" Jayson sliced a look Emmy's way. "We used to be pretty darn good together."

"That was a long time ago…another lifetime." She shook her head. "We were young and…"

"And what, Emmy?"

"Never mind."

"That won't cut it. Because I *do* mind." Jayson refused to let it go. He'd speak his mind this time around, and not leave a single word unspoken. "You only get one go-around. This life is not a rehearsal for the big show, you know. This *is* the big show."

"I have no regrets concerning the choices I've made."

"No?"

"No."

But she didn't sound so sure of that. Her voice faltered, and was that moisture causing her eyes to shimmer like dew-kissed gemstones?

"So this is how it's going to be?" Jayson turned the corner and headed toward the rear theater lot, designated for staff and cast parking. "Why are you sabotaging this?"

"Sabotaging what?"

"The show...us."

"There is no us, Jayson."

"Regardless, it's no secret that you can dance like a prima ballerina, Emmy. I know because I've danced with you—a lot. You may have forgotten that, but *I* haven't forgotten the way that feels." He lowered the volume on the radio before shutting it down altogether. Temper bit at him, and he fought against it. "You're acting like you never laced up a pair of dance shoes and miscuing at every other turn. Why?"

"I'm running on fumes...jetlag, just like Aunt Dahlia said." Emmy dismissed the question with a wave of her hand, but there was more lurking beneath the surface, he was sure of it. "I've just finished a gauntlet of auditions and I'm tired."

"We're all tired. It's more than that." He turned into the lot, snagged a parking space.

"Like I said before, I didn't expect..." She shook her head.

"You *did* miss me, didn't you?"

"Even if I did, what does it matter now?" She caught her lower lip between her teeth as her jaw trembled. "Jayson, what happened between us—"

"What, exactly, *did* happen between us?" He killed the engine. "What would you call it, Emmy...the dates, the talks...the kisses? Did it mean anything to you? Because it sure meant something to me."

"Whatever you feel led to call it, it ended a long time ago, and it's not bound to be resurrected. Too much time has passed, too much water has run under the bridge." As if trying to convince herself, Emmy shook her head. "You have your life now, Jayson, and I have mine. The paths don't meet."

"They've met here, now." He swept one hand across the cab. "What do you make of that?"

"Merely a temporary detour." She ran a hand through her hair, refusing to look at him as she unlatched her seatbelt. The passenger door popped open and frosty air rushed in as she exited the car. She grabbed her purse and backpack from the seat and slung them both over one shoulder. "Thanks for the ride."

"Emmy, if you'll wait a minute I'll walk you in."

"No worries. I can find my way into the theater." She lifted a pair of fingers to her mouth and whistled. "Come on, Max."

# 5

**THEY'D BEEN REHEARSING FOR THREE** full days, and Emmy's muscles screamed in protest, but she'd finally nailed the choreography.

"You're looking fantastic," Aunt Dahlia called out her approval from the second row of the theater seats. "It's much better than I had hoped, judging from our rocky start. I'd say that's a wrap for the day. We're ready to go with tomorrow's opening show."

Whoops of joy rang out, and Emmy crossed the stage to gather her towel and bottled water. She wiped beads of sweat from her forehead and then drew a sip from the bottle as she settled onto a wrought iron bench that served as a prop in the shows outdoor scenes. The rehearsals had been brutal, and she knew it was mainly due to her lack of concentration. Rep after rep had been taken, until finally both the songs and the steps clicked into place.

"That was great." Jayson seemed to have come to terms with the fact that their renewed partnership was for the Christmas show only—nothing personal. "Perfect."

"Thanks, but I wouldn't go that far." Emmy had spent days leading up to her return to Hope Creek singing along with Harvey via the preview video Aunt Dahlia had emailed to her. But despite the hours of practice and the fact that their voices matched pitch, something was missing. She couldn't quite put her finger on the element that seemed to be lacking, but when she sang with Jayson, their harmony proved truly magical. "What's perfect is this set you've designed. It's beautiful."

The colors proved vibrant and cheerful, and the balcony complete with a rail adorned by cheerful velvet bows stood sturdy against her weight. Emmy thought about how thoughtfully it had been constructed by Jayson to ease her fear of heights, and gratitude warmed her.

"Manny and the crew sure came through." Jayson slipped into the seat beside her. Wasn't that just like him to give credit to others? She knew he'd worked tirelessly on his designs for the set, and had also pulled double duty as he burned the midnight oil over the past week leading the team to get things done. But then, he'd always been humble and giving, which was one of the reasons she'd fallen in love with him in the first place.

*Fallen in love…*

The thought jolted her. Where had it come from? She'd best keep her mind from wandering. Such ramblings would only serve to lead to doors better left shut tight.

Jayson's voice brought her back.

"I hope this winter storm that's bearing down doesn't throw a wrench into the show's opening." He twisted the cap from his water bottle and drew a sip.

"Me, too." Emmy offered him a peanut butter cracker from the pack she'd opened. "It sure has been toying with us for the past day or so."

The clouds had gathered and thickened to an angry beast, spitting and churning. Emmy watched them at midday as she and Jayson shared take-out from the deli next door. The changing textures fascinated her.

And now, she also found herself fascinated by Jayson. He seemed so comfortable in his own skin while she felt as if her world had been tossed into a blender with the switch set to puree. So many emotions sprang up, ones she thought had been laid to rest many seasons ago.

Why were they all rising to the surface now…especially those she still harbored for Jayson?

Emmy chalked it up to the holidays. Christmastime always made her feel nostalgic. But somehow this year seemed different, the nostalgia magnified.

Jayson shifted in the seat, and the movement drew her back.

"It would be a shame to have to refund the ticket costs." He swiped a hand across his mouth, seemingly unaware of the storm that churned through her. Or was he aware, and simply trying to assuage her uneasiness? "So many people—so many children—are counting on us to get that new pediatric wing funded."

"Maybe the storm will change direction, miss us completely." But Emmy had listened to that morning's weather reports, and the meteorologists seemed convinced that Hope Creek sat in the direct path of the storm track. There was no avoiding it, just as there seemed to be no hope of avoiding Jayson—or the feelings that refused to work their way out of her system. "You know what a good snow can do to East Tennessee."

"Cripple the roads, shut down businesses...sometimes for days." Jayson paused thoughtfully before adding, "At least we would be sequestered at the inn. There are worse places to be stuck during a storm. Generators, at least, will keep the power flowing in case of an outage. And the guests keep things interesting—never a dull moment."

It almost sounded like he *wanted* to be snowed in—with her? Suddenly a flush of heat spread through Emmy. She couldn't take that chance. Maybe she should rent a room at the motel next door to the theater and hunker down before the storm rolled in, to put distance between them.

Or better yet, she could just hop a plane back to California before McGhee Tyson airport started posting weather delays—or worse yet, closures—and leave this whole misadventure behind. After all, she was the one who'd been duped into performing the lead with Jayson. It wasn't the deal she'd agreed to. So, no one would blame her for running, would they?

"I think I'd better grab my things and get ready to head back to the inn," Emmy stood, not quite sure what to do next. Her pulse hammered in her chest. Time was wasting. She had to take action, put a measure of distance between her and Jayson, and quick.

"Are you OK, Emmy?" Jayson stood to face her. He reached out to brush a strand of hair from her eyes. His fingers lingered at her brow. "Your face is flushed."

"I'm good." She lifted a hand to one cheek and felt the heat radiate as she took a step back from him. "Just a little overheated from rehearsal."

"OK...if you're sure." Yet he seemed unconvinced as he drew his car keys from his pocket. "We can head back to the inn together. I'll bring the SUV around front and pick you up beneath the awning so you don't have to cross the lot through the wind."

"There's no need for you to do that. I think I'll take a cab back today."

"Emmy, that's not necessary. It's a bear outside and we're going to the same place, for goodness sake."

"I know where I'm going." Suddenly, it was important for her to go it alone, without Jayson's help—and without his distracting presence beside her in the SUV. She needed time to think, and to sort out the feelings that churned inside, mirroring the storm that brewed along the backdrop of Smoky Mountains beyond the theater walls. "And I said I'll take a cab home today."

She tossed her water bottle into the trash and stalked off to the dressing area, her senses on overdrive. How could she be so conflicted, at once wanting to be close to Jayson while fighting the urge to run? He seemed determined to pick up where they'd left off, a course of action that could only lead to disaster. History repeats itself, right?

*Not always,* a tiny voice inside her spoke. *Not always, Emmy.*

She grabbed her backpack, wrapped a scarf around her neck, and without so much as pulling on her coat turned toward the rear exit that led to the parking lot. A blast of cold air slapped her face and the wind whipped, turning her damp skin to ice. She thought of retreating back into the warmth of the theater, but nixed the idea. Instead, she forged with resolve toward the parkway.

She'd made it to the sidewalk before she realized Max was behind her, following her step for step.

"You fool," she muttered. "Go back inside where it's warm. Jayson will be worried about you."

The dog refused, keeping pace at her side as if protecting her from rush hour traffic that darted back and forth along the winding road. How far, exactly, was the inn? Two miles? Three? Or was it farther? She hadn't paid much attention on her drives to and from the theater with Jayson. She'd been too busy reminiscing with him, sharing conversation…enjoying time with him.

*Why, oh why do I still care? Why can't I make these feelings stop?*

Max nipped at the air, and Emmy realized snowflakes had begun to fall. And not the little, wispy kind but big, fat plops of moisture. She wished she'd thought to snatch her coat from the hook in her dressing room. Her fingers were already numb, her teeth chattering. She hunched her back in an attempt to ward off the wind that sliced through her. She was miserable, pure and simple.

*You're a fool, Emilee…a fool for coming back here. What were you thinking…what were you hoping for?*

A car honked and Emmy turned to see Aunt Dahlia's limo inching up to her with Louis at the wheel. Was Aunt Dahlia perched in the backseat?

That question was answered when the rear window lowered and a head sporting teased, blonde hair leaned out.

"Emilee Marie, I've seen you do a lot of foolish things, but this has got to take the blue-ribbon award." Leave it to Auntie not to sugarcoat. "Have you lost your ever-loving mind? What on earth are you doing?"

"Walking." Emmy gritted her teeth.

"I see that." The limo continued to creep along behind her, heedless of the parade of traffic growing behind it. "I meant, what on earth are you *doing*?"

What *was* she doing…running away like a three-year-old? Suddenly, Emmy felt like a fool, but the stubbornness she was famous for had taken hold, and she refused to relent. She crossed her arms over her chest and set her jaw against chattering teeth. "Just let me go."

"You know better than that. You're going to catch your death of cold, and then who will your mother blame—yours truly." Dahlia jabbed a finger toward her chest. "Then there'll be all sorts of explainin' to do that I'd just rather not get into."

"I'm an adult. I can make my own choices."

"No one's arguing that point. But right now you're acting like an obstinate child."

"So?" Emotions boiled to the surface, and Emmy's voice rose with them. "Maybe I just want this all to go away. Maybe I'm more than a little confused and just trying to sort this all out."

There. She'd said it. Jayson had done something to her...opened a vault that she'd sealed tight a long time ago. She thought the key had been tossed away, but here she stood, proof that the past had nine lives.

"Yes, life has a way of knocking the wind out of us sometimes. But we have to get up, we have to keep pushing on. So get in the car, Emilee." Aunt Dahlia's voice was insistent...and losing patience. Cold had to be taking over the cab, chilling her to the bone. Auntie had never liked to be chilled. "At the very least, think about Max. The poor dog is freezing, and so loyal to you that he wouldn't return to the warmth of the theater. You wouldn't want *him* to catch pneumonia, would you?"

That did it. Emmy stopped in her tracks and did an about-face. She stepped from the curb and rounded to the passenger side of the limo. She opened the rear door, quickly tossed her backpack to the floor, and then whistled and motioned for Max to get in. He launched himself into the backseat and without another moment's hesitation, she followed. She slammed the door behind her.

The warmth was immediate and welcomed. Holiday tunes that sang from the limo's speakers soothed the jumble of nerves that had balled in her belly until they finally began to release. For the length of a few blocks, she sat in the plush leather seat without voicing a single syllable. And for once Aunt Dahlia refrained from her well-honed verbal sparring.

"I'm sorry," Emmy finally offered, clasping her hands

together in her lap in an attempt to warm them. "I know I'm being unreasonable. I just can't seem to help it. I don't know why all this is driving me crazy. I'm off kilter, swept into a storm. Jayson..."

"Yes, it all boils down to Jayson, doesn't it?"

"He gets me stirred up, riled up. I don't know how to feel."

"You know, Emmy, I'm an old woman who's traveled the globe and seen a lot of places and my share of things. I certainly don't have all the answers. But one thing I know for sure is that fear never got me anywhere."

"I'm not afraid."

But the words came too quickly. Who was she trying to fool? Even Max, who'd laid his meaty head across her lap, could see through the fib. Emmy buried her hands in his thick fur, trying to work numbness from the tips of her fingers.

"The charity show only lasts six days, and then you can be on your way back to California...if that's what you truly want." Aunt Dahlia patted Emmy's knee and studied her with a gaze that spoke volumes. "You never have to see or speak to Jayson again if you don't want to."

The thought jarred Emilee. A sadness swept through her. Life without Jayson—again. Could she bear it?

"And if I want to stay?"

"I'm still seeking a lead for the spring show. And after that, who knows? You don't have to decide right now. Why don't you give thoughts about the show—and Jayson—just a little more time?"

"I suppose I could do that." Relief flooded her, followed by a shiver of uncertainty. After the way she'd behaved back at the theater—not to mention the past several days—would Jayson still want to give *her* more time? Even he must have limits.

"Let's head to the inn, then. I'd like to see you safely ensconced there before this storm hits. And judging from all of the signs, I'd say it's going to be a doozy."

# 6

**JAYSON PARKED THE SUV AT** the top of the snow-dusted drive. The white stuff was coming down pretty hard now, covering tree branches and rooftops. The inn appeared to be sequestered inside a snow globe that had been given a hearty shake.

He noted with dismay that Emmy's room at the end of the inn's second floor wing stood dark. He hoped Dahlia had found her, and would bring her home safely.

He'd go after her, but she'd made it clear that she didn't want him around. Still, it took every ounce of resolve not to turn the SUV around and head out again.

No. Dahlia could handle things. If he knew anything about the big-hearted singer, he knew she was all fluff and polish on the outside but tough-as-nails on the inside.

Besides, Emmy would have to sort out her feelings on her own. Dahlia couldn't do that for her.

He couldn't either.

Jayson leaned into the wind as he made his way to the cottage entrance. Inside, he shrugged from his jacket and tossed it over the arm of the recliner before stacking a few logs in the fireplace along with some kindling, and then laying a match to it. As the flames danced to life, he drank in the heat. His whole body felt as if dampness had taken root, and he'd lost the feeling in his fingers. The sharp chill in the air outside proved uncharacteristic for mid-December in East Tennessee—even rarer for snow to fall with such gusto.

When he'd had his fill of the warmth, he headed into the kitchen.

A loaf of bread sat on the counter, and he knew he had cold

cuts in the fridge. He thought about making a sandwich, but an appetite that had raged from the grueling day of rehearsals had fled right along with Emmy.

*Where is she? Why did she leave in such a rush? What have I done to make her want to run again?*

*How can I convince her to stay?*

His thoughts seemed to echo along the walls of the small kitchen, lonely without Max curled up beneath the table, waiting for food scraps to fall. He'd watched the dog follow Emmy out the back door and across the parking lot of the theater, and he'd let him go, thankful that Emmy wasn't alone.

He'd let Emmy leave, as well, because there was no point in trying to hold on to something—some*one*—who didn't want to be held. No good could come of it, simply a delay of the inevitable. He'd learned that the hard way—finally.

It was over, for good. Any hopes that he'd harbored to make a second go of it with Emmy had fizzled there at the rear exit of the theater as the arctic blast of air rushed in.

So, he'd watched her leave. Again.

Jayson filled the kettle with water, set it to boil on the 1980-era gas stove and rooted through the cabinet for a mug. He'd spotted a box of hot chocolate in the pantry, and a steaming cup of the sweet stuff just might chase the remaining chill from his bones…and his heart.

Again, his thoughts drifted. Was Emmy OK? Had Dahlia found her and brought her home?

*Home…*

Jayson reminded himself that Hope Creek was no longer Emmy's home. Her home—the place she thought she belonged now—lay more than two-thousand miles away.

He sighed as he waited for the water to boil. A knock sounded at the front door as the kettle squealed. Jayson turned off the burner, removed the pot from the heat, and crossed back toward the living room. A series of staccato, low pitched barks signaled that Max waited on the stoop. A moment later, Emmy's face appeared in the glass.

Her cheeks were flushed with cold, and damp eyelashes framed eyes dark as smoky onyx. She offered a little wave along with a lopsided smile, and he noticed her teeth chattered uncontrollably.

*Beautiful...she's so beautiful.*

The thought leapt before Jayson could tamp it down. He tugged on the door and Max barreled in, bringing a flurry of snowflakes along with him.

"May I?" Emmy asked softly.

She wore only a scarf and the clothes she'd donned for rehearsal. She must be freezing. Jayson stepped back, allowing her entry. His heart raced ahead of rationality, and he fought to bring the two back into sync.

He longed to wrap his arms around her...to chase away the chill. Instead, he said softly, "Thanks for returning Max."

"Of course." She tugged at her scarf, but didn't remove the fabric. Silence danced around them as Max watched from the floor where he'd curled before the fireplace.

"Your teeth are chattering." Jayson took her hand and felt the sheath of cold along her skin. "You're freezing. Come stand beside me by the fire."

She didn't argue as he led her across the room. Heat enveloped them like a soothing blanket and the pine kindling wove a pleasant aroma around them. For several moments, they simply stood side by side, in silence.

Then Emmy slanted him a look as if she wasn't quite sure what came next. She murmured, "I'm sorry, Jayson."

Her words, not what he was expecting, choked the breath from him. He gathered his bearings.

"I'm sorry too." The admission burned, yet the words were necessary. Emmy wasn't the only one at fault here. It was time he shouldered his share of the blame.

"But you didn't run away today." Emmy's eyes grew wide as she studied him closely. "You didn't—"

"You're right, I didn't do a lot of things I should have—like go after you that day you announced you were leaving." The memory choked him, turned his gut to smoldering embers. "I should have, and I regret not telling you…"

"What, Jayson?" She lifted her free hand to his shoulder, then ran her fingers along the length of his arm. "What do you regret not telling me?"

The question, coupled with her tender touch, melted any reserve he had left in the tank.

"I should have let you know, Emmy…how much I loved you."

\*\*\*\*

*Loved…*

The single word cut Emmy to the quick, and brought back so many memories of the times she and Jayson had spent together. Those had been good days, carefree days full of happiness and laughter. Why had she let them go?

"Storm's brewing." Jayson motioned toward the bay window that overlooked the gardens. The inn glowed like a lighthouse beyond, a thousand twinkling beams of color cutting through the oncoming darkness.

"Yes." *In more ways than one.*

Jayson released her hand, and a chill crept in once again. Emmy shivered.

"I was just about to make a cup of hot chocolate." He bent to add another small log to the fire. "Would you like one?"

"Yes, I'd like that—a lot."

She followed him into the kitchen and slid onto a chair at the scuffed wooden dining table. He riffled through the cabinet for a second mug. One already sat on the counter beside a cheerful marigold-colored stovetop, waiting to be filled.

"I remember how much you like marshmallows." As if to prove the point, Jayson filled the cup with a handful of the minis before tearing the top from a pouch and dumping chocolate powder into the mix. He added steaming water and a splash of milk before topping it all off with a generous dollop of whipped cream.

Max wandered into the kitchen and settled at Emmy's feet. He lay his head across her dancing shoes, now damp and soiled from tromping through the snow. Good thing she'd packed a second pair to wear for performances.

The scene proved idyllic...the dog, hot chocolate...Jayson. She remembered that as much as she liked marshmallows, he didn't. And while she liked seafood, steak was his weakness. She enjoyed pop music, he was a fan of country.

But they both loved to dance, especially to the slow songs that sent a message straight to the heart.

Did Jayson remember that as well as she did?

"Thank you," Emmy accepted the filled mug from Jayson. "It looks better than what they make at the coffee shop down the street."

"I aim to please."

And he did, without fail. How had she so easily forgotten that?

She took in her surroundings as Jayson gathered his drink. The kitchen was modest yet comfortable, with a coat of bright yellow sunshine along the walls. Somehow the dated appliances and time-worn cabinets worked together to welcome with a homey touch. Scents of crackling wood and cinnamon drifted as Jayson placed a plate of cookies on the table. Emmy's belly yapped as he settled in across from her.

"Oatmeal raisin." He said as if he sensed her stomach yowling. "Try one. They're good."

As Emmy reached for a cookie, laughter rang out in the yard beyond the cottage. She lifted her gaze to see a couple, along with a child, dashing through the falling snow. The child, bundled in a snowsuit, dropped to the ground and swept the snow aside as she lay on her back, arms and legs stretched wide. When she rose again, her shouts of delight danced from the mountaintops and Emmy grinned at the small angel print left behind. So sweet, but also evidence of the amount of snowfall already on the ground.

"They're having fun," Jayson noted.

Emmy turned to see him staring out the window alongside her. "Evenings like this were made for laughter and a few shenanigans along the way."

*Shenanigans...*

That's what Jayson had dubbed their high school escapades that leaned more to the mischievous side—like the time they stood outside Old Man Whittaker's place sporting a birthday cake while they belted a rousing rendition of *Happy Birthday*, because they knew he had no family to speak of. By the time they finished, half of the neighborhood had joined in and someone even brought a small ice cream cake. Mr. Whittaker had cried happy tears as he blew out the birthday candles.

Or the time Jayson talked her into performing in the Hope Creek High talent show with him. They'd done a comedy sketch, complete with song and dance, and had captured the winning prize—a one-hundred dollar gift card. The next day, at Jayson's insistence, they'd headed to the five and dime together, and purchased enough coloring books and crayons to supply every child shut in at the hospital with a Christmas gift. They'd made the delivery and spent the day playing tricks on the nurses while entertaining the kids. It had been so much fun.

There were other times...many of them. Suddenly, Emmy's heart ached with the bittersweet memories.

"You're wearing these." Jayson lifted his fingers to her right earlobe. "The earrings I gave you that last Christmas, before you left for California."

They were a pair of angels fashioned of silver. "One guardian to watch over each shoulder," he had told her. Emmy hadn't worn them in ages. What made her think to tuck them into her suitcase as she left California, and to put them on today?

Beyond the window, laughter continued to ring through the air as the child chased snowflakes beneath a whisper of dusk that settled in. Chapel lights glowed in the distance, and Emmy thought once again of the first kiss she and Jayson had once shared on the steps leading to its entrance. She'd heard a Christmas Eve gathering in the sanctuary was planned, and delighted in the idea of sharing the holiday with Jayson.

Then reality settled in, stealing her delight. Would she still be here in Hope Creek for Christmas…or back to California by then?

# 7

EMMY SET THE MAGAZINE SHE'D been reading aside and rose from the arm chair where she'd spent the past hour lounging in her room. A walk to the window told her what she already knew—snow was still falling. It settled along the inn's gardens and piled like cotton batting along the roof of the chapel. Even Jayson's cottage was not immune to the burial. Bushes along the front walk had been transformed to oversized humps while his SUV sat motionless as a grounded ghost. Max's paw prints from his last outing had already disappeared beneath a fresh layer of crystals.

Aunt Dahlia had canceled today's performance, and tomorrow wasn't looking any better. Although she loved the beauty of it, Emmy prayed the storm would soon pass. It would take a miracle to raise the necessary funds for the pediatric wing with only a handful of salvageable shows and a sparse audience, at best.

She'd spent the afternoon alternating between the arm chair and gazing from her window as guests played in the side yard, making snowmen and engaging in a playful fight with handfuls of the white stuff. Even Jayson had gotten into the merry chaos at one point, hauling a sled he'd found in one of the outbuildings to offer up rides for little Chrissy Sheridan, who was stranded at the inn with her father and nanny. He'd run in circles over the packed snow with the child bundled and seated, holding on for dear life as Max romped alongside. Emmy was sure his muscles screamed for relief, but Chrissy's shrieks of laughter proved a testament to her enjoyment at being treated like a little snow princess for the afternoon.

That was so much like Jayson to put his needs aside for the good of others. He'd done it his entire life, and Emmy had taken his acts of kindness for granted. The realization sliced through her, cutting to the core. She closed her eyes, sighed as she massaged an ache from her temples, and then stood to pace the room.

Angels watched as she walked. The Christmas family had seen to it that each room at the inn was decorated with a fitting theme, and hers was graced with angels of all sorts and sizes. One suspended from the ceiling over the bed, keeping watch as she slept. Another fashioned of delicate crystal hovered from the fan pulley at the center of the room. A mischievous pair peeked from potted ferns along the wall near the window, seeming to drink in every move Emmy made.

She lifted a hand to each ear and felt the angels seated along her lobes.

*"One guardian to watch over each shoulder…"*

How fitting that she'd settled into the Angel Room. Was it a sign of some sort…a portent of things to come?

Emmy paused at the door leading out to the landing, opening it a sliver. Muted, merry voices drifted from the lobby below. Ari Christmas and a guest chef had promised a dinner buffet of sorts to those who were stranded, which proved to be virtually everyone who had not high-tailed it home at the first signs of snow. Making good on their word, they'd set the food along a sideboard and rang the dinner bell. The tangy aroma of a lobster mac and cheese filled Emmy's senses, and her belly launched into a series of defiant growls. She'd skipped lunch and was now paying the price.

She glanced in the dresser mirror and smoothed her hair before applying a dab of lipstick. It wouldn't hurt to head downstairs and enjoy a bit of company. Being snowed in had dislodged memories, bringing with them a sense of melancholy that proved difficult to shake. The inn's festive decorations—especially the grand and brightly-decorated fir tree that graced its foyer—would surely chase away the sadness.

Emmy opened the door and stepped onto the landing, where she found Jayson climbing the stairs toward her. The sturdy cadence of his boots along the wood, matching the tempo of carols that hummed from below, proved a song to her soul. Immediately, the gloom lifted and her heart began to sing.

"Hey, Emmy." He paused just below the landing, his gaze lifted to hers. Damp hair fell in crisp, coiled waves across his brow. He brushed flakes of white from the crown. With his blue eyes bright from the cold, she thought he'd never looked so handsome. "I was just coming to check on you. Have you had dinner?"

"No." She could barely gather her voice. She felt seventeen all over again, as if he'd come for her for the very first time. "It smells scrumptious. I was headed that way."

"Perfect. May I join you?"

"Of course." She nodded. "I'd love that."

He took her hand. "Let's go."

****

Their dinner conversation proved easy and light. Emmy laughed softly at one of his jokes, and Jayson remembered all over again why he'd fallen in love with her.

"How on earth did you talk Ari Christmas into allowing Max into the inn—not to mention the dining room?" Emmy asked as she lifted the edge of the linen tablecloth and peeked beneath the table where Max lay at her feet, curled up and snoozing as if he hadn't a care in the world.

Lucky dog.

"I didn't ask. She offered." Jayson was thankful for the kindness the Christmas family had shown him over the past several weeks, allowing him to bunk at the cottage. Originally designed to house a caretaker, the outdated building had stood vacant for the past few years. The family planned to update it for rental this coming summer, but had made Jayson feel welcome in the meantime. "Max seems to have a way with people."

"I suppose he takes after his master." Emmy reached for the sugar and added a teaspoon to her second cup of coffee. "You made little Chrissy Sheridan's day, pulling her all over the hillside on that sled. I thought you were going to drop right there in the snow from offering up so many rides."

"You saw that?"

"Yes, I certainly did." Emmy chuckled. "It was hard to miss the child's gleeful shouts from my window. I expected at any moment you would tear off your coat to reveal a Superman cape and emblem."

Jayson joined in her laughter as he sliced a look to his left. Soft carols hummed along the dining room, mingling with the thrum of after-dinner chatter. Guests lingered, enjoying each other's company. The inn, with its hospitable, easy charm proved the perfect place to pass the time during a winter storm.

His gaze alit on Chrissy, who sat across the room, nodding off in her father's arms. The day's activities with their fresh air and laughter had taken a toll as her bedtime neared. One tiny palm curled along her rosy cheek as her lips pursed in a dream.

Jayson's heart lurched. At one time he'd thought he and Emmy might make a family together. They'd talked about it on more than one occasion, often tossing about names as well as their respective wishes for the number and gender. He'd always longed to be a father, and he felt certain Emmy would prove a doting, loving mother alongside him. Together, they'd make countless happy memories.

If only she'd give them a chance.

"Can you believe it's still snowing?" Emmy's voice drew him back.

"It's crazy, isn't it?"

"At this rate, it will take days to dig out."

"I know. Dahlia has canceled tomorrow's show." Jayson tapped the cell phone tucked into his pocket. "The message came through just before dessert."

"Oh, I figured as much." Emmy sighed and sipped her coffee, watching him over the rim of her cup with those alluring, dark eyes. "What will we do if this storm keeps up? No shows mean no funding for the pediatric wing."

"It will be OK." Jayson reached over to shelter her hand in his. "God is in control, and He'll work it all out."

"Yes, I had forgotten that." She squeezed his fingers gently. "I'm glad you haven't."

"You know Aunt Dahlia is a prayer warrior and she always has a trick or two tucked up that sleeve of hers."

"I know. Remember the time right after you adopted Max that he ran off and we thought he was lost for good, but Aunt Dahlia insisted he'd return?"

"She told us to sing as we searched, because he liked the harmony of our voices together. So we did just that, walking to the four corners of the countryside."

"We'd scoured and sang into the evening before we found him sitting right here on the chapel steps as if he'd been waiting for our arrival all along."

"You were so happy you burst into tears."

He'd wrapped his arms around her as Max looked on, and he hadn't been able to contain his feelings for her any longer—he'd kissed her for the first time. His head had spun and a wave of longing swept clear to the tips of his toes.

At the time he'd thought Emmy felt the same. She'd leaned into him to return the kiss, sighing from somewhere deep down inside as if a whole new world had opened before her. The chapel bells had clanged in a gusty breeze, making them laugh...and wonder.

But now he questioned if she even remembered standing on the chapel steps beneath the glow of a harvest moon. Hard to tell from the faraway look in her gaze. Was it the subtle wash of overhead lights or memories that caused her eyes to take on a sheen of moisture?

Jayson's coffee cup clattered as he returned it to the table with a not-so-steady hand.

"If we're going to be snowed in here again tomorrow, we'll need some entertainment." The timbre of his voice mirrored the confusion that churned inside him. "Ari Christmas has gone above and beyond to keep us comfortable. It would be a nice gesture to give her a break."

"I agree." Emmy drained her coffee cup and placed it on the table beside his. "What do you have in mind?"

"Let's take a walk and consider it." He rose from his seat, tugging Emmy along. "I'm sure we can come up with a plan."

# *8*

**MOONLIGHT SPILLED OVER NEW-FALLEN** snow as a slight breeze caused whispers of dampness to dance over Emmy's hair. She followed Jayson down a walking trail toward the Christmas Inn chapel on the far side of the sprawling property. The scent of pine and burning firewood swirled through the treetops, evoking visions of holiday cheer. Max romped alongside them, burying his snout in the snowdrifts as he sniffed for fallen hazelnuts and pine cones.

Every so often a lone cardinal or blue jay flitted by, stealing Max's attention and causing him to dart off and give chase. His enthusiastic barks rang across the mountaintops.

Dusk deepened to night and the temperature dipped into the twenties, but with Jayson at her side Emmy felt only a sense of warmth. Their breath swirled out in puffs of white as they navigated the snow-laden path, and Emmy realized that she hadn't seen a storm such as this in years.

Southern California rarely saw a winter day when the temperature dipped below the mid-forties. She'd missed the excitement and anticipation of watching billows of ominous clouds gather to dump their load over the undulating landscape. The world seemed to stop spinning and she lavished in the brief time-out from life's hectic pace as the community spent a string of days snowed in before digging out from beneath the blanket.

She lifted her gaze toward the horizon, framed by the rugged landscape of snowcapped mountaintops. Pinpoints of light beckoned from the chapel's majestic steeple, drawing like a beacon in a storm.

Emmy and Jayson made their way toward the glow.

"Oh, it's so beautiful here." The words escaped before she

even realized she'd spoken. Their boots crunched in unison along the packed snow and the air felt so crisp, so clean, that each whisper of sound seemed magnified. "Look at the lights shimmering along the gazebo in the gardens. And I think those are candles glowing from the chapel windows across the way. I'll bet they mirror the battery-operated candelabras I've seen shining from the guest room windows at the inn."

"Beautiful antiques." Jayson's breath curled like smoke from a pipe. "The inn is really shaping up. By this coming summer, the place will have been completely restored to its original grandeur. I'll be out of the caretaker's cottage by then and in a place of my own."

"Oh? Where will that be?"

"Close by." Jayson's attention drifted to the pasture beyond the inn's boundaries. He seemed deep in thought, lost for a moment before turning back to Emmy. "An easy commute to the theater, yet far enough off the beaten path to feel secluded."

"Sounds perfect."

"Oh, it is." He nodded vigorously, sure of the statement, and opened his mouth to say more, then seemed to think better of it. "Lots of things are changing around here, Emmy, and just as many are remaining the same."

Cryptic. She wasn't sure what to make of such a statement. The inn was transforming, and the community itself seemed to have grown up since she'd left several years ago. But the hometown feel remained the same.

Her heart seemed to mirror the sentiment. She'd done some growing up as well, yet her heart retained a myriad of feelings for Jayson. She needed only to sort them out—to fit all the pieces together.

What about his feelings...for her?

"Hopefully the inn will be so popular and so booked to the gills they'll need to bring on a groundskeeper and staff, like in the old days." Jayson's voice, soothing as the velvet sky, drew her back.

"That would be fantastic."

What had he been thinking of moments before as he gazed toward the wooded pasture? Was he considering the time they'd spent there during their wanderings together years ago? Emmy had often thought the property would provide the perfect site for a home, both tranquil and functional—not to mention gorgeous.

"I've always loved this area."

"Me too." With its lush green landscape framed by rolling foothills, one might easily become lost in the beauty. "The inn is such a historical landmark here in Hope Creek. So many good times...so many memories. I'm glad Aunt Dahlia thought to book me a room here."

Jayson paused as the path curved and turned to face her.

"Are you sure about that—enjoying this even though I'm also here and we're trapped in this snowstorm together?"

"Yes." She didn't hesitate, but voiced the single word with her whole heart.

Being here with Jayson proved the one point she *was* sure of. The storm that only yesterday had seemed to be a curse, now proved a blessing in disguise. How else might she have been afforded the time to sort out her feelings...to come to terms with it all?

"Good. At least we have that." Jayson's smile spoke volumes. He brushed snowflakes from the damp swatch of hair that swept across her forehead to blur her vision. "It's a start...a very good start."

"I'm enjoying the break from our work schedule and, for the record, I don't feel trapped." Emmy returned his smile. His tender touch had loosened the knots in her belly. "I feel...just right. I know I haven't been very gracious, but this storm has given me time to reflect."

"And what sort of conclusion have you come to?"

"I'm still sorting that out." She refused to offer a more direct answer—not until she felt completely certain herself. "But there's starlight at the end of the tunnel."

"Yes." Jayson followed her gaze, saw the stars lifting their sleepy heads, and nodded slightly. He reached for her hand, sheltering it in his as they resumed their walk alongside one another in a comfortable silence, simply listening to the night sounds and drinking in the expanse of sky. "Does that starlight include me?"

"I'm not sure how everything fits together." Hoping for something that couldn't be would do neither of them any good. So many variables stood in their path. Her dreams—her home and future—were in California now.

But would those hopes and dreams remain there?

"It's OK, Emmy." Jayson's gentle voice lacked the overtone of reproach that she expected. Had their roles been reversed—had he made such a statement to her—she would have felt wounded. Yet he put those feelings aside for her sake. "We've got time."

His lack of censure eased waves of nervous impulses that fired along her spine. She paused as they approached the gazebo set into gardens with a grand, tiered waterfall near the center. Though the fall stood dry and silent in the midst of the winter storm, her mind recalled the beauty of its sprawling flow.

She spied the oak where she and Jayson used to picnic together on warm summer days when they were both able to get away from school and work obligations. Limbs bowed beneath the weight of snow, but she recalled the glorious, leafy summertime umbrella that lent shade from the heat of the sun. "Do you remember how we used to sneak over here and go exploring?"

"We'd sit right here in the grass and listen to the song of the creek—Jingle Bell Creek, you called it." He nodded. "Max would tag along and romp in the water, then hop out and sun himself on one of the rocks over there, as if he hadn't a care in the world." He motioned to the large outcropping of boulders that framed part of the shoreline.

"Right." Emmy pictured the scene in her mind's eye, and despite the stiff north breeze the sounds of summer came alive again. "The squirrels drove him crazy, racing by his snout to gather nuts and berries, and then scurrying just out of reach along the tree trunks to hide their wares."

"He never caught one, despite his enthusiastic attempts." Jayson belly laughed. "You know, your name for the water— Jingle Bell Creek—stuck. I believe it's on all the promotional materials for Christmas Inn."

"I've noticed that." She'd seen the wording in pamphlets at the inn's welcome desk. "We always ate well on those picnics. You'd pack turkey and tomato sandwiches on slabs of homemade wheat bread from your grandmother's kitchen and a thermos of her sweet sun tea for us to share."

"The tomatoes came straight from her garden and oh, how I miss that tea." Jayson paused as a faraway look overtook his gaze. "It sported just a splash of lemon for a tang and enough sugar to turn our blood to molasses."

She wondered if he was thinking of his grandmother, gone now for half-a-dozen years, and the way she'd waggle a finger at him as he led Emmy off on another adventure. *"Bring sweet Emmy home safe, Jayson. Bring her home safe."*

He'd done just that, time and time again. He'd laughed with her, protected her. Brought her home.

Loved her.

"I miss Granny's tea, too." In truth, she missed more than the tea. A sense of nostalgia wove through the fibers of her heart and she did her best to tamp it down, refocus. "There's none other like it."

Some things in life could not be duplicated. Was her relationship with Jayson one of them? She'd gone to dinner and to the occasional show with her fair share of men in California, but none of them had gained her admiration enough to warrant a second date.

Only Jayson had ever managed as much.

They passed by a merry display of colorful holiday décor and then crossed the North Pole Bridge over Jingle Bell Creek. Emmy drew a deep breath as they approached the chapel, a devout and ready sentinel overlooking the countryside.

The wooded expanse of rolling hills beyond lay undeveloped, and the scene could not have been more perfect if it had been captured on a postcard. She'd often wondered what would become of the land, and was surprised to find it had not yet been developed. Again, a sense of longing laced with nostalgia bubbled to the surface. What a perfect place to build a home…to raise children.

Last she'd heard, the Christmas family owned it. Perhaps she'd speak to them and see if they were willing to bargain. Perhaps one day…

"Have you ever seen anything so magnificent?" The words formed on a sigh from deep inside her.

"Yes, I have." Jayson paused and turned to her. He stroked a finger along her cheekbone. "You, Emmy. You're magnificent—top to bottom, inside and out."

Her pulse raced at the tenderness of his touch and the sincerity in his tone. She leaned into him and tilted her head to find his gaze. For a moment she hoped he'd kiss her just as he had for the first time, right here on the chapel steps.

She longed to hear the song of the bells once again.

He skimmed his hand along her back and paused at the base of her spine, cradling her against the cold.

"Jayson, I think…I want…" She could hardly speak, could barely utter a sound. The words lodged in her throat.

"What do you want, Emmy?"

She wanted him to kiss her, to take her back to the happy, carefree days that they'd shared.

She wanted forever with him.

The need washed over her in a wave that nearly swept her under.

Then fear crept in, causing her to shiver, and pinpricks of reality banded together and surged into focus.

There was no going back to the way things once were—only moving forward into what they might become. Could she take that leap of faith? Was it fair to Jayson—or to her—to give either of them the impression she was ready to do that?

For a moment she stood paralyzed, unable to move, simply to be.

Then she found her lungs, inhaled deeply. She took a step back as her throat tightened and her vision blurred with the threat of tears.

"We should keep walking." She drew her hand from Jayson's and swiped at her eyes before she tucked a fist into her coat pocket. "And find what we came for before the next squall blows in."

**\*\*\*\***

Jayson saw Emmy's gaze wander to the chapel and then the partially-wooded pasture beyond. He knew what whispered to her heart, although he'd also determined she had yet to acknowledge it.

So he'd wait to tell her the property that she loved so much, that she'd chattered on and on about during their dating days, belonged to him now.

And that he longed to share it—to make a life together and raise a family—with her.

Ari Christmas and her family had sold him the five-acre swatch, tucked into the wooded cove and set far enough back from the road to seem as if it existed in its own tranquil universe. The location proved convenient for daily commutes to and from work at the theater, yet perfect with its measure of solitude.

"This will only take a minute." He climbed the steps to the chapel entrance and pushed open the door. A portable karaoke machine, once used for outdoor weddings and the receptions that followed, was tucked into one of the hall closets. Ari Christmas had mentioned so in passing. "Come stand in the foyer while I gather a little entertainment for tomorrow's snow day."

"OK." She followed him through the chapel's heavy double doors, fashioned of solid wood that had just been polished and cheerfully adorned with festive wreaths laden with holly. Warmth welcomed and he switched on a panel of lights, casting the sanctuary with an angelic glow.

Though the interior was beautifully decorated in anticipation of an upcoming evening service, Emmy paid the intricately woven wreaths and silver-glazed angels little mind.

Instead, she wandered to the side window that overlooked the pasture beyond. With her forehead pressed to the glass, she resembled a child longing for Christmas treasures.

With a little help Jayson would bring those treasures to her. Whether or not she chose to accept them was entirely up to her.

But he hoped she would do just that.

# 9

"WOW, THAT WAS CUTER THAN sunshine," Emmy said to Jayson as Chrissy Sheridan finished a rousing rendition of *Santa Claus is Coming to Town* at the karaoke machine. For a six-year-old, the child had a big voice and an even larger personality. She was sweet as granny's sun tea, with a smile that charmed the socks off a crowd.

Applause sounded and the little girl curtsied on the makeshift stage at the front of the dining room. Jayson had fashioned the raised floor that afternoon from a piece of plywood and several two-by-fours. Their idea to host a karaoke concert had proven a hit.

Now that her turn was finished, Chrissy made her way to Jayson. The smile on her cherubic face framed two rows of pearly-white baby teeth.

"That was fun!" Chrissy brought her hands together in a flurry of claps.

"Great job, sweetie." Jayson patted her head.

"Do you think Max liked it?" She eyed the dog, curled at Emmy's feet. His jowls were splayed across her toes as if holding her there so she couldn't escape.

Not that she wanted to.

"I think he loved it," Jayson assured Chrissy, garnering a giggle.

"Thanks, Mr. Jayson." Chrissy patted his cheek with her chubby hand. "You're the best. I love karaoke."

"It was Emmy's idea. She loves to sing, too."

Only partially true, since they'd come up with the idea together. But it was just like Jayson to deflect credit to others.

"Thank you, Miss Emmy." Chrissy climbed onto her lap long

enough to press a quick kiss to her forehead, then scrambled down again and skipped one table over to join her dad.

Kids and dogs loved Jayson, Emmy knew this with certainty.

She loved him too. But was it too late? He'd been a little standoffish today, and she wondered what was rambling around inside his head.

"It's your turn now, Mr. Jayson and Miss Emmy," Chrissy called. "Sing for me."

Soon, she had the others in the dining room chanting in unison, "Sing, sing, sing!"

"Well?" Jayson tilted his head to slice a look her way. "Shall we?"

His chair scratched along the tile as he pushed back from the table. He reached for her hand as he stood.

"I suppose we shall."

There was no getting out of it. Emmy rose from her seat and wound toward the stage with Jayson.

A duet was in order. Perfect.

Jayson thumbed through the playlist until he found a familiar song. He waited as Emmy read the title. She nodded her approval of the ballad they both knew well by memory, since it was included in their lineup for Aunt Dahlia's holiday show. No need to worry over words.

He cued the music.

Sharing the only microphone, they stood close together as the harmony portion approached.

Emmy tried to focus on the words.

They'd practiced the ballad a hundred times, but the sound had never meshed quite so beautifully. All eyes focused on them, yet as Jayson turned to her, she felt as if they were the only two in the room.

Then she was completely swept away when he took the microphone from her, set it aside, and drew her into his arms.

The room swirled as he sang to her—only to her.

The words were at once familiar yet also magnified in their

message. They spoke to her heart...to her very soul. She could only listen and try to breathe.

Time seemed to stand still as the world around them disappeared.

"Jayson..." The single word—his name—proved a vessel that coiled all of her emotions together and decoded them in a single moment in time.

As the song closed and the music faded, he pulled her close and kissed her.

In the distance, carrying ever-so-faintly on a breeze, came the joyful toll of church
bells.

\*\*\*\*

The room went silent following the fade of music. Completely silent.

A strangled sound rose from Emmy's throat to spill over and only then did Jayson fully realize what had happened. He'd kissed her. And she'd kissed him back. Without hesitation.

But then she took off running through the dining room doors and out onto the deck, down the steps and across the grounds that were turning sleepy beneath the first hints of dusk.

He watched her go, too dumbfounded to move. But not for long.

"Emmy!" He took off after her, grabbing his coat from the hook by the door. She'd left hers hanging over the back of her dinner chair, and he snatched it up on his way. "Wait!"

She'd made it as far as the gazebo before he overtook her.

"Jayson, please let me go."

"Not like this." He blocked her path. "Talk to me."

Her baby blue sweater made her dark eyes pop and the familiar scent that clung to her skin had his senses reeling. He vaguely wondered if she could read his mind. Did she know how much she undid him?

"I-I can't." Her teeth chattered beneath the bite of darkness.

"You can't or you won't?"

"Does it really matter?"

"Yes. It matters to me."

He draped her coat over her shoulders, and she shoved her arms through the sleeves, diving into the offered warmth. The snow-covered ground glittered like starlight beneath a full moon, mirroring her shimmering eyes.

"I'm sorry." She sounded miserable. As if she was being torn in two. "I'm so sorry, Jayson, for everything. For...this."

The words cut him to the core, and for the first time since she'd returned he felt a nip of anger.

"Well, I'm not." He refused to allow the cold to overtake him as he forged ahead. "I'm not sorry I kissed you, Emmy. In fact, I want to kiss you again."

"How? Why? How could you want—?"

He leaned in, captured her mouth as he drew her close. The world stood still, as if shuddering on the brink of something both exhilarating and terrifying. There was no turning back now, merely a quick plunge into the future—for better or worse. Warmth wove through as the kiss deepened.

"If you're intent on walking away again, at least you'll walk with a memory of this." His words were clipped as he came up for breath. "Think of it, Emmy—deny it if you can. But whatever you decide, know I loved you then, I love you now, and I'll love you with my last breath.

Before she could protest, he pressed his lips to hers one last time. Then, without another word, he turned and left her standing there with nothing but the melodic thrum of church bells and an angel at each shoulder.

# 10

**EMMY FINISHED HER CLOSING NUMBER** for the final performance of Aunt Dahlia's Christmas charity show, and exited stage right. Instead of a sense of satisfaction and euphoria, she felt only a wave of deflation.

Tomorrow was Christmas Eve and her flight was scheduled to take off just before midnight. She'd be home by daybreak.

*Home...*

Why didn't the idea of snuggling beneath the covers in her very own bed warm her more? The thought of luxuriating in the California sunshine as she sipped coffee on the small patio in her apartment complex should fill her with glee, but it didn't. She already felt homesick for Hope Creek and she hadn't even left yet.

She was tired. The show schedule had proved grueling as they attempted to recover missed performances. When the storm had finally cleared and people were able to putter down the road once again, Aunt Dahlia had arranged two-a-day performances to accommodate the record crowds. After three days of being relentlessly snowed-in, everyone seemed eager to return to the hustle and bustle of holiday cheer.

"I've just spoken with my accountant. We've met our goal and then some," Aunt Dahlia announced as she came around the corner to join Emmy in the wings. "The hospital will break ground on the pediatric wing this spring."

"That's wonderful." Emmy threw her arms around Aunt Dahlia and hugged tight. "I never doubted you for a minute."

"Nor have I doubted you, dear." She nodded. "You've been a trooper. I suppose you'll be on your way now?"

"I...Yes, I suppose." She glanced around the room. "Have you seen Jayson? I think I'll ask him for a ride back to the inn to gather my things."

"Oh, he's gone and took Max with him. He mentioned something about meeting up with an architect. Something to do with the parcel adjacent to the inn that they were going to take a look at together."

"I'm sorry I missed him."

She'd hoped to say goodbye, at least.

"Yes, but I'm sure you have packing to do. I'll leave you to it. Louis will take you to the inn, and then on to the airport when you're ready."

"Thank you."

"Merry Christmas, Emmy." Aunt Dahlia leaned in to hug her, and the familiar scent of her perfume caused a pang of regret.

Tears burned Emmy's eyes. She had stubbornly booked the red-eye flight before she left California for Hope Creek, despite Aunt Dahlia's oft-repeated invitation to stay for the holidays. She'd thought she'd be more than eager to return to the sanctuary of her modest loft as soon as the final performance ended. Now she had only to gather her suitcases and head to the terminal. Things were going exactly as she'd planned.

So why did she feel so miserable?

\*\*\*\*

Moonlight spilled across the field as the last of melting snow purged itself from rooftops with its soft, melodic symphony. Jayson's meeting with the architect had gone well. Together, they'd rendered a seamless design for the lay of the land.

Everything seemed perfect. Everything but—

"Jayson?"

Barely a murmur. Jayson swung toward the soft voice, certain he was dreaming.

Emmy stood awash in starlight and more beautiful than he'd ever seen her with her hair flowing and her eyes shimmering dark as midnight.

"You're supposed to be gone." He could barely speak for the

breath that caught in his throat. His pulse thrummed along his jawline to march around the nape of his neck. "I figured your flight would have taken off, that you'd be over Nashville—"

"I'm not going."

"And home by morning." His words plowed right over hers. "That I'd never see..."

His voice trailed off. What had she said?

"I *am* home."

Soft as a whisper, her assertion filled his ears.

"You're not...going?" He couldn't wrap his brain around it. "You're staying...*here*?"

"I'm staying home—with you here in Hope Creek." She stepped in, pressed her head to his shoulder. "I've been a fool to drag this out so long, to allow fear to overtake my heart. I don't know what the future holds, Jayson, but whatever it may be I can't imagine letting another memory go by without you in it—without sharing it with you."

"Emmy..." His heart raced like a piston in his chest. She probably heard it clear as the night sky overhead. Suddenly the future—everything he'd imagined and hoped for—fell into place.

"After all this time and despite my stubborn pride, do you still love me, Jayson? Do you still want me...want *us*?"

"Do I love you...want us...?" he murmured, pressing his lips to her crown with a hint of merriment because his heart felt so full he was sure it would burst wide open. "Those angels...I knew they'd watch over you, and bring you home to me."

"Yes, home...with you..." She pressed a palm to his cheek and leaned in for a kiss. "...forever."

# ~ About Mary ~

**MARY MANNERS** is a country girl at heart who has spent a lifetime sharing her joy of writing. She has two sons and a daughter, as well as three beautiful grandchildren. She currently lives along the sunny shores of Jacksonville Beach with her husband Tim.

A former teacher as well an intermediate school principal, Mary spent three decades teaching math and English to students from kindergarten through middle grades. While growing up in Chicago and as a coed at the University of Illinois, Mary worked her way through a variety of jobs including paper girl, figure skating instructor, pizza chef, and nanny. Many of these enriching and challenging experiences led to adventures that continue between the pages of her stories. Mary loves long sunrise runs—she's completed three marathons—ocean sunsets and flavored coffee.

Connect with Mary at her website:
**www.MaryMannersRomance.com.**
"Like" her author page on Facebook:
**www.facebook.com/MarysReaderPage/**
Follow her on Twitter:
**www.twitter.com/MaryManners1**

# ~ More Titles by Mary Manners ~

*Sweet Summer Love (Christian Romance for the Ages)*

## Wildflower Wishes Series

*Magnolias and Mercy*
*Tulips and Truth*
*Gardenias and Grace*
*Poinsettias and Promises*

## Miracle Cove Series

*Miracle Cove: The Collection*
*Christmas in Miracle Cove*
*Mischief in Miracle Cove*
*Secrets in Miracle Cove*
*A Miracle Cove Reunion*

## Honeysuckle Cove Series

*Sunrise at Honeysuckle Cove*
*Beyond the Storm*
*Honeysuckle Cove Secrets*
*Showered by Love*
*Moonlight Kisses*
*Sweet Tea and Summer Dreams*
*A Pair of Promises*

*Honeysuckle Cove: The Collection*
*Honeysuckle Cove Collection 1 – Print*

## Diamond Knot Dreams Series

*A Tender Season (Diamond Knot Dreams Prequel)*
*Veiled Gems*
*Jeweled Dreams*
*Precious Fire*
*Crystal Wishes*
*Diamond Knot Dreams: The Collection*

## The Mulvaney Sisters Series

*Love on a Dare (The Mulvaney Sisters: Alana)*
*Captive at Sea (The Mulvaney Sisters: Claire)*
*Landing in Love (The Mulvaney Sisters: Erin)*

## Serenity Lake Series

*Dream Come True*

## Christmas Collections

*Love at Christmas Inn: Collection 1*
*Love at Christmas Inn: Collection 2*

## Stand-alone Titles

*Promises Renewed*
*Tragedy and Trust*
*Hopes and Kisses (A Sweet Little Sequel to Tragedy and Trust)*
*Proven Love*
*A Pocketful of Wishes*
*Winter Wishes and Snowflake Kisses*
*Seasoned Lies*
*Honor's Reward*

# ~ Connect with Mary Manners ~

I hope you enjoyed reading *With Bells On*. If you did, please consider leaving a short review on Amazon. Positive reviews and word-of-mouth recommendations honor an author while also helping fellow readers to find quality fiction to read.

Thank you so much!

If you'd like to receive information on new releases, please follow me here:

**www.amazon.com/Mary-Manners/e/B004AL16YY/**

Want to join the fun on my street team and help spread the word about my books? Find information here:

**www.facebook.com/groups/MaryMannersPageTurners**

Please visit my website for more of my books:
**www.MaryMannersRomance.com**

Follow me on Bookbub:
**www.bookbub.com/authors/mary-manners**

You can also find me on social media:

**www.amazon.com/Mary-Manners/e/B004AL16YY/**

**www.facebook.com/MarysReaderPage/**

**https://twitter.com/MaryManners1**

# Love at Christmas Inn

## Bells on Her Toes

# DELIA LATHAM

# Bells on Her Toes

## Delia Latham

*"Make pomegranates of blue, purple and scarlet yarn
around the hem of the robe, with gold bells between them.
The gold bells and the pomegranates are to alternate around
the hem of the robe. Aaron must wear it when he ministers.
The sound of the bells will be heard when he enters
the Holy Place before the Lord..."*
*~ Exodus 28:33-35 (NIV) ~*

# *1*

**"WE'RE EARLY." KARYNN MICHAELS GLANCED** at her cell phone screen. "By a whole two hours. How could we have over-estimated driving time by that much?"

"We didn't." Her sister swung her luxury sedan into a small shopping center a few blocks from their destination and slid smoothly into a parking slot. She shot Karynn an impish grin and opened her door. "I got us here early so you could get a head start on unwrapping your gift."

"Savannah!" She climbed out, and then stood for a second, listening for the beep that assured her the doors were locked. "What are you up to now?"

Her gaze swept the storefronts lined up side by side. The little strip mall boasted only a half dozen or so businesses. Which of them was her sister all set to dash into and lay down more money?

Savannah could afford to spend lavishly, now that she'd married Dr. Darren Quinn, brain surgeon extraordinaire. Karynn rejoiced in the couple's happiness and was thrilled for her sister—who grew up right along with her in the school of hard knocks, hard work and staying hard at it to keep the wolves from the door.

Still, despite her genuine joy in Savannah's happiness and

financial security, she cringed when the younger woman tossed money around like game board cash. This trip to Hope Creek, for instance. Why couldn't her sister be like everyone else and just wrap up a bathrobe or a good book for her birthday? But no…nothing would do but to bring Karynn here—several hours from their hometown of Quillpoint—for a ten-day vacation at Christmas Inn. They'd be in Hope Creek all the way through Karynn's birthday on December 25th. Darren would join them on Christmas Eve.

She didn't dare think about the fact that Hearth & Home, the bed and breakfast that was her livelihood, would be closed for two entire weeks. She'd manage the loss of income by cutting corners for a while. Growing up poor taught a person how to live on less than most people thought possible.

Savannah rounded the hood of the car and pulled her into a tight hug. "Sis, just let me do this for you. Please? Darren *wants* me to. He gave me specific instructions to pull out all the stops and show you the time of your life." She batted her long lashes like a preening prima donna. "He said he owes you for taking such awesome care of his 'Precious' until he could take over."

They both burst out laughing, despite the truth of the exaggerated presentation. Dr. Quinn adored his wife and always referred to her as 'my Precious,' never mind the negative connotations brought about in recent years by a popular book-turned-movie. Unlike Karynn, Darren didn't waste time and effort trying to please everyone.

Savannah grabbed her hand and tugged her along as she stepped out of the parking slot and onto a wide sidewalk. "Seriously, Karynn, my husband thinks you're pretty special, and he's right. You are. So this year, we want to pamper you for your birthday. Will you just let us do that without fretting the entire time?"

"Oh, sweetie…I promise to try, but you know how I am." Karynn heaved a hopeless sigh. "If life were to roll along without a single kink in the works, I'd fret because there's nothing to fret about."

"Well, then I'll consider it my job to foil your frets. See this?" Savannah whirled in a circle and pivoted to a stop directly in front of Karynn, who came close to barreling into her.

"Vanna!" She brushed off her sweater, which didn't need brushing. Still, it made her feel better to administer a stinging slap to *something*.

"Sorry, Sis. But look at me." Savannah tilted her head forward, raised one perfect eyebrow and dipped the other one. "When you see me do this, you'll know you're being an old fuddy-duddy fretter."

"What are you, eight years old?" Karynn tried to give her sister a stern look, but when Savannah only repeated the 'fuddy-duddy' alert, she burst out laughing instead. "Fine. I will try to behave more like my crazy, lighthearted, totally irresponsible little sister. Now, will you stop doing that?" She cast a furtive glance around. "People will think you're strange."

"Uh-uh…that's fretting!" Still, Savannah stopped rolling her eyes, linked arms with Karynn and they were on the move again. "Anyway, I am strange."

"Well, you got that right." Karynn giggled, and then blinked. Twice. *Giggling? Really? Now who's the eight-year-old?*

"This is it!" Savannah trilled. "We're here."

Karynn read the sign on the window and suppressed a sigh. *Nail It.*

"I take it we're getting manicures?"

"And pedicures—a double-digits treat. And we're right on time for our appointment." She opened the door, enacted an exaggerated bow, and waved Karynn inside with a flourish. "After you, birthday girl!"

\*\*\*\*

Later that evening, Karynn started to slip one foot into a brand new, strappy red heel, but paused to consider. She loved the shoes, in spite of the scary price tag they'd worn when she spotted them.

But the bright, cheery bells, one on each of her toes....

"Maybe I should wear something else. Don't get me wrong...I loved the mani-pedi, but my sweet, little Bohemian toe tickler might have gone a bit over the top. I'm not sure I want to hang these showy toes out there for everyone to see."

"*What?* No way, Sis. You're wearing those heels. And your toes look fabulous!" She crossed the room to stand in front of Karynn. The silver sequins around her dipping neckline caught the light and sent out a myriad of bright sparkles as she moved. "Honey, they're not gaudy at all. You asked for a soft, nearly transparent background. What's so showy about that? And the bells are beautiful—not large or distasteful in any way. You look stunning, Karynn, and I love that your finger-and-toe designs match so perfectly."

Karynn sighed and slipped on the shoes. Savannah would throw a fit if she refused to wear them, and it wasn't worth an argument. At least her hands sported tiny bells only on the ring fingers.

Moving to the full-length mirror, she took in her completed look for the formal dinner downstairs. She hadn't dressed up for anything in such a long time...maybe this was too much.

"Oh, no, you don't." Her sister stepped up beside her and used the fuddy-duddy alert for the first time since they'd left the salon. "You look absolutely beautiful. Not in the least pretentious or overdressed." She laughed when Karynn's eyes widened. "What? I've known you all my life, remember? You always think you have to live in someone else's shadow. Well, not tonight. Tonight you shine!"

Savannah reached up to touch Karynn's hair, arranged in a loose coil behind one ear, with wispy strands hanging free. Tiny, pearl-tipped pins sparkled from within the twist.

"You look like Italian royalty. Do you seriously not know how lovely you are?" She kissed Karynn's cheek—lightly. "Don't want to mess up the little touch of makeup you allowed yourself. Thing is, on you it's enough. You look amazing completely *au naturale*, but this—a bare touch of cosmetics to highlight your beauty—it's perfect." She shook her head. "I can't believe some guy hasn't scooped you up and carried you away, long ago."

"Oh, stop it." Karynn gave her sister a quick hug, and then ran both hands over the deep red fabric that hugged her hips and flowed like a silky river to her ankles. "I don't need a man to sweep me off my feet, and I'd never leave Quillpoint. You're the only family I've got, kiddo. You're stuck with me."

"Hmmm...what if Daniel showed up again?"

A quick intake of air, and then Karynn regained the composure she'd lost for half a second. "If Daniel had wanted to return, he would have by now. Let's not talk about him."

"Then let's talk about the box of Daniel-memories you still keep in your closet."

She rolled her eyes and busied herself putting on a pair of her sister's triple-strand diamond earrings. Savannah had insisted they—and the matching necklace—were perfect accessories for her outfit, but Karynn wouldn't be comfortable until the expensive trinkets were back in the safe.

"Savannah..."

"I know, I know. But tell me about them, and I'll leave it alone." Savannah settled on the side of her bed to watch Karynn finish getting ready. "Although..." She lowered her voice to a mutter. "I think I know why every single man who's tried to win you over in the past decade has 'lacked that certain something.'"

Karynn chuckled. She'd almost heard herself in Savannah's silly impression. "Oh, do you now?"

"Yep. That 'certain something' they all lacked? They weren't Daniel Sheridan."

Karynn turned to face her pesky sister, both earrings swinging. "What does it matter?"

"It matters because you have to move on, Sis. Or maybe we could find Daniel!" Savannah's blue eyes took on a gleam that knotted every nerve in Karynn's body. "We'll hire a private investigator and—"

"Savannah! Listen to yourself!" Karynn snatched up the soft, white wrap spread across her bed and pulled it over her shoulders. "Daniel was my high school sweetheart. He and his family left, and we eventually lost contact. It happens. We were kids, honey."

She perched on the edge of the bed and took her sister's hand. "I keep the box in my closet because it holds memories that are still sweet, even though things didn't work out for Daniel and me—not because I'm still weeping over him, or dreaming of the day he returns." She stood, tugging the younger woman up beside her. "Now let's go down to dinner."

"OK." Savannah crossed to the mirror for one last look at herself. "Oh, wait! You're supposed to ring your bell."

Karynn's 'Bells on Her Toes' mani-pedi package had included a beautiful handheld crystal bell...and a series of ten 'promidictions'—some promises, some cheesy predictions. She'd been instructed by the petite, flower-child pedicurist to ring the crystal bell once a day, after reading that day's 'wise words.' Karynn preferred to call it a daily slice of absurdity.

"You don't expect me to play along with that silly bell-ringing ritual?"

"It'll be fun!" Savannah reached for the box in which the crystal bell resided. "May I?"

"Knock yourself out."

Savannah lifted the bell from its satin bed. "It's lovely."

"Yes." *And a good part of why that mani-pedi package was so expensive.* Karynn bit down on her bottom lip, and then made a deliberate decision to share something of herself with her sister. "You know, there's a bell in that box of 'Daniel-memories' in my closet. Just a cheap, glass one, but Daniel gave it to me the day he left Quillpoint." She stared off into the corner of the room, remembering how he'd used his thumb to brush away her tears, and pulled her in for a sweet kiss before he handed her the bell. "He said to ring it and think of him when I was lonely."

"Did you?"

"Many times." Karynn tucked a small, sequined clutch under

her arm and headed for the door. "But he mustn't have heard, because ringing that bell never brought him back. After a while, he didn't even call anymore. Let's go eat."

"First you have to ring this. I insist—and read the first promidiction."

Karynn laughed and joined Savannah in the vanity area.

Ten small envelopes lay beneath the satin cushion on which the bell had rested. Karynn removed a single half-sheet of paper from the one marked "Today," and read the beautiful, flowing script aloud, for Savannah's benefit. "*You will come into contact with someone from your past. Whether the relationship was romantic, familial, or a simple friendship, its revival will impact your future in unforgettable ways.*"

Karynn rolled her eyes, but she picked up the bell and swung it back and forth, enjoying the sweet, high tinkle in spite of the ridiculous situation. "There. Now let's go." She reclaimed her evening bag and widened her eyes. "Perhaps this mystery person waits in the dining room even now."

Savannah gave her another fuddy-duddy face, but said no more.

The sisters admired the lovely Christmas decorations as they made their way downstairs. A dainty garland of holly berries and silver bells wound around the baluster, from the newel post at the top to the identical one at the bottom of the staircase. Over the fireplace, a large clock boasted elves that popped out every quarter hour to chase each other behind the timepiece and back inside.

Darren's family had wonderful memories of Christmas Inn, where they'd often spent brief vacations. "It never mattered what time of year we were there," he had told them. "The place is like having Christmas all year round. It's beautiful, and the décor is breathtaking. I was a kid—and a boy, so I didn't really notice particulars, but it did make an impression. You girls will love it."

Karynn did love it. While retaining the all-important elements of welcome and home, the inn also possessed an unmistakable touch of class. She was eager to explore the gift shop. Perhaps she'd find something to enhance those same elements at Hearth & Home.

A faint smell of paint, varnish and new carpet hung in the air, lending a clean, fresh ambiance. Had the place fallen into disrepair at some point? Many clues pointed to a recent facelift...but then, Karynn's efforts to maintain her bed and breakfast made her aware that keeping a place like Christmas Inn in this kind of condition would be a constant, ongoing effort.

"This is it." Savannah spoke in an awed tone, so unlike her usual fun-at-all-costs persona that Karynn bit back a grin. Her sister was impressed with their surroundings, as well.

They stood in the door of the dining room, getting their bearings.

White linen cloths topped six round tables, each of which boasted a three-arm candelabrum. Candlelight played over bright Christmas baubles and gleaming silverware.

"Each table has its own holiday theme," Savannah noted.

Karynn lifted an eyebrow. "And each room is assigned to a specific table, based on theme?"

"Right. Ours is the bell theme." She laughed. "So is our room—and your toes. We'll be hearing bells in our sleep tonight, won't we?"

Karynn glanced down at the painted-on bells peeking from beneath the hem of her gown. They were growing on her. "That's OK. I like them. Let's find our table." She gave Savannah a quick, mischievous grin. "Or perhaps we should close our eyes and follow the sound of tinkling bells."

"Ha! I'm game, but you'd never make such a spectacle of yourself. Oh, I see it." Savannah pointed out a table that sported a bell-adorned wreath around the base of its candelabrum. "Only one other guest at our table, at least for now."

An older gentleman stood as they approached, a broad smile lighting his face. "Ladies." He pulled a chair out for each of them before returning to his own. "I am Gabriel D'Angelo."

They introduced themselves and Gabriel shone that sunny smile again. "It is an honor to meet such lovely sisters."

Karynn couldn't put a finger on why, but the man's presence calmed her. Gabriel D'Angelo wasn't just any sweet, elderly man from...where? Certainly not America, judging by his beautiful accent. She'd enjoy getting to know this guest.

"Gabriel, I'm guessing you are perhaps from...Italy?"

"Ahh...you are as perceptive as you are lovely. Venice."

"I thought so. What brings you to Tennessee?"

"I've come to deliver a message for an old friend." He smiled, but seemed disinclined to reveal more about his mission.

Karynn didn't pry. The man's purpose in Hope Creek was his own business.

"Savannah, may I be so presumptuous as to guess that you are a newlywed?" Gabriel ventured.

Savannah laughed outright. "How did you know?"

"It is easy to see beneath the surface, if one tries. You are quite young, yet you wear a beautiful wedding ring. You are glowing, so your heart is happy. It was a reasonably safe assumption."

"You had me going for a second!" Savannah said. "I was starting to think—"

A petulant female voice cut into their conversation. "I take it this is the bell table."

Something unpleasant coiled its way up Karynn's spine, and her breath caught in her throat. She'd experienced it before...the same instinctive, soul-deep, gut-wrenching aversion on first contact with an individual. Over time, she'd come to recognize the powerful inner reaction as more than the instant dislike some humans experience now and then toward one another. This wasn't a personality clash or adverse chemistry. Karynn called them Spirit-warnings, and she no longer downplayed their existence or their importance. They'd proven true and accurate one hundred percent of the time.

She fisted both hands, as if by tensing her fingers she could school her facial muscles to hide the war raging inside. Then she lifted her eyes to see what kind of person could call forth her Spirit-warrior by voice alone.

Copper-colored hair. Green eyes—up-tilted, almond shaped and narrowed to slits, like a cat on the hunt. A face that might have been lovely but for its bored, dissatisfied, self-indulgent expression. The newcomer held the hand of a small, blonde-haired girl whose sunny smile made up for her mother's lack of one.

"Please...join us." Gabriel stood once again and waved an arm toward the empty chairs.

"Thank you, but we're waiting for my daddy." The child's voice was as sweet as her smile.

"I'm here, Chrissy." A tall man with a trim, medium brown beard and slightly longish hair strode toward the table. "It's crazy cold out there, and the snow is—" He broke off and stopped as if frozen in place, sapphire-blue eyes wide, shocked...and fixed on Karynn.

"I, uh...I don't...Karynn? Karynn Michaels?"

The cat-eyed woman cast a waspish look at Karynn, and then back at her husband.

Savannah's soft laughter held a touch of pure wonder. "This is unreal."

Karynn refused to look at her sister. She forced a smile that felt wooden and dredged up every ounce of courage she possessed to hold the man's startled gaze. She prayed her eyes did not reflect the mixed emotions creating utter turmoil in her heart.

"Hello, Daniel. It's been a long time."

# 2

**STUNNED TO SILENCE, DANIEL COULD** only stare. Once upon a long time ago, he'd thought this lovely creature would one day be the mother of his children. Even now, she sometimes stole into his dreams…a sweet whisper of memory that lingered upon awakening to brighten his day and bring a smile. What unbelievable coincidence had brought them both to Hope Creek at the same time?

Someone discreetly cleared a throat.

Daniel blinked—once, and then again. This time, he was wide awake and fully alive. He hurried around the table to claim the chair next to Karynn.

After seating Chrissy between her nanny and himself, he met the copper-haired woman's slit-eyed gaze and tilted his head toward his daughter. She acknowledged his silent directive with a stiff smile. He'd half regretted bringing Lena along, but thank God she was here. Someone would need to keep his six-year-old occupied while he drank in the sight of the beautiful woman who had somehow, by some miracle, appeared in his waking world.

Introductions were made around the table, and by the time Daniel's turn rolled around, he felt a little less like he was muddling through dream-muck.

"Savannah? Little Vanna?" He grinned at the pretty blonde he remembered as a gangly pre-teen with braces and a super-sized attitude. "Look at you, kid! You're gorgeous, and judging by that rock on your finger, some lucky guy's already staked a claim."

"Still a charmer, aren't you, Daniel Sheridan? Some things never change." Savannah's sweet, natural laughter brought out answering smiles on every face around the table…except Lena Hinson's. The nanny appeared anything but charmed. "I was old enough, even back then, to notice. And yes, I am married, to the most amazing man on the planet—Quillpoint's own Dr. Darren Quinn."

"Our fair city's one and only brain surgeon." Karynn spoke softly, with an unmistakable satisfaction in her sister's happiness. "They are the most adorable couple ever, and I must agree—my brother-in-law is beyond wonderful."

"Well, he certainly has the most eye-stopping publicity team possible." Daniel smiled, and then tore his gaze from hers—deepest brown, like rich, dark chocolate, just as he remembered—and introduced his party to the other diners.

He liked Gabriel D'Angelo instinctively. The guy smiled, and the tightness in Daniel's gut relaxed a bit. Pure coincidence, of course. Gabriel's voice, while pleasant, couldn't have spoken peace into his muddled emotions. But something had, and he welcomed the lessening of tension in his gut.

Lena made no effort to greet anyone in response to Daniel's introduction. Puzzled, he turned toward her, only to find her narrowed gaze on Karynn. The set of her mouth, and the almost visible sparks shooting from her eyes sent little darts of...something—something he didn't like—deep into Daniel's psyche. He shook it off as a momentary glitch of consciousness, but it left a vague discomfort in his mind.

When she realized Daniel's gaze was on her, the nanny's instantaneous change of demeanor gave him another disconcerting jolt of...what? Warning? He felt sucker-punched, as if he'd watched someone don a new face, like some kind of shapeshifting thing. How could one person display two remotely different visages in almost the same second?

He frowned, but decided it was probably nothing. Caught up in the undeniably emotion-laden shock of running into the woman a part of him had never quite stopped loving, he'd probably read a whole lot of something into a little bit of nothing.

Time to get past it and enjoy what time he could with Karynn. He issued a stern mental reminder that their relationship—the all-

or-nothing, over-the-top whirlwind of young love—had lived and died over a decade ago. A quick glance at the six-year-old daughter he loved more than life was enough to bring his world into crystal clarity. A whole lot of water had rushed and tumbled and crashed under the bridge since he kissed Karynn goodbye on the football bleachers at Quillpoint High. At the time, he'd thought his heart would surely crack wide open and never mend.

*But that was then. This is now.*

Karynn might be curious about him, about who he'd become since they last saw each other—just as he was about her. But they'd both moved on, and survived without the other. He'd be careful not to interpret polite interest as anything more.

With introductions over, he was finally free to focus on her, and prayed the others would find their own paths of conversation. "I caught a glimpse of you in the parking lot this afternoon. You seemed familiar, but at that distance...and after all this time." He shook his head. Too bad he couldn't shake it hard enough to loosen the fog of disbelief still clouding his brain.

Karynn Michaels had been a knockout in high school. She'd wowed him even then. Now she was drop dead gorgeous, with a timeless beauty and a natural grace that stole his breath.

"I didn't see you. Not that I would have recognized you, with the beard." Her gaze moved over his face and head. "Is that snow in your hair? I thought the sky looked rather threatening when Savannah and I checked in, but we haven't been back outside."

"It's snow all right. I went outside to bring in a couple of things we might need tomorrow, since it might be a challenge to get to our vehicles by then. I believe it's ten degrees colder than when we arrived. The snow's coming down hard, and it's pretty windy."

Karynn glanced at her sister, a troubled frown between her eyes. "I'm pretty sure Savannah and I brought everything in..."

"We did, Sis." Savannah fixed her gaze on Karynn, tilted her head, and did something weird with her eyebrows. Then she plowed ahead as if she hadn't just given her face cartoon-character attributes. "We have everything we need, and the inn is probably well stocked in case of emergency. They don't serve dinner every night, and lunch not at all, but if we're housebound, I'm sure they'll improvise."

"I can assure you, no one will starve or suffer hypothermia within the walls of Christmas Inn." Gabriel's hearty laughter wove over and around the table like a soothing balm, and he gave Chrissy a special smile, for her alone. "It'll be an adventure, won't it, little one?"

"It'll be fun, fun, fun!" His daughter's tiny voice warmed Daniel's heart to a ridiculous degree. She clapped her hand, clearly enthralled with the idea of being snowbound. "If we have to be stuckted somewhere, Christmas Inn is the bestest place of all. Did you see, Daddy? There are elves in the clock! There's a Santa too...'cept he changed clothes, and now he's wearing a pretty white robe with silver stuff, 'stead of that ol' red thing he usually has on." Her nose wrinkled and she seemed puzzled for half a minute or so. Then she wrinkled her tiny nose. "Even Santa has to change clothes *sometimes*. He prob'ly has to brush his teeth too. *Ick!*"

Almost everyone laughed. Lena was the one exception, and she didn't appear likely to find anything funny any time soon. She couldn't have looked more sour with a lemon stuck between her teeth.

Daniel made a conscious decision to ignore her attitude, and didn't notice the nanny again all through dinner. All he could see or think about was the woman at his side. Quiet and even a bit stand-offish at first, she opened up like a rosebud in morning sunshine as they made their way through the meal. By the time a waiter took away their dessert plates and surprised them with small glasses of apple-flavored *digestifs*—and a mug of hot chocolate for Chrissy—Karynn glowed.

A long, soulful note of music filled the air, and Daniel looked up, surprised. He'd dashed inside in a rush, and then been knocked sideways when he found Karynn at his table. In all the excitement, he'd failed to notice the small stage in one corner of the room.

Two young women occupied the raised platform. Mirror images of each other, they both wore beautiful white gowns that shimmered beneath the lights. One sat next to a harp, fingers still poised over the strings, one of which she'd stroked to gain the attention of the diners. Her sister held a violin tucked beneath her chin. With the room silent and every eye fixed on them, the identical musicians sailed into a slow tune with underlying vibrations of sorrow, loss and longing, countered by higher notes of joy...victory...unconquered love.

The unexpected pairing of the two instruments created a phenomenal effect. Daniel glanced at Karynn, to find her entranced with the instrumental. Naturally rose-colored lips slightly parted, chocolate-brown eyes wide and bright. A vision.

Her gaze swung from the musicians to him, and Daniel's breath caught. Karynn in any color of the rainbow was a treat for the eyes. Karynn in red had always hit him like a thunderbolt. How could he have forgotten? Tonight the effect packed a double jolt. His breath took a brief vacation.

"Daniel? Are you all right?"

He made a herculean effort to regain his composure. "Yes, of course. Just...good, sweet Lord above, Karynn...you're stunning!"

She lowered her eyelashes, but a smile tugged her lips upward. Daniel waited...and there it was. The rosy blush that had always crept into her cheeks when she was pleased, or embarrassed, or just shy.

"You were always prone to exaggeration," she murmured.

"Not at all. I was just always trying to find ways to say how beautiful I found you. Even then."

"See? There you go again."

A glance toward the stage revealed a few couples swaying together on the dance floor. *Thank you, Lord!*

"Would you like to—?" He broke off. Huffed out a breath and shook his head. "I'm afraid to ask, because I don't want you to say no."

"But if you don't ask, I can't say yes." Was that a bit of mischief in her gaze? He'd seen it now and then when they were kids, but not often. And something told him she'd almost forgotten that side of herself.

"In that case...may I have this dance—and maybe another dozen or so?"

She bit down on her full bottom lip, sending hot bolts of something electric through Daniel's body. How long had it been since he'd experienced this kind of reaction to any woman?

"Oh! I don't—." She lifted one shoulder. "I haven't danced in absolutely forever."

"Then it's time, don't you think?"

She hesitated a moment longer, and then nodded. Once. As if the gesture would convince her she was doing the right thing.

"Yes. I'd love to dance."

Daniel turned to address Lena. "Please take Chrissy upstairs and get her ready for bed. I'll be up in time to tuck her in."

A quick, hissing intake of breath met his request. He ignored it.

"Chrissy, go with Lena. I'll be up soon to say goodnight."

"Yes, Daddy." She stood to wrap both arms around his neck, and then addressed the rest of the table's occupants in that sweet, innocent voice that never failed to grip Daniel by the heartstrings. "Goodnight, everyone. I have to go to bed now."

Lena stood and held out a hand. "Come, darling. Let's go."

Daniel frowned. Her hand shook. Was she drunk? But no one at their table had anything alcoholic to drink, except the complimentary *digestifs*, most of which still sat untouched beside their plates. Still, he had to remember to look a little deeper into tonight's behavior.

"I know the way." Chrissy sailed past her nanny's trembling hand with her tiny nose in the air and a frosty bite to her tone. "You don't need to *lead* me, Miss Lena."

Daniel blinked. He'd never heard his daughter address an adult with such blatant disrespect. He'd nip that in the bud before another day passed.

But not right now. He stood and held out a hand to Karynn, who shone that stunner of a smile and laid her fingers in his. Daniel escorted her to the dance floor, confident every man in the room experienced a twinge of envy...because every man there would have loved to dance with the beauty at his side.

****

Karynn's heart banged against her ribs with such force she wondered if she'd actually be sore the next morning.

Seriously? Twenty-seven years old and still behaving like a teenager with a massive crush? She wanted to give herself the biggest eye roll ever, but she'd look pretty silly doing that. Instead, she lifted her chin and smiled when Daniel pulled her into his arms on the dance floor.

*Breathe*...that was important, so she didn't swoon to the floor in front of all these people. But Daniel's unswerving gaze made it hard to remember to pull in a new breath after each exhale.

Enough. She had to say something to ease the unbearable awareness. "The music is heavenly, isn't it?"

"You're heavenly."

She'd been trying so hard to maintain eye contact...to not look away like a kid in the throes of puppy love. So much for that.

She looked over his shoulder in time to spot Chrissy in the doorway, her bright eyes fixed on the dance floor. The child's rapt expression spoke to her love of music, and her fascination with the rhythmic sway and bend of the dance. As Karynn watched, horrified, Lena snatched the child's arm in a talon-like grasp, thrust her face nose-to-nose with the little girl and said something. Her lips barely moved, and her green eyes glittered. Chrissy's lips quivered, but she didn't cry—she glared at Lena. Karynn saw the tug-of-war as the child attempted to pull her hand free.

Then Lena dragged Chrissy away, with the little one quick-stepping to avoid being thrown to the floor.

Karynn closed her eyes and forced air in and out of her lungs, fighting an anger that threatened to make her do something she'd regret later. Surely Daniel wouldn't entrust Chrissy to that woman's care if he were aware of Lena's mean streak. She'd noticed how the nanny's expression changed during dinner—from sour to sickly sweet, depending on whether Daniel was looking her way.

Would she hurt Chrissy?

No. Karynn hadn't been around Daniel in over a decade, but somehow she knew he wouldn't abide anyone laying a hand on his daughter. The child was unhappy at the moment, but Lena wouldn't dare harm her. Besides, this was none of Karynn's business. Daniel was lavish with compliments, to say nothing of far too handsome for her peace of mind. But he wouldn't appreciate her interference in his private life.

"What are you thinking?" He pulled away a little, his vivid blue gaze tracing her face. "You look troubled."

"Nothing. Really." She needed to think of something to say. Fast. "My sister's never going to let me forget this."

"Forget what?"

"Maybe I can tell you about it tomorrow? Right now, I just want to dance and listen to the harp and the violin. These ladies are fantastic!"

"They are." He pulled her a little closer. "You still fit perfectly under my chin."

She laughed. "You always used to say that. I'd forgotten."

Daniel's smile faded a little. "I hoped you hadn't forgotten me. I mean, you know, not entirely. We shared some special moments back in the day."

"We did, didn't we? I could never forget you, Daniel. You were my first love." *And my last.* "I thought for sure my life was over when you went away."

"Believe me, it wasn't easy for me either." He shook his head. "What happened to us, Karynn?"

# 3

"IT ISN'T THAT HARD TO piece together." She tried to maintain a steady voice, even as her heart pounded a timpani rhythm. "We were kids, Daniel. Long-distance relationships rarely work for young people."

"I should have tried harder."

"Perhaps we both should have." She offered a deliberately lighthearted smile. "I admit I shed a few tears when ringing my little bell a hundred times over didn't bring you running back to Quillpoint."

He grinned. "The bell! Oh, how I labored over what to buy you as a parting gift. I'm sure you eventually gave up and threw it against the wall."

Karynn gave him a high-browed glare. "Bite your tongue! That bell is in my closet—completely intact, I assure you—in a little box of what Savannah refers to as my 'Daniel-memories.'"

"You have a box of *me*-memories? So let me think." He swung her around once as the musician temporarily upped the tempo, and then settled back into a steady sway, much to Karynn's relief.

She could handle simply moving to the music, with Daniel's strong arms supporting her. But anything more complicated and she'd fall on her face. Her mother had seen to it that Karynn and Savannah knew all the basic dance steps, so the problem wasn't a lack of know-how—more an absence of strength. Her legs seemed noodle-weak, almost as if they didn't belong to her. A dance that required her to stand up on her own strength could prove disastrous.

"There might be a poinsettia in that box." Daniel was nothing if not persistent. "Although I'm sure it's crumbled by now."

"Entirely possible." Her lips curved into a smile all on their own. He had given her a single poinsettia when she turned sixteen, saying a rose just wouldn't work for a Christmas birthday. "But if there *were* a poinsettia in that box, it would not be crumbled. It would have been sprayed with a thick coat of hairspray—just as my mother taught me—and then hung upside-down to dry in the basement. Afterward, it would have been arranged ever so artfully in a shadow box frame, where it would—in theory, of course—remain intact…well, mostly intact…even now."

"Hmm." He tugged her closer and placed his lips close to her ear, where his warm breath shot a volley of delicious shivers through her entire body. "I wonder if somewhere amongst that box of treasures there might also be a class ring that once belonged to a lovesick high school quarterback?"

"Let me think…" She laughed when his vivid blue eyes widened. "I'm all but certain there's some small, hard item rolling around in there. But I'm getting older by the minute, you know, and I have slept more than once since I last looked at my Daniel-memories."

He laughed. "Well, I'd say that's probably because your husband doesn't much like you mooning over me-memories, but then, you're not wearing a ring on that pretty left hand of yours."

"No." She shook her head and put on the saddest of mock-sad expression she could manage while looking into sapphire eyes that still haunted her dreams. "Alas, you left me a broken woman. How was I to give someone else the heart you never returned?"

He chuckled. "You're a regular comedienne, aren't you? But I really want to know. Why aren't you married? And don't say no one's asked, because I'm not about to believe it."

Karynn raised an eyebrow. "I plead the fifth. A girl's got to have a few secrets."

The music stopped, and when it didn't start again, she looked around at the empty room.

"Everyone's gone!"

He laughed. "So they are. I guess we got a little carried away up here."

"You think?" She eased herself out of his arms and whirled toward their table. "I wonder if Savannah left my evening bag...and my wrap, of course. Oh, and we didn't say goodnight to—"

"Karynn."

She stopped when his voice broke through her rambling prattle, but refused to turn back. He might see something in her eyes that wasn't meant for his.

Strong arms circled her from behind and turned her to face him. A finger lifted her chin.

"Look at me."

She shouldn't have listened. But she raised her eyelashes, and found his gaze so full of longing...

He pressed his lips to the corner of hers and lingered there, creating havoc with her senses. "You taste the same," he murmured. Then he pulled away—oh, bittersweet relief!—and drew her hand through his arm. "We should get upstairs. I promised to tuck Chrissy in. You will be here tomorrow, won't you?"

"No, I plan to steal away during the night...in the storm...while my sister lies asleep in the bed next to mine."

She burst out laughing when he narrowed his eyes to slits and managed to hike one brow halfway to his hairline at the same time. Stopping for a moment at their table, she slung her wrap over one arm and picked up her purse. "This trip is my birthday gift from Savannah and her husband. We'll be here all the way through Christmas."

"We're spending Christmas here, as well. I try to do something special for Chrissy every year during the holidays. With her mother gone..." He trailed off, cleared his throat. "Well, it helps to have people around. I heard about Christmas Inn from friends, so here we are."

"And you came here from...?" They were on the stairs, but neither of them seemed in a hurry to get from the lobby to the upstairs landing.

"Tulsa."

"Oh, my! That's a great deal longer road trip than Savannah and I made."

"Road trip? Not a chance. We get super prices on airline flights. Our trip probably didn't take as long as yours." On the landing, his gaze danced from door to door. "Which room are you in?"

She stiffened, her mind filled with pictures of Daniel and that sweet child sailing through the air in a gleaming silver monster, many miles above the ground.

"Hey, you OK? You're a little pale."

"I'm fine." She hauled in a breath and pointed to a door only a few feet from where they stood. "Suite 2."

With a little chuckle, Daniel held out his hand. "Your key, m'lady."

He unlocked her room, leaned in to kiss her cheek, and then grinned and moved to the neighboring suite. "Suite 1. Goodnight, Karynn."

"'Night." She slipped inside and leaned against the door.

Even as her body thrummed with the unexpected pleasure of having been in Daniel's arms for the first time in over a decade, she felt the effects of a long day. Still, she dared not sleep. She'd had various versions of this same dream before, but never in such vivid technicolor. Karynn couldn't bear the thought of waking up to find she'd dreamt this entire, beautiful night with the man she'd never stopped loving.

\*\*\*\*

"Daddy! Wake up, Daddy! Come look outside!"

Chrissy's excited and insistent voice pierced through several foggy layers of sleep, and Daniel sat up with a huge yawn.

"What's all the hullaballoo, Princess?" He blinked at the clock. "How long have you been up?"

She giggled. "You woke me. You make choo-choo sounds when you sleep."

"Choo-choo sounds?" He widened his eyes, and then crept from beneath the covers and across the room with his hands curled into claw-like shapes. "Choo-choo trains can't tickle a fairy tale Princess 'til she screams, can they?"

Chrissy backed into the nearest corner, her blue eyes huge. Pink, bow lips twitched on each end as she tried not to laugh, already anticipating a tickle fest.

"No! No, Daddy. Please? I want to show you something."

Daniel stopped and narrowed his eyes. "Lock up the tickle monster?"

Her head bobbed up and down with vigor. "Uh-huh."

He crossed his arms and twisted his body back and forth as if struggling against an invisible opponent. Finally he dropped his hands to his sides and heaved a few breaths in and out. "I think I've got the Terrible Tickler locked away, but he's pretty slippery, you know. He could show up again any minute."

"I know!" Her eyes went even wider. "He always gets out."

"Well, he's not tickling anybody right this minute. What did you want to show me?"

She climbed into an easy chair in front of the window and stared outside. Daniel grinned at the sight she made. Fuzzy, footed jammies sported various depictions of a grinning, doltish-looking snowman from one of her favorite animated films. Long, blonde hair stuck out in a dozen places, as it did every morning—and no wonder. The child rolled and tumbled in her sleep as if she physically chased a dozen dreams.

Far too huggable to resist. Daniel caught her in his arms from behind, eliciting a delighted shriek. He turned her around, planted a big kiss on her cheek and squeezed her tight. "I love you, munchkin."

"To the moon and back, to infinity and beyond, and more than life," she spouted.

"Me too...all of that, plus I love you forever and like you for always."

She giggled. "That's lots o' love, huh, Daddy?"

"You got that right, little one." He shifted her to one arm and stepped to the window. "So what's so fascinating out there?"

"Snow!" She squirmed, her excitement almost uncontainable. "Lots and lots and *lots* of it!"

Daniel blinked. She couldn't be more right. It appeared someone had used a paintbrush the size of Texas to slap a coat of pure white on the entire world. Tall shapes that had been trees yesterday now looked like skeletal white creatures, frozen in place with their multiple arms spread wide—some outward, some upward, and still others pointing toward the ground. The Christmas Inn gardens slept beneath a white blanket that revealed nothing more than humps and bumps of various size and shape. Even Jingle Bell Creek, which ran behind the Inn along the length of the property, had surrendered to the storm. The narrow, winding waterway lay frozen beneath a layer of frosty white.

"Can I make a snow angel, Daddy? Can I, please?"

"May I, Chrissy."

She giggled. "'Course you can, but yours will be huh-*uge*."

Daniel laughed. "Thank you for that, Princess. What I actually meant was...oh, never mind." He set her on the ground. "Let's get dressed and go play in the snow."

"Yes! Yes, yes, yes!" She hop-skipped into the restroom.

Half an hour later, Daniel locked their door and pulled his phone out of his pocket. Maybe Karynn liked to make snow angels too.

He glanced toward room four, but didn't bother to knock. Lena hated getting up early, and always took full advantage of the days he was home to look after Chrissy. The nanny wouldn't be downstairs until at least noon. Maybe later. If a good night's sleep hadn't improved her sour mood, he prayed the woman slept all day.

****

Karynn and Savannah sat at the bell table. The inn's Continental breakfast, normally served outdoors on a lovely patio complete with several space heaters, was set up in the dining room this morning in deference to the frozen world outside. This kind of cold made space heaters about as effective as candlelight in sunshine.

"Savannah, that's not breakfast." Karynn sighed. "Three bites is not a meal."

"Depends on three bites of *what*." Savannah shot the fuddy-duddy at her, then grinned and forked another piece of the boiled egg she'd sliced into three parts. "Eggs are protein. One is enough to take a person through to lunch. If I get hungry, I'll eat an orange." Grinning, she hooked a thumb over her shoulder, where three large bowls filled with oranges, apples and bananas took up a portion of the food counter.

"You're hopeless." Karynn picked up her cup and sipped at the steaming beverage. "This is amazing peppermint coffee. I have to find out where they get it. Hearth & Home guests deserve a cup of heaven, don't you think?"

"If you say so. You know I don't drink coffee. Although, I have to admit, if it tasted as good as it smells, I'd be a java junkie." Savannah nodded at the small glass of pineapple juice beside her plate. "Juice is good, though. Hey, I wonder who has a message for you today?"

"No one." Karynn laughed at her sister's obsession with the silly promidiction ritual. Savannah'd insisted she ring the crystal bell again this morning, and read the Day 2 promidiction aloud. As expected, she'd found another generic bit of typical fortune cookie fare.

Someone has an important message for you. But listen closely...the message may hide in the words.

"Remember what it said yesterday? And look what happened."

"Coincidence."

"Don't believe in it, and neither do you."

Karynn's cell phone rang and Savannah grinned. "Wanna bet

I know who that is?"

"I don't gamble, little sister. Besides, I've already got 'promidictions.' I don't need a fortune teller, as well." She grinned when her sister's tongue protruded like a sassy child. "It's probably some poor soul who'd hoped for a room at Hearth & Home, and found the place locked and boarded up."

"Locked and boarded?" Savannah rolled her eyes. "And you accuse me of exaggerating!"

Karynn winked at her sister. But when Daniel's name showed up on the ID screen, she sucked in a breath.

"Told'ja so." Savannah gloated better than anyone.

She shot the younger woman a sarcastic eye roll as she accepted the call. "Good morning, Mr. Sheridan. This is your wake-up call."

"Wait. I called you. That doesn't work."

"Are you awake, sir?"

"Well, yeah, but—"

"Then it worked, didn't it? You know, if you plan to feed your daughter anything for breakfast, you'd best shake a leg. The dining room's filling up, and the pancake pile is going down. Fast."

"Then I hope it's all right if we join you ladies." He spoke from directly behind her chair.

Her phone clattered onto the table and she shrieked as both hands flew to her cheeks. She glanced around to see how much attention she'd drawn.

"Daniel! Don't do that!"

# 4

**KARYNN COULD HARDLY BLAME CHRISSY** for giggling at a butterfingered adult. Daniel and Savannah, on the other hand…

"I'm sorry." Daniel's apology lacked a certain sincerity, since he couldn't quite stop laughing. "I didn't mean to startle you. Well…not much, anyway."

He settled his daughter next to Karynn. "Do you mind if the munchkin sits with you while I get us something to eat?"

"Chrissy, do you mind if your daddy leaves you with me?"

The little girl giggled. "Nope. It's OK."

Daniel chuckled. "Be right back."

"Have you looked outside, Chrissy-cake?" Savannah asked.

"Yep. We're going to make snow angels after we eat." Chrissy's excitement was almost palpable, and completely contagious. "Wanna come with us? Daddy says snow angels can be big too. He's going to make one, and his will be huh-*uge*."

"You're right, it will." Karynn widened her eyes. "That will be something to see, won't it?"

"Uh-huh." The child's eyes shone like blue stars.

Savannah shook her head. "Karynn doesn't know how to make snow angels."

"What?" She glared at her sister. "Of course I do."

"I've never seen you make one. Not even when we were kids." Savannah twisted her lips, mockingly doubtful. "So I've got no proof."

"You've got no—why, you little upstart!" Karynn shook a finger in Savannah's face. "I'll show you 'proof,' little sister. I'll make the best snow angel you've ever seen. You just watch me."

"It'll for sure be the best one I've ever seen you make."

Savannah winked at the little girl, whose wide eyes bounced back and forth between the adults. "She doesn't play. Just works. All the time. Work, work, work."

Chrissy lifted a wide gaze to Karynn. "How come you like to work so much, Miss Karynn? Playing is fun! You gotta have fun sometimes, don'tcha?"

Karynn bit back a grin, and Savannah placed a hand over her mouth. Ha! She wasn't so good at "biting back."

"You really think so?"

The child's long pigtails bounced when she gave a vehement nod. "Uh huh. I think I know so."

Hiding their amusement became impossible. Both women laughed outright.

"Well, then I'll play today and see what I think."

"Yay!"

A plate slid onto the table in front of the child, and Daniel dropped onto the chair beside hers. "Yay later, Princess. Eat now."

"'K." She picked up half of an orange muffin her father had already buttered. "Miss Karynn's not going to work, work, work today, Daddy. She's playing with us instead."

"Really?" Daniel opened a little packet of grape jelly and spread it on his daughter's toast. "Hmmm... What if these ladies don't know how to make snow angels?"

Chrissy rolled expressive blue eyes. "All they have to do is lie down in the snow and wave their arms and legs."

Karynn narrowed her eyes as if deep in thought. "We should be able to do that."

Savannah crinkled her whole face and shook her head. Had Karynn not known better, she'd have thought her sister was really worried. "I don't know, Chrissy. I can wave my arms. See?" She stuck both of hers in the air and moved them back and forth. "But I've never waved a leg before."

Karynn and Daniel laughed at her silliness.

Chrissy gave them both a stern look. "That's not very nice."

Savannah stuck her nose in the air and glared at Karynn. "No, it isn't. Thank you, sweetie."

"You're welcome, Miss Savannah. We're not supposed to laugh at others." The little girl reached for her mug of hot chocolate and shot Savannah a sympathetic look. "Even if they're not very smart."

****

Heavy coats and several layers of clothing proved little defense against the frigid cold outside. Still, Karynn couldn't remember ever having such a good time.

They braved the weather long enough to make a couple of snow angels each. Their first efforts didn't pass Chrissy's inspection, which necessitated another try. Through chattering teeth, the child deemed the second set "b-b-bee-*you*-tiful!"

The bite in the air seemed like a playful nip at first, but soon became downright painful. With Chrissy's approval of the snow angels—and Savannah in possession of far too many photos—Daniel scooped his daughter up and hefted her slight weight onto one arm.

The other he slid around Karynn's waist.

"We should take the munchkin back inside, where it's warm. I spotted a stack of games in the lobby. Anyone care to take me on at a word game? I saw Scrabble—hint, hint—but I'm sure there are others to choose from."

Savannah shook her head and blew warmth into the palms of her hands. "Not me. Karynn's the word guru."

Karynn watched her sister breathe into her hands again. "You're wearing gloves, Vanna. Blowing your hands isn't helping."

"It's worth a try." Savannah dashed around Karynn to Daniel's other side. "I happen to be pretty good at Candyland. Maybe I can find someone to play with."

"Me, me! Would you play Candyland with me, Miss Savannah?"

"What a great idea, kid!"

After changing clothes, the sisters headed back downstairs. As Savannah locked the door, she stole a sideways glance at Karynn. "Having a good time, Sis?"

"The best ever." She let the younger woman slip the room key into her jeans pocket, and then pulled her into a hug. "Maybe I'm enjoying myself too much—to the point of being slightly delirious. I keep thinking I'm going to wake up, and—" She stepped back and swallowed hard. "You know. None of it will be real."

"It's real, Karynn. Daniel is here, and the two of you are...magic. Just like you always were. You've waited so long. God knows you deserve a little happiness, and sweetie, it's your time." Savannah leaned in and lowered her voice. "I've been watching Daniel. The man is beyond help...completely under your spell."

"Sis. Don't." Karynn shook her head and held up both hands in a warding-off gesture. "He's an old friend, and it's been all kinds of wonderful to run into him again. But that's all we are. Friends. The sooner you get that through your overly romantic noggin, the better."

"Mmmhmm." Savannah arched an eyebrow. "I'm not above saying 'I told you so' later."

They stepped onto the staircase, only to be greeted by a shrill shriek from the bottom step, where Chrissy waited. Excitement rolled off her in waves, and she bounced on the tips of her toes, unable to be still.

"Yay! You're here." The child grabbed Savannah's hand. "I found Candyland. See? I put it on a table for us. Mr. Gabriel's saving our place. Can he play too? Please, can he?"

Savannah tweaked the excited child's nose. "Sure, Mr. Gabriel can play. Come on, kiddo, let's hit the candy trail."

Karynn smiled as Savannah took the little girl's hand and hurried toward Gabriel, who warmed the whole room with his smile.

"Over here, Karynn!"

She joined Daniel near the fireplace. He'd spread a jigsaw puzzle across the surface of a card table and set up two folding chairs.

"Let me guess." She eyed the jumble of puzzle pieces. "You realized you didn't stand a chance at Scrabble."

"Not even close—and if that's a challenge, honey, you are on." He shot her a playful, don't-mess-with-me glare. Then he grinned and cocked his head toward a nearby table, where a beautiful, dark-haired young woman sat opposite a well-muscled man with a rugged air. "Those two beat us to the Scrabble game, and...well, look at them. They're having such a great time, I can't even dredge up a hint of resentment."

Daniel's crooked grin was so reminiscent of the boy he'd been in high school that Karynn's mouth went dry, and her heart set up a ridiculous clamor. She fixed her gaze on the Scrabble players, seated herself and gathered her dwindling composure. The man and woman laughed and teased back and forth as they laid tiles on the board, clearly caught up in the competition, and in each other. "I think someone blinked them both out of a pretty people magazine."

Daniel chuckled. "That's Ariana Christmas. Her family owns this place."

"And her husband?"

"Rumor has it her *friend* over there is Taylor Knox, the contractor responsible for revamping Christmas Inn."

She laughed. "Did you say you got here yesterday, same as me? You're a regular fount of Christmas Inn knowledge."

"I just listen and learn, m'lady. Anything else you'd like to know? I'd tell you about the chapel bells, but it's a sappy little tale. You wouldn't like it. Too sweet. Too...magical."

She planted both hands on her hips. "I'll have you know, sir, that I happen to love fairy tales. Tell me now or later, but I intend to hear about those bells."

Daniel took the other chair. His low laughter rumbled across the table. "I did not say 'fairy tale.'"

Already busy sorting pieces according to color, Karynn grinned. "Sure you did. You said 'sappy,' 'sweet' and 'magical,' all in the same breath. What else could it be?"

"OK, you've got a point." Daniel fit two pieces together right off, and reached up to pat himself on the shoulder. "If this were Scrabble, I'd already be in the lead."

Karynn chuckled, and then cast a glance around the room. "Can you believe how well the staff has responded to having everyone stuck inside? Last night's weather report confirmed the incoming storm, but their snowfall prediction fell a long ways short. There's no way the Christmas Inn powers-that-be were prepared for all this."

Daniel's low response was half growl, half irritation.

She cast a curious glance across the table. "Daniel?"

He glanced at her from beneath lowered brows. "I'm either going blind or my clumsy fingers are getting in the way."

A little giggle surprised Karynn. "Or maybe those pieces just don't go together." She picked through the little pile of bright orange she'd accumulated, eyed the troublesome cardboard piece Daniel couldn't give up on, and handed him one of hers. "Try this."

The new piece slid into place on the first try. She gave him a saucy thumbs-up, then returned to sorting…and talking.

"This many people—strangers, mostly—with no choice but to be in close quarters, all day. It's a recipe for disaster, but everything's moving along without a hitch. I suppose some folks are a little antsy, but listen…" She closed her eyes. "Hear that?"

"What? Ten different conversations under one roof?"

"No." She shook her head, and then opened her eyes to meet his puzzled gaze. "The sound of zero arguments, and no loud demands to see a manager. Everyone seems mostly all right with spending at least one entire day of their vacation pretty much stuck here."

"I noticed the lack of obvious friction between workers or

guests." Daniel did a cocky head dance when first one piece and then another came together beneath his busy fingers.

She chuckled. "Maybe it's the magic of Christmas."

He waggled his eyebrows, and his grin turned outright wicked. "Or we're trapped in a sappy sweet fairy tale."

"Ha, ha."

Daniel pushed back from the table. "Let's go see if one of the benches in the foyer is open. I'm going a little stir-crazy."

No one occupied the small entry area. With the connecting doors between foyer and lobby closed, the clatter of tumbling dice and whisper of shuffling cards died away. Even the conversation and laughter faded to a quiet buzz.

For a moment, they stood at the double glass doors, looking out onto the stark, white beauty of the winter world. Then, as if by unspoken consent, they moved to one of the benches.

Suddenly Karynn didn't know what to say or do. For the first time today, she was alone with Daniel. She still suspected she might be dreaming, and yet...he was so warm, so real. He sat close, tucking her against his side in a gesture so familiar, so precious in her memory...

As if he'd been snatched right out of her dreams and plunked down into her life.

She sneaked a sideways glance and caught him doing the same. Warmth flooded her face, and she caught her lip between her teeth to still a sudden, slight tremble. "Uhm, Daniel..."

"Uhm, Karynn..." He stroked a finger down her cheek and touched it to the corner of her mouth. "You're biting your lip. You used to do that when you were nervous." His gaze traveled her face and settled on her eyes. "Are you nervous, Karynn?"

"N—no. Why would I be?"

He hiked one brow and said nothing.

"OK. I guess I am." She sighed. "This is all so surreal. The two of us here, together. In some ways, it feels like no time has passed at all. But it has, and we really don't know anything about each other, do we?" She hesitated. "May I ask you something personal?"

"Ask away. I'm an open book."

"Well, you have the lovely Lena in tow, so I assume Chrissy's mother isn't…in the picture?" She blinked as a thought flashed through her mind. "Where is Lena? I haven't seen her today."

"Sleeping? Pouting?" He shrugged. "I apologize for her behavior last night. When we get home, I'll need to rethink her place in our lives. I'm away from home a lot with my job, so I have to keep someone on hand to take care of Chrissy. Trouble is, she's never quite connected with Lena." He heaved a heavy sigh. "Sometimes I think I'm doing everything wrong. Being a single dad…it isn't easy." A subtle tightening of his lips tugged at Karynn's heart. "In answer to your original question, we lost Tina to cancer four years ago."

"Oh, Daniel, no! I'm so sorry…I shouldn't have asked."

"Of course you should. If you didn't wonder about her, I'd wonder about you."

That made some kind of crazy sense. "Does Chrissy remember her?"

The twist of his lips couldn't quite be called a smile. "She thinks she does, but I'm pretty sure she only remembers the things I tell her. She has a photo of Tina in her room, but…" He shook his head. "She was barely two. How much can she really recall?"

Karynn blinked against a sting in her eyes. "It must be so hard."

"At first, I was…adrift. Just wasn't sure how to stay anchored, you know? But I had to, because Chrissy needed me. That little girl saved me, Karynn. Just by being there, she kept me together." He drew in a breath, and the exhale that followed seemed to come from his very core. "It's gotten easier though. God's been with us, and we're doing all right—moving on, just as Tina ordered." A crooked smile now teased at his lips. "She was bossy, just like her daughter."

Karynn laughed softly. "Well, if Chrissy looks like her, then she was lovely. If nothing else, that would've made her…uhm, assertiveness…easier to take."

"She was attractive, although I can't say it made her *bossiness* easy to take. Not all the time." He chuckled, and slanted his gaze toward Karynn. "Still, we had a good life. We were happier than I deserved."

"Why would you say that?" She studied his expression. "Of course you deserved to be happy."

"Tina told me once that there was a part of me she didn't know, and couldn't ever hope to know." He cleared his throat. "A part of me that would never be hers."

"What…? What does that even mean?" She didn't understand. At all.

For the first time since Karynn asked about his wife, Daniel lifted his head and looked full into her face. His eyes pierced deep, as if seeking her soul. She was certain they found it because something within her leaped in response. Her heartbeat went from gentle canter to racing gallop in an instant. Her toes curled so tight she imagined the tinkle of tiny bells.

Daniel took her hands. He held one against his face, and closed his eyes as if to absorb her touch. Karynn's breath caught when an electric tingle shot from her fingertips to her shoulder, and arrowed straight for her heart.

"You already know, Karynn…I see it in your eyes." He squeezed the fingers of her other hand. "But I'll answer, since you asked. Tina knew about you. I told her myself…why wouldn't I? She knew I hadn't seen you since high school, and that, in all probability, I'd never see you again." He looked away for an instant, and then recaptured her gaze. "She also knew—although I swear I never said so—that a part of me never stopped loving you."

# 5

**HAD THEY TRULY BEEN TRAPPED** in a fairy tale, perhaps Daniel could have unspoken those words. Wrong time. Wrong place. Wrong context.

Just wrong. Karynn's wide eyes and shocked expression said it all.

"Daniel, I don't think—" She blew a couple of panicky breaths in and out. "We shouldn't—"

From inside the lobby, a loud, ringing sound startled them both.

"Hold on." He raised one finger, halting her choked response, and strode to the lobby door. By the time he shoved it open, Karynn was at his side.

An old-fashioned, triangle dinner bell hung from a cord gripped in Ariana Christmas's fingers. With obvious delight, she moved a striker around the three-sided opening, creating a surprisingly musical 'ringing' effect. With every eye fixed on her, she set the bell aside and grinned. "I've never been able to resist a chance to play with that thing."

Amongst scattered snickers and laughter, she clapped her hands to keep their attention. "I appreciate that you're all making the best of a frustrating situation. Right now, the snow has slowed considerably, and so has the wind. But according to local weather reports, it's just a lull in the storm. So how about a little time outside before the next wave hits? Let's have a snowman contest!"

Before the enthusiastic applause died all the way down, Ariana had divided them into teams and shooed everyone upstairs to bundle up and gather supplies.

Daniel, with Chrissy in tow, joined Karynn and Savannah on

the landing moments later. They hurried through the empty lobby and foyer, and pushed through the glass doors into the frosty air.

"Look, Daddy, a doggy!" Chrissy squealed.

He followed her gaze to the circle drive. A huge mastiff rode like a canine king on a sled pulled by a tall man with a dark beard. The animal's tail beat hard and fast as the crowd milled about outside the inn. His taut muscles indicated a wild desire to dash into their midst, but a low command from his master, along with the man's hand on his collar, kept the dog on the sled.

Daniel took a vice-like hold on Chrissy's tiny hand. Fully clothed and soaking wet, she didn't weigh as much as one of that creature's hind legs.

Ariana stepped close and laid a hand on Daniel's arm. "That's Jayson—the man, not the dog. He lives in a cottage here on the property, and he's ten kinds of wonderful. I would trust him with my life." She tilted her head at Chrissy, still focused on the man and dog. "Jayson's letting Max run off some doggy energy, after being cooped up all day. He's offered to let your little sweetheart join them while we adults are playing rough-and-tumble games."

Where was Lena? Daniel wouldn't have to make this kind of decision if his nanny were earning the ridiculous salary he paid her. Why would anyone think he'd let his little girl out of his sight with a man he'd never met—not to mention a dog the size of Paul Bunyan's blue ox?

Jayson pulled sled and dog through the milling guests, and Ariana bent to give the mastiff a strong rub behind the ears. "Max looks scary, but he's gentle as a lamb. Chrissy couldn't be in safer hands—or paws."

Daniel turned to Karynn. She was watching Savannah, perched on the sled with her arms around the big dog's neck. None of the women seemed to have a problem with the size of the creature. Still, Karynn must have sensed his concern, because she turned, looked straight into his eyes and gave him a barely perceptible nod. "She'll be safe."

She had always possessed an uncanny "knowing" where

people were concerned. That she trusted this stranger all but clenched the deal. Even so, he was relieved when Jayson removed a pair of reflective sunglasses, offered his hand, and introduced himself. His quiet, sincere smile and open demeanor erased the last of Daniel's concerns.

"Max sure could use a little company. He's been stuck in the cottage with me all day. Look at him." Jayson's laughter rang across the cold air. "He loves kids. We'll take good care of Chrissy, if you'll allow her to come with us, and I guarantee she'll enjoy the ride." He nodded toward a low hill well within sight of the inn. "We'll do a couple ups-and-downs over there, and you'll be able to see her the whole time."

"Daddy?" Chrissy's pleading blue eyes broke down the last of his resistance. "Please, please, *pleeeease*, can I go?"

"All right, I—I suppose so. Thank you, Jayson." Daniel grinned. "You too, Max."

Jayson strapped Chrissy onto the sled. She waved, grinning ear to ear, as they set off toward the distant rise. The mastiff trotted alongside the snow vehicle.

Karynn slid her hand in his. "He's a good man. He'll protect her with his life, and so will Max."

"Yeah, I get it, but still." He huffed out a breath and turned, so he couldn't see Chrissy moving further away. "Let's go, before I change my mind."

Getting everyone outside the inn was a great idea. Crisp, cold air and the welcome release of pent-up energy took the edge off an underlying tension that had been building beneath the surface calm.

Besides himself, Daniel's three-man team included Gabriel D'Angelo and Ariana's friend, Taylor. They worked well together, and after their snow creature won them the Christmas Inn Snowman Champs title, they pounded each other's backs, enjoying their victory.

Taylor enjoyed it too much. He caught Ariana's eye and fist-pumped the air. She responded with a snowball that smacked him in the face—and the two were off and going with a vigorous snowball battle. Then Taylor let loose a big, wet snowball that sailed over Ariana's shoulder and hit Karynn. The man froze, along with everyone in the immediate vicinity—including Daniel.

Karynn's mouth formed a perfect "oh." She brushed a hand across her snow-splattered features in slow motion. Then, without a word, she bent, packed a fast snowball of her own and let it fly.

Now it was a free-for-all, and everyone got in on the fun.

Daniel tried to participate, but he couldn't keep his eyes off Karynn. Finally he stepped away from the 'war zone' and watched her turn into a livewire. Caught up in the excitement of the game, she let her guard down, released her inner child, and just…played. He found her more beautiful with every musical burst of laughter, more tantalizing with each mock-frightened scream and excited squeal, more endearing with every clumsy tumble and roll.

At last, energy waned and the bevy of flying snow slowed to a stop. As folks moved back toward the inn, Karynn turned her head one way and then the other. Searching. For Savannah?

Her restless gaze locked onto his and stopped.

He smiled, and her full lips curved upward in a slow, sweet response that stole his breath and left him reeling. She trudged through the snow toward him—and he set off in her direction, helpless to wipe the dizzy grin off his face.

Maybe…just maybe he hadn't ruined everything after all.

Even as he'd raced alongside Taylor and Gabriel, rolling huge balls of feathery white flakes to build a decent snowman before Ariana's Aunt Lizzie clanged the dinner bell, he'd given himself kick after mental kick, called himself all kinds of a fool. Why hadn't he answered Karynn's question about Chrissy's mother and let it go at that? There'd been no need to bare his whole soul.

Every conversation since they both showed up in the dining room last night had centered mostly around him—*his* life since he left Karynn in Quillpoint a decade ago. All he knew about her in the here-and-now was that she owned a box of 'Daniel-memories.'

She reached his side in the trampled snow. Daniel slipped his hands around her waist and drew her close, and his anguished questions found an answer in the chocolate-colored depths of her eyes.

He'd spouted a whole decade's worth of living because that's what Karynn meant for him to do. Even as a cocky, over-confident high school jock, he'd melted like butter on a fresh-flipped flapjack when she turned those big, brown eyes his way. When she amped up the voltage with a smile, his spine turned to jelly. He'd never stood a chance against anything she wanted.

Not then, and not now.

But it was her turn to open up, and Daniel intended to make it happen soon. Upwards of ten years' worth of questions churned in his mind. Did she still live in her old neighborhood? What kind of work did she do? Did she ever play? Who were her friends—did she hang with any of the old crowd, the kids he'd known back then? How were Mr. and Mrs. Michaels? Karynn had been close to her parents, and yet he'd been so caught up in the present that he hadn't even asked about them.

The things he didn't know about her could fill a dozen books. But one thing he did know, without even a whisper of doubt. Karynn Michaels was back in his world, and Daniel knew a miracle when he saw one. He wouldn't walk out of her life again unless she ordered him out.

\*\*\*\*

Karynn stared into the flames of the fireplace. After a day of forced company, the other guests had chosen to spend the evening in the privacy of their own rooms. She'd accepted Daniel's request to sit with him in the quiet lobby and enjoy a bit of time together, just the two of them and the crackling fire.

The joy in his eyes when she said yes touched her in a deep place—a place that belonged only to Daniel. As a teen, he'd been incapable of deception. Even when he tried to tease her with a 'little white lie,' his eyes gave him away. Every time. That soul-deep honesty was one of the reasons she'd loved him so much.

Where Daniel was concerned, the familiar phrase about eyes being the windows to the soul held enormous truth. His soul shone through his eyes like a beacon of all things right, and pure, and clean.

He was upstairs now, tucking a worn-out little girl into Karynn's bed. She'd sleep there, in the room with Savannah, until Daniel returned for her. No one expected her to awaken, even during the move from one bed to another. The child had nodded off over dinner, exhausted from a grand day of sledding and romping with Max.

Karynn pulled one foot up under her on the sofa and tugged a light throw over her shoulders. Jayson should sleep well tonight too. He'd climbed the little hill he'd pointed out to Daniel at least a dozen times, and rode the sled down with Chrissy, who begged for 'one more time' upon every stop at the bottom. When he finally brought her back to the inn, Jayson wore a smile as broad and delighted as the child's.

Daniel thanked Jayson—and Max—but he confessed to Karynn that he'd had to squelch an unworthy stab of jealousy when Chrissy looked at the man with stars in her eyes.

"Karynn?"

She jumped when the quiet voice shattered her reverie. "Gabriel! I thought everyone had called it a night."

"I planned to, but decided to stretch my legs a bit." He indicated the other end of the sofa. "May I?"

"Of course." She welcomed his company. Every conversation with this man had proved enjoyable. His wide smile remained a source of inexplicable calm. Had his presence contributed to the day's surprising absence of temper and trouble amongst the shut-in occupants of the inn? "Tell me about yourself, Gabriel. We haven't had a real opportunity to chat."

"Oh, you don't want to hear an old man ramble—not when you're waiting on a young one to join you."

Karynn's cheeks warmed, but she didn't mind the Italian

man's gentle teasing. "Of course I do. I have a feeling you've led a fascinating life."

He nodded, and his dark eyes twinkled when he hiked one eyebrow. "I'm very old, you know. Over the years, I have experienced many things. But none of them are to be shared tonight."

"Maybe another time, then?" She watched the man's expression—somber, at the moment. His kind eyes reflected the flames leaping and dancing in the fireplace. "I have to say this. There's something wonderful about your smile. It spreads peace and calm like a soul-salve." She reached across the center cushion to touch his shoulder. "But you're more than a nice man with a magical smile, aren't you, Mr. Gabriel D'Angelo?"

"We're all more than we appear to be, my dear. In the deepest part of ourselves, we each have our own little worlds of wonder and hope, as well as hidden hurts, secret longings, fears and failures…things most of us seldom talk about. Some people never share that innermost, heart-part of themselves—not really." He hesitated, and then turned his entire body toward Karynn. His gaze captured hers.

Her breath caught on an audible gasp. She couldn't look away. Was it a reflection from the firelight that made Gabriel's eyes glow golden? Might the dim overhead lights have cast a white aura around his form?

"Our Father has such wonderful plans for you, Karynn. Be careful lest your will interferes with His as He brings them to perfection. Trust Him. And remember this, my dear." Gabriel rose and stepped between Karynn and the fireplace, blocking her view of the dancing flames. Not that it mattered, as she remained fixated on his impossibly glowing form. "When past and present collide, the impact carves out a road to the future—one laid in place by Divine hands. Take that high road, Karynn. All other paths lead backwards."

Gabriel's aura began to dim, along with the golden glow in his eyes. When the last bit of beautiful light disappeared, Karynn blinked once, and then again.

The throw around her shoulders fell to the floor as she leaped to her feet and turned in a slow circle. Where was the Italian gentleman?

He'd stood in this very spot, and she'd been mesmerized by the glow that undulated around him, captivated by the golden light in his eyes. Then he was gone. Vanished, as if he'd never been there at all.

Karynn's heart set up a genuine fuss at the excitement whirling in her soul. When at last her racing pulse slowed and settled into a normal pattern, she relaxed onto the sofa again and tried to laugh off her vivid imagination. She'd dozed off, that's all—dreamt the entire encounter. No other explanation made any kind of sense.

Lost in thought, she didn't hear Daniel's approach.

He joined her on the sofa, slipped one arm around her shoulders and coaxed her closer. "Sorry I took so long. I had to take a phone call."

"No problem. I wasn't alone long. Gabriel stopped by for a moment." The statement startled her. Why had she said such a thing, after deciding she'd dreamt the encounter? "I hope everything's all right. Your phone call?"

"I may have to leave for a couple of days. They'll find someone else if they can, but it may not be possible, this close to Christmas." He sighed. "My company tries not to interrupt our scheduled vacations, but still, it happens too often. These sudden calls and hasty departures are why I'm forced to hire live-in child care."

A chill gripped her heart. "L—live-in?"

# 6

UNLESS HE WAS READING HER wrong—and Daniel didn't think so—the thought bothered Karynn. Did it mean she cared enough to be concerned about his living situation?

He chuckled and gave her shoulders a little squeeze. "Lena *lives in* a studio apartment above my garage."

"I see." A tiny frown creased her forehead, and she caught her lip between her teeth. "Daniel, I don't want to interfere—" She broke off and shook her head. "And I shouldn't. Never mind."

"You're nibbling on that luscious-looking lip again." He traced their soft outline with his fingertip. He longed to cover them with his own, to taste their sweetness. But she wasn't ready, and he could wait. For now. "You do it when you're feeling shy, and when you're worried about something. You can say anything to me, Karynn. Anything."

She sighed. "I don't like the way Lena treats Chrissy."

Daniel frowned. "Until I saw you and Savannah with Chrissy, I never noticed the lack of connection between her and her nanny. Now I can't un-see it. Lena's not a good match, and I'll be letting her go when we return to Tulsa. For now, however, given the call from my job...." He huffed out a breath. "She's certainly not affectionate, but you don't think she'd hurt Chrissy, do you?"

The crackle of burning wood and the hiss of flames filled a brief silence while Karynn stared into the fireplace. Then she sighed, and her shoulders drooped as if in surrender to an inner battle. "I saw something I didn't like, but maybe it's just me. I can be over-sensitive when it comes to children."

"Karynn." He stroked her cheek with his fingertips, and then gently turned her face toward him. "What did you see?"

Still she struggled, and every muscle in Daniel's body

tightened. If she decided to talk, he wouldn't like what he heard.

At last, she nodded, and the single, determined dip of her chin said she'd won some kind of inner battle. Now she'd leave nothing unsaid.

Daniel had seen Karynn in the middle of a soul-struggle before. Even as a quiet, shy teen, something strong and fearless came to the fore when she felt strongly about a cause. He'd considered her an indomitable warrior of all things right and true. How was it that, after all these years, she still didn't know her own strength?

"We were dancing." Her voice lacked any hint of the hesitance she'd shown moments ago. "You'd asked Lena to take Chrissy upstairs."

"I remember." *I couldn't wait to hit that dime-sized dance floor and hold you in my arms.*

"I was facing the doorway, and…oh, Daniel, I'm so sorry. In retrospect, I should have done something…said something right then. But I didn't want to interfere in your personal life."

"Karynn, don't apologize. I can see that you were in a sensitive position. Tell me."

"Chrissy stood in the doorway, watching everyone dance." Karynn's eyes softened with the memory. "She loves music, you know. And she believes in fairy tales…in 'love like that.'"

"She's her mother's daughter."

"If you say so." Karynn's dark brown eyes softened to burnt caramel, and he saw in them an impossible knowing. This woman, to whom he hadn't spoken in a decade or more, knew that he—even more than Tina—believed in 'love like that.'

Her beautiful smile faded, and a razor's edge of fury surged through Daniel's body. The petulant, self-absorbed woman he'd hired to care for and protect his child had done something to Chrissy—something despicable enough to steal Karynn's smile. He clenched his jaw hard, and pain lanced through his temples. His heartbeat roared like an angry ocean, shoving blood through his veins in pounding waves.

*God, I'm afraid of myself. If Lena's hurt my daughter in any way, You'll have to take the reins of my emotions. Please...breathe Your refreshing peace into my soul, and Your wisdom into my heart.*

"Daniel." Karynn sat up straight and placed a hand on each side of his face. For a moment, he couldn't draw a breath. Her spirit reached out to his in tendrils of soothing serenity—invisible, and yet with enough substance that he almost felt their touch against his skin. Even in the midst of her own turmoil, Karynn possessed a core of inner peace that wound its way from her soul to wrap around him like a gentle Spirit-hug.

The awful roar in his chest quieted, and his runaway heartbeat slowed to normal. He hauled in one deep, fortifying breath, and then another as snarled webs of emotion loosened and untangled in his mind.

In the next instant, Karynn's eyes widened. Her hands lifted off his face, and she stared at them as if confused. Then she eased back into the curve of his arm.

"Uhm...anyway." She seemed a little disoriented, but picked up where she'd left off.

Daniel remained calm, still warm in the glow of that unexpected, miraculous moment of contact with her pure spirit.

"Lena grabbed Chrissy by the arm—rough, and hard enough that I almost—" She shook her head and drew in a long breath, as if to keep from drowning in the memory. "Chrissy winced a little, and tried to pull away, but Lena wouldn't let go. She bent close to that sweet little face...oh, Daniel..."

Tears shimmered in her eyes. She blinked, and they spilled down her face. "What happened then, even more than her claw-like grip on that tiny arm, horrified me. Lena went nose to nose with Chrissy, and her face—" A shudder shook her entire body, and she squeezed her eyes shut, as if to un-see the memory. "It was a mask of vile hatred. She said something—gritted words between her teeth. Poor little Chrissy! She didn't cry, but her lips trembled. Then Lena yanked her away from the door and dragged her across the lobby. Chrissy had to run to stay on her feet."

By the time she finished, Daniel struggled to maintain the calmness of spirit he'd been gifted. What had Lena done when no one was around to see? Why hadn't Chrissy told him about the incident?

"I wish you'd said something." He pushed the words through stiff, numb lips.

"I should have, Daniel. I'm so, so sorry."

*Breathe. Just breathe.*

He sent up another silent plea for control. None of this was Karynn's fault. Chrissy was *his* daughter. Why hadn't he seen that something wasn't right?

"I'm not angry with you. You couldn't have known whether I condoned Lena's behavior."

"That's not true. My heart told me you would never allow anyone to mistreat her, but I was so sure you'd resent my interference. We hadn't seen each other in over a decade, after all. No one appreciates a stranger inserting herself into—"

"Stop. Just stop." He turned to pull her close, and rested his chin on top of her head. Even now, having heard the worst, her nearness leveled out his anger. "You and I are not strangers, sweetheart. Never that. Even after a decade of separation, the moment I saw you again, I knew you—and I don't mean that I recognized your face. I *knew* you, as if we'd never spent a day apart."

"Me too." Her hands made a slow journey across his shoulders. "But I couldn't be sure you experienced that same knowing." She pulled away enough to look into his eyes. "Please forgive me."

"There's nothing to forgive." He bent his head to kiss her temple. A soft wisp of dark hair tickled his face, and a thrill of something he hadn't felt in far too long coursed through his veins. But this wasn't the time for such thoughts, or such feelings. "Now that I know, I can't leave Chrissy with her again, not even for a moment. I'll have to tell my boss—"

"Savannah and I will take care of her while you're gone."

Startled, he drew away, so he could see her face. Her clear, steady gaze met his without flinching.

Daniel gave a firm shake of his head. "No. You're on vacation. You shouldn't have to worry about taking care of someone else's child."

"Please...I'd like to help. Will you trust me with Chrissy while you're gone? Only..." Determination warred with something else in her gaze. "Only don't leave Lena here. I don't know how to say this delicately, so forgive me if I sound petty, or unfeeling. I don't mean to be. When you let her go, her reaction will be extreme. She'll unsheathe some pretty sharp claws—which won't matter for you, at all. You're tough."

Daniel threw his shoulders back and expanded his chest in a playful show of pride. Karynn's lips teased upward, but not enough to form a real smile.

"But Chrissy's just a little girl. She's not strong, or tough, and she doesn't have an ounce of meanness in her. If you leave Lena here, watching someone else in what should have been her role, she'll take it as a public slap in the face. I'm certain—absolutely, without a doubt, chillingly certain—she'll seek revenge in one way or another." She shrugged one shoulder, but maintained steady eye contact. "I can't prove it, and of course there's a chance I'm wrong. I hope I am. But I don't think so, Daniel. I don't want Lena anywhere near Hope Creek after you fire her, especially if Chrissy's in my care."

The truth in her words was unmistakable. Why was it that now he clearly saw in Lena what he'd never noticed before? *Dear Lord, I've been so blind.*

He nodded. "You're right, of course. She shouldn't be here. If it turns out I have to leave, I'll take her to the airport. I'll be going there anyway."

Karynn blanched. Had she gone a shade paler in that bare instant? "I—I hadn't thought about that. You'll...fly...home to your job."

"Well, I'll fly, but not home." Daniel wanted to kick something. He'd asked Karynn to join him by the fireplace tonight so they could talk…about her, this time. He'd wanted to hear all the little details of her life, to watch her expressions as she shared them with him. But once again, the conversation had revolved around his issues. "We haven't even discussed our occupations, have we? What do you do, Karynn?"

"Nothing exciting." She shrugged one shoulder. "I inherited a bed and breakfast from my aunt. God knew I'd need it after my parents died. Because Hearth and Home was a viable, income-rendering business, I was able to be Savannah's legal guardian, even though I was barely twenty-one. She wasn't quite seventeen at the time, and without that source of income to my benefit, she'd have gone into the foster system for at least a year. I don't think I could've taken that…and I'm not sure she'd have come home the same, sweet girl she was before."

Daniel had to clear something scratchy from his throat before he spoke. "You're the most incredible woman I've ever met. How can you not know how special you are?" He hugged her, and then touched his lips to her forehead. "I remember your parents well, and I'm so sorry for your loss. They…both died?"

"Yes. A—a plane crash." Something flickered in her eyes, and Daniel's stomach gave an empathetic lurch. She shivered, and a chill scurried up his spine. "I miss them every day."

"I'm so sorry, honey. I wish…" What did he wish? That he'd been there for her? When Karynn lost her parents, he'd been married to Tina. He'd loved Chrissy's mother. Wishing he'd been there for Karynn felt like a betrayal of his wife. "I wish I'd known."

"Things happened as they were meant to. Don't second guess God's plan. He had a reason for all of it. The good and the bad."

"You're right." He smiled and traced a finger down her face. "Maybe someday I'll be as wise as you are, and trust like you do."

"Oh, Daniel! I'm nobody's role model of grace."

"Well, I suppose we can agree to disagree on some things."

She laughed softly. "So now you know I'm a boring lodge owner who fills the roles of maid, doorkeeper and billing manager. What about you? Where do you work?"

He tipped an invisible hat. "Captain Daniel Sheridan, at your service, ma'am. I'm a commercial airline pilot." Grinning, he touched a finger to the tip of her nose. I soar through the clouds on a silver steed. Does that make me a knight in shining armor?"

\*\*\*\*

Karynn's vision faded for the barest of half-moments. She breathed a silent prayer of thanks that she was sitting, otherwise she would have wilted to the floor in a humiliating puddle.

"Karynn?" Daniel's frantic voice cut through the haze in her mind, but she couldn't find her voice. "Karynn!" He slid to his knees, took her by the shoulders and gave her a tiny shake. "What's going on?"

"I'm OK." She forced enough starch into her spine to sit up straight. "I must be more tired than I realized. It's late, and we should call it a night. You may have to leave early."

He helped her to her feet, and then pulled her against him. "You were so pale…" The tremble in his voice hurt her heart, and she clenched her hands to keep them from sliding around his neck and through the soft hair that curled around his collar. If she stayed where she was, no amount of determination would keep her hands at her sides.

She eased out of his arms. "I'm fine. Really. I just need to sleep."

Disappointment clouded his gaze, but he nodded. "Then let me help you up the stairs."

Before she could protest, he'd slipped an arm around her waist. Within a couple of steps, she was grateful for his assistance. His playful announcement had noodled her legs. She couldn't have managed the staircase on her own.

At her door, Daniel pulled her close against his chest. Karynn allowed the embrace…sank into it. She inhaled the faint smell of woodsy cologne…absorbed the ripple of muscles in his arms…committed to memory the wonderful sense of being cherished.

Blinking back hot tears, she determined to remember every tiny detail about these moments. After tonight, she couldn't let it happen again.

Then she raised her face and looked into his beautiful sapphire gaze. That sparkle of life and fun in their depths would haunt her dreams. Savannah was right. Every other man who'd tried to find a hole in Karynn's defenses had failed because he wasn't this man. Daniel would forever be the love of her life.

He kissed her forehead. "Are you sure you're OK?"

"I'm sure. Thank you for helping me upstairs. My legs feel a little boneless."

"My pleasure. Always." He winked, and a teasing grin caught her by surprise. "I'll dial back the charm a little next time. At least enough to keep you on your feet."

She laughed and took his face between her hands once more. On tiptoe, she brushed her lips over his. Too brief to be called a kiss, the fleeting touch nevertheless sent a zip of something powerful through Karynn's body. She pulled away with a tiny gasp. "Goodnight, Daniel."

He blinked, his eyes dazed and unfocused.

Karyn slipped into her room and closed the door between them. The latch barely had time to click into place before she gasped, startled by a soft knock. Heartbeat racing, she jerked it open again.

"I forgot my kid."

"You—? What?"

"Chrissy. She's sleeping in your bed."

"Oh." She stared at him a moment before comprehension drew a burst of soft laughter. "I forgot too. Come on in."

He moved easily through the dim suite and gathered the sleeping child into his arms. Karynn swallowed hard, touched to the core by his gentleness, and the overwhelming love that rolled off him in near-palpable waves as he settled her on his shoulder, all the while whispering soft reassurance into her ear.

*Oh, God…how can I lose him again?*

At the door, he peered over the blanketed bundle in his arms to give Karynn one of his trademark, self-assured grins and a slow wink. Then he was gone.

Locked inside the quiet suite once more, Karynn slid to the floor and buried her face in trembling hands that would not be stilled. Silent tears trickled through her fingers and down her arms.

Much later, she gathered her strength and stumbled across the room. Her clothes fell in a sad, crumpled heap beside the bed. She left them there, and slid between the sheets without bothering to find a gown.

All the hopes and dreams that had begun to take root in her heart lay in shattered disarray. What she'd seen in Daniel's eyes today echoed what had been there when they were kids—he loved her, just as she loved him.

Yet, even now, they couldn't have a future together.

She still had nightmares of her parents' plane going down, still screamed out for them in the night, begging them not to die. She couldn't survive that kind of loss again. For Karynn, Daniel's "silver steed" was a monstrous metal beast, set on ripping the life from anyone to whom she gave a piece of her heart.

Despite the clamor of raging emotion, exhaustion won against the wide-awake tension in her soul. Sometime in the wee hours of a new day, she drifted off, to the quiet whisper of Gabriel D'Angelo's voice in her mind. *When past and present collide...take the high road, Karynn. All other paths lead backward.*

## 7

**KARYNN GROANED AND PULLED THE** covers up over her head. "Leave me alone."

Savannah persisted. "Are you saying you don't want to come down for breakfast, or you want to spend the day in bed?"

"Both."

"Then I'll be back after I eat. If you're not up, I'll do it your way....and you know what that means."

Karynn's eyes snapped open. "You wouldn't dare."

Savannah sailed across the room and opened the door. "Are you brave enough to test me?"

Then Karynn was alone. She turned her back on the door and closed her eyes. Maybe her sister would chicken out and leave her alone. They weren't kids anymore, and she was on vacation, after all. If she chose to spend the day huddled beneath the covers, alone in this suite, then that was her right.

On the other hand, she didn't much like the idea of cold water in the face. Despite her fierce desire to stay in bed and mope, the thought brought on a little burst of laughter.

Savannah'd never been easy to get out of bed and off to school. Their mother used to accomplish the task by dribbling cold water on her forehead until she sat up, piping mad, but awake. The task sometimes fell to Karynn, but she never followed Mom's kinder, gentler example. She gave her sister one loud yell of, "Rise and shine!" If Savannah didn't drag herself out of bed within five minutes, Karynn dumped a full cup of iced water in her face. She had to get herself ready for school too. Who had time to coddle the spoiled baby of the family?

She lay a little longer, drifting in and out of sleep, wishing she really could get by with snoozing the entire day away. But, while her sister probably wouldn't go so far as to drench her in icy water—at least, she didn't think so—Savannah would demand an explanation for such out-of-character behavior.

She wasn't ready to talk. Not today. Maybe never.

One last, loud groan, and then she stretched, angled onto her elbow and lifted out of bed. When she stood, her feet tangled in something, and she glanced down. Her clothes, piled on the floor in a messy heap, brought on a deluge of fresh pain. She rushed into the shower and stood beneath a stinging, hot spray until it turned warm, and then tepid, and finally grew cold.

As she wrapped a huge towel around her shivering body, she remembered.

"No. No, no, *no!*"

She'd promised to take care of Chrissy if Daniel had to leave. Had he been called in, and forced to leave his daughter with Lena?

Karynn whirled around the suite, and was ready in record time. She reached the top of the staircase in time to see Savannah headed up with Chrissy in tow.

"Hi, Miss Karynn!" The child trilled a sunny greeting and ran ahead of Savannah to wrap both arms around her legs. "Are you all better? Miss Savannah said you were not having a rise-and-shine morning."

Karynn managed a smile she hoped was reassuring, and drew the little one into a warm hug. "I'm all better now. Did you have breakfast?"

"Uh huh." Chrissy grinned, and her ponytail bounced up and down in time with her chin. "I had a boiled egg with Miss Savannah."

"One boiled egg?" Karynn sent her sister an outraged look. "Your daddy didn't make you eat more than that?"

"Daddy went bye-bye with Miss Lena."

So Daniel was off to work, and Chrissy was here. He'd chosen to trust Karynn with his most precious possession...even though she'd failed to be on hand to accept the responsibility.

"Vanna, thank you for filling in for me. I should've said

something before you came downstairs, but I—" She broke off. No excuse was good enough. She'd let Daniel down and put her sister in the position of accepting shared responsibility without advance notice. "I'm so sorry. I should've come down with you."

"You're not making sense. What is it you should have told me?" Her sister pulled out the fuddy-duddy face, and Karynn almost laughed. She'd forgotten about the silly alert because she hadn't seen it since…when? She couldn't remember. Perhaps she'd been less fretful than either of them expected.

Which had everything to do with Daniel.

She ignored the painful pinch in her heart. "I volunteered the two of us to take care of Chrissy, but you were asleep when I came upstairs last night. I didn't get a chance to tell you, and I forgot this morning."

"Oh. So what's the big deal?" A little crease marred Savannah's smooth brow. "Chrissy didn't want to go, and I said she could stay with me. Are you sure you're all right, Sis? If you need to go back to bed, do it. Seriously. I promise I won't drown you in ice water." She hiked one eyebrow and managed to look downright wicked. "Although it would be such an awesome payback!"

Karynn laughed. "That's almost too kind. Thanks, but I'm up. I just need to get something to eat."

"Chrissy and I want to take a drive through Hope Creek, and see what fun we can find. You coming?"

Chrissy tugged at Karynn's hand. "Come with us, Miss Karynn. Please?"

"I want to grab a banana first, and…do you think I might find one more of those very popular eggs in the dining room?"

"You can find three more. There were four, but I ate one all up. Hurry, Miss Karynn, a'fore someone else gets 'em all."

"I'll take the pipsqueak upstairs for a visit to the little girl's room while you're finding food." Savannah eyed Chrissy's outfit. "And we need to get her coat and mittens. Come on, Chrissy-cake." She dug a hand into first one jeans pocket and then the other. "Ah, here it is. What do you think, kiddo? Will your daddy's key work for me, or only for him?"

"You're silly, Miss Savannah." Chrissy giggled.

"Silly? Me?" Savanah took the child's hand and the two hurried for the stairs, where—despite their supposed rush to be off and going—they stopped.

Karynn frowned. What now?

"One. Two. *Three!*" Woman and child jumped into the air and onto the first step. They hopped upward, one stair at a time.

The center section of the facility rose all the way to the second-floor ceiling. A U-shaped landing fronted the guest rooms on the upper floor, providing a grand view of the beautiful lobby below. With the high ceiling and open layout, sound carried well, and Chrissy's high, sweet laughter echoed throughout the inn.

Karynn watched them all the way to the top. The child's elated giggles touched the hurting places in her soul like healing fingers. And Savannah...she'd never been prouder of her sister than in that moment—whole-heartedly lost in Chrissy's world, willing to be a child herself to give a little girl a friend.

"That's the sound we love to hear at Christmas Inn—any time of year, of course, but especially during the Christmas season."

She whirled toward the reception desk, where a young woman stood with her elbows on the high counter. Dark brown eyes complemented beautiful, creamy skin and long, straight, dark hair. Adorable dimples played hide-and-seek with a warm, natural, open smile that reached out to Karynn and drew her toward the desk.

"Chrissy's a special child. My sister and I have both fallen in love with her. And this place...well, I think it's meant to ring with the voices of happy children."

"Well, she's certainly happy." The woman's soft laughter wrapped around Karynn's heart like a sweet, familiar hug. As if, although she'd never met this woman before, she'd always known her.

"I'm Karynn Michaels. Suite 2." Introducing herself to

strangers didn't come easily to Karynn, but she did it now without hesitation. "I haven't seen you around before."

"Lydia Cutler, IT tech. My job is to drag this delightful, but technologically backward facility into the twenty-first century. I'm behind the scenes most of the time." She opened a gate at one end of the reception area and rounded the counter to stand directly in front of Karynn. "Would you think it terribly strange if I said I'd like to hug you, Karynn Michaels, Suite 2?"

Karynn opened her arms. Lydia did the same, and then they were heart to heart. Karynn felt as if they'd been in this moment a thousand times before. She knew nothing about Lydia Cutler except her name and occupation, and that she enjoyed the laughter of children. Yet, in some impossible way, she knew her as well as she knew Savannah.

In this woman, with her beautiful, dimpled smile, she'd found a soul sister.

Lydia pulled away and then lifted both hands and touched her fingertips to Karynn's face. "We're going to be friends, you and I."

"We already are. I think…we've been friends forever."

"Oh!" Lydia blinked. One dimple peeked out, and then the other. "Oh, my. You're absolutely right." She looped an arm through Karynn's. "I was getting ready to take a break. Walk with me? I know it's cold, but I love winter in Hope Creek. Besides, we have a lifetime to catch up on, don't we?"

Karynn hesitated. She wanted to accept the invitation, but Chrissy was so excited about exploring Hope Creek…and Lydia wasn't going anywhere.

"I wish I could, but—"

"Hey, Sis!" Savannah called from the top of the stairs. "Change of plans. It'll be an hour or so before we leave. Chrissy's already wrapped up in one of her favorite movies. Want to join us for some fairy tale fun?"

Darren must've called. Savannah wasn't one to carry on about missing her husband, but Karynn had noticed periods of

301

uncharacteristic quiet, and far-off expressions at odd moments. She was feeling this first lengthy separation from her adored hubby.

"You two go ahead." She stepped to the bottom of the staircase. "I'll meet you here, an hour from now."

"Alrighty then." Savannah narrowed her gaze and studied Karynn for a moment, then raised hands and eyes to the ceiling. "I won't ask. See you later."

Karynn made a quick trip up to grab a jacket, and then she and Lydia set off through the snow-covered grounds, arm in arm.

"Have you seen the chapel?" The sparkle in her new friend's eyes rivaled the glitter of sunshine on snow. "It's small, but jam-packed with charm. And the bell tower! You have to hear the legend of the Christmas Inn Chapel bells."

The bells. Daniel had teased her about the 'sappy, sweet, magical' bell tale.

Lydia squeezed her arm. "And you'll tell me why you look so sad. Off to the chapel!"

They headed north on a walking trail that followed a narrow, meandering waterway on their right—Jingle Bell Creek, Lydia informed Karynn. On their left, bright Christmas lights reflected off icy surfaces in the garden area, turning the frozen world into a kaleidoscope of refracted color.

Karynn noticed a huge, bright red, sleigh-shaped structure on the far side of the gardens. Complete with a slide, several swings, and a maze of climbing equipment, the cheery, over-sized vehicle clearly catered to the enjoyment of children. She'd have to make sure Chrissy visited the big sleigh.

A narrow footpath wound through the garden's snow-laden bushes, trees and flowerbeds. Benches bordered the path at regular intervals, and Lydia pointed out statues of various heights and diverse style. They stood between and peered from behind the foliage—angels in one area, a number of happy-faced elves and a large Santa in another. A full, life-sized nativity scene held majestic reign near a tiered waterfall that, even with all three levels frozen in place, was stunningly beautiful.

Just past the gardens, they came to an arched walkway spanning Jingle Bell Creek. "This is North Pole Bridge." Lydia laughed. "Don't you just love the little touches of Christmas everywhere on this property?" She pointed back the way they'd come. "South Pole Bridge crosses the creek at about this same distance on the other side of the inn." They crossed the short bridge, and Lydia made an abrupt left. "Here it is."

Karynn couldn't hold back a tiny gasp. She'd never seen anything so perfect.

Tucked into the edge of an enormous wooded area, a small white clapboard church stood like a sentinel of righteousness over the ice and snow-covered corner of Christmas Inn property. Karynn's charmed gaze raced over the tiny, one-story building. The most striking feature of the chapel soared into the sky from directly over the double oak doors—a bell tower, crowned at its topmost point by a white cross.

From where the two women entered the glade, they had visual access to only one side of the church, but Karynn caught her breath at the three stained glass windows along its length. Sunlight caught the varicolored, multi-shaped panes and spilled beautiful prisms of blue and green, red, yellow and purple onto the pristine snow surrounding the building.

"Oh, my…this is perfect. It's just…absolutely…stunning!"

"It is, isn't it?" A touch of huskiness in Lydia's voice reflected her deep love for the little chapel. "Come look inside."

They stepped through the double doors and into the smell of fresh paint, wood polish and cleaning products.

"Ariana's been working out here every free moment. She's determined to make it ready for a Christmas Eve prayer service— the first in…well, far too long. When I was a kid, Hope Creek families looked forward to meeting here in this little church on Christmas Eve. But the doors have been closed and locked for years. I'm so excited that Ari and her family are bringing back the old tradition."

"It sounds beautiful."

"It is." Lydia swung in a slow circle, her appreciative gaze sweeping the small sanctuary. A long, full skirt flowed around her legs in graceful waves. "Don't miss it, Karynn, even if you have to change a dozen different plans to make it happen. You'll be blessed, I promise."

The wood floors creaked and groaned as they made their way to the front of the room. Karynn was pleased to see the stained glass windows she'd admired from outside were duplicated on the opposite wall. Antique pews gleamed with freshly applied elbow grease and wood polish, but also bore a deep sheen created by years of churchgoers sliding on and off their surfaces.

They sat on the first row, and Lydia filled Karynn in on the chapel's history. "Ari's great-great grandfather, Angus Christmas, was among the first to settle in Hope Creek. He and his wife lived in a small, split-log cabin while he built this chapel. He went to great expense to have the bells shipped in so folks could 'hear the call of the Lord.'" She chuckled. "I can't help wondering how his wife felt about the bells, considering her home was subpar, while her husband focused all that labor and love—and money—on the house of God."

Karynn slanted her a guilty, sideways glance. "I hope she was a better Christian than me. I'm afraid my attitude might have been less than desirable for a minister's wife."

"You and me both. Still, Angus' bells were used for lots of things besides announcing services. They tolled for births and deaths, weddings, funerals…any time folks needed to know about something, the bells called them together to hear the news. This bell tower played a big part in Hope Creek history." She nudged Karynn's arm. "Legend has it that the bells took on a life of their own. If a couple was destined to fall in love, the bells tolled when they kissed."

Karynn glanced at her companion, surprised to find Lydia's big eyes full of wonder. "You—you don't believe that?"

"I don't disbelieve it. Too many things in life are beyond

explanation. Nothing's impossible."

"Well...I guess that almost makes sense."

Gabriel's mysterious disappearance last night flashed through her mind, but she shoved the memory aside. Dreams didn't count. And Daniel was right. The whole Christmas Inn bells legend rang of sappy, sweet and magical—ergo, the stuff of fairy tales.

"So, you know the bell story." Lydia spoke into the short silence following Karynn's doubtful concession to possibility. "Now tell me what I want to know. Why are you so sad, Karynn?"

# 8

KARYNN DREW A DEEP BREATH and then...talked. More than she'd talked to anyone since she and Daniel used to share their every thought for hours on end.

She told Lydia about high school in Quillpoint, and about Daniel...how much she'd loved him, and the awful, lonely place her world became when he and his family moved away. She shared her parents' death, and the horrific nightmares that followed, and continued even now. Tears fell, and she didn't even mind that show of weakness, because Lydia cried with her.

She recounted her surprise when Daniel showed up at the bell table her first night at Christmas Inn, and mentioned Gabriel, sharing with Lydia how the man's sweet smile poured peace and calm into even the most tense of situations. She even shared her strange encounter with the Italian gentleman by the lobby fireplace, what he'd said and how he'd disappeared the moment he'd given her that strange, cryptic message.

She caught her breath, barely able to believe she'd become so chatty with someone she'd met less than an hour ago. For the first time since she started spilling her heart, a twinge of self-consciousness struck, and she lowered her eyelashes.

"Of course, I'm pretty sure I dreamed that last little bit."

"Really? Because I don't think you did."

Karynn chuckled. "You think he really went 'poof' and disappeared?"

"Uhm...I'll say it again. All things are possible. You know, I spoke to Gabriel when he checked out."

"He—what? Gabriel's gone?"

"He left early this morning. He was so pleasant, and you're right about his smile—it felt like someone poured a cup of calmness into my spirit. I had the weirdest inclination to beg him to stay…maybe forever."

"I wish I could have said goodbye."

"Well, I'm sure there's a reason it didn't happen." Lydia's dimples winked in and out. "I asked why he was leaving so soon, and out came that glorious smile. He said he'd done what he came to do, and it was time to go."

Karynn nodded. "The night my sister and I arrived, Gabriel told us he was in Hope Creek to deliver a message from an old friend."

After a moment of contemplative silence, Lydia took her hand and gave it a squeeze. "And you don't see a connection between your visit with Gabriel last night and that special delivery message of his?"

"Connection?" She frowned a little, even as her heart picked up speed. "What are you saying?"

Lydia swiveled on the pew so she could look square into Karynn's eyes. "Maybe Gabriel visited you last night in a dream. Or perhaps he really was there with you beside the fireplace. It doesn't matter, does it? What he said though…that matters, Karynn. He brought you what could be the most important message you'll ever hear in your lifetime. And you know what else?"

"Wh—what else?" Karynn spoke through numb, uncooperative lips.

"You know exactly what it meant, but you don't want to accept it. We never have to decode messages from God, sweetie. He always speaks in a language we understand."

"You think Gabriel came here for me?" Karynn shook her head. "Why? To tell me about past and present and future? About high roads and paths that go backwards?"

"I do. I believe he came to tell you all those things." Lydia leaned in to kiss Karynn's cheek. "And don't forget the part about not letting your will get in the way of God's." She stood. "As much as I hate to leave right now, I really have to get back to work."

"Of course—and I kept you here while I ran on and on. I hope it doesn't cause you any trouble at work."

Lydia laughed. "I couldn't talk them into getting rid of me, not with my mother and Lizzie set on making me a lifetime fixture at the inn."

"Maybe they will. When I go back home, I'll enjoy thinking of you here, listening to the laughter of children inside the inn, and making special trips here, to the chapel, on your breaks." She stood to give Lydia one last, quick hug. "Do you mind walking back alone? I'd like to sit here for a while."

"Not in the least. This is a good thinking place. We'll talk again soon, my new old friend."

Then Karynn was alone, with Gabriel's words ringing in her heart like carillon bells, tolling a message of utmost importance.

****

Daniel left Lena at McGhee-Tyson Airport and navigated heavy traffic out of the terminal.

Back on the 35 freeway, he relaxed against the seat and huffed out a breath. No more exits until he reached US 411, and that was a straight shot into Hope Creek. Barring any unpleasant surprises, he'd be there within the hour.

Back to Karynn.

He could enjoy the drive, now that he'd rid himself of the so-called nanny's constant yapping. When he told her he no longer required her services, she'd turned into a human bomb packed with pure hatred. Vindictive threats spewed from her lips and turned a face that should've been more than slightly attractive into an ugly mask. Daniel shuddered to think she'd been alone with Chrissy for days at a time. While he piloted plane loads of people safely to their destinations, he'd trusted that madwoman with the care of his precious daughter.

No more. He wasn't sure how to handle the time in between the coming transition at work, but he now knew how to respond to a proposition he'd been pitched by airline bigwigs just before he left for Tennessee.

He punched a single number into speed dial on his cell phone, then touched the speaker button and laid the phone on the console.

"Perry Calvert."

"Perry, it's Daniel."

"Daniel, my man! This is a surprise. Did you get my message? We found someone else. Tell me you're not on your way in."

"I got the message. This is about…the other thing we discussed before I left."

A short silence followed, and Daniel almost forgot to breathe. *Please, Lord, don't let them have changed their minds.*

"Have you made a decision? Already?"

"I'll do it. And, Perry, I don't know what the timeline looks like on your end, but don't delay on my account. The sooner the better."

A short bark of laughter filled the car's interior, and Daniel grinned.

"You got me this time, man. I didn't expect you to go for it, but I'm glad you did. It'll be good for the airline—and for you, I think. Just be sure it's what you want. There's no going back."

"I understand. No U-turns."

"Well, then, welcome to a whole new world. Catch you on the flipside—and I'll want to know what brought about such a sudden decision."

The line went dead, and Daniel chuckled. The man never wasted words. They were good friends, as close as brothers. From the time Perry invited Daniel to join his bowling group five years ago, they'd fallen into an unspoken agreement—keep things professional at work, and never discuss the job in private. Maybe that's why their friendship remained strong.

Having accepted the airline's surprising offer, he felt the lightening of a load he hadn't known he carried. Now, if he could only figure out what he'd said during his fireside chat with Karynn that made her draw into herself like a frightened clam. He'd gone over the conversation too many times during the night to count, and hadn't found an answer. Nor had Lena's yammering all the way to the airport given him a chance to mull it over while fully awake.

Daniel dragged his mind off Karynn. A couple more phone calls, then he could focus on her to the exclusion of everything else.

He reached a Tulsa locksmith, who agreed—at a hefty fee for emergency service—to change the locks on every entrance at Daniel's address before Lena's plane set down at the local airport.

Then he called Tina's brother—a big, burly, teddy bear of a guy who adored Chrissy. Bert owned a gym and took fitness to heart. The man was built like a linebacker. After a quick rundown on the situation, he promised to be at Daniel's place in time to accept the new keys from the locksmith. He'd stick around and keep an eye on Lena while she packed. That wouldn't take long— not with a bulldog-faced, gorilla-sized man watching her every move. Bert would help load everything into her vehicle and watch her drive away. Then he'd make sure everything was locked up tight before taking the new keys home with him.

With everything back home squared away, Daniel's thoughts homed in on Karynn. Whatever he'd said to put her off, he'd figure it out and fix it. He had to. Losing her, now that he'd found her again, wasn't an option.

*A little help here, Lord? I'll fight for Karynn to the final breath, but I need to know what she's running from. What is the enemy I'm battling against? How do I win? And, Lord...I have to win.*

His hands cramped, and he loosened their grip on the wheel. A quick glance at the speedometer showed the needle hovering too far to the right. He lifted his foot off the accelerator and told God again, just in case He hadn't heard the first time.

*I have to win.*

He pulled in a deep breath, let it out nice and slow, and then took himself back through last night's fateful conversation. One word, one sentence, one inflection at a time. Again and again.

Fifteen miles outside Hope Creek, the puzzle fell into place.

Daniel swerved off the road, too stunned to drive for several minutes. How had he not put two and two together right off? Given the circumstances, what else could the problem have been?

He laughed aloud, amazed at God's simple, yet profound ways. Easing back onto the road, he shook his head. "You are amazing, Lord! By the time I found the problem, You'd already delivered the solution."

****

Alone in the chapel, Karynn slid to her knees, desperate to find peace. Was she really going to let the love of her life, her very heartbeat, walk away again? This time, they had a choice…and Daniel had already made his. She saw it every time he looked at her.

Karynn longed to give him that same reassurance. Why, of all the possible career fields he might have chosen, had he become a pilot? She could never survive the horrible, bone-chilling dread every time he climbed into a metal monster and soared off somewhere too far above solid ground. The thought alone turned her mind to mush.

"God?" She spoke through the tears that clouded her vision and the lump that closed her throat. "I need help, if I ever hope to find happiness with Daniel. Thank You for sending Gabriel with such a beautiful message. Forgive me for trying so hard not to hear it. But You knew I would hear it, didn't You? You were pointing me toward Daniel, and I know that's where happiness lies for me. But how do I find the courage to face this choking, drowning fear of losing someone else I love?" A sob tore past her throat, and she dropped her head onto folded arms atop the pew. "Why can't everyone just keep their feet on the ground?"

*I am God, daughter.*

Karynn opened her eyes, but dared not raise her head. Something holy washed over her, leaving gooseflesh along the length of her body despite the warm jacket she still wore in the chilly chapel. Her mind filled with words…still, quiet words that were not her own.

*Am I not your God?*

"You are my God. Always."

*On sea and on land, I am God.*

She shook her head. Of course God was God. She'd never doubted that.

"Yes, Father. I know You are God."

*Below the earth, I am God.*

"Even there, Lord, I know You are God."

*And in the sky, above the clouds, I am the same God."*

Karynn froze. Her heart thudded hard against her ribs, and she struggled for breath.

*Daughter. Can you trust Me only in your familiar world?*

She crumpled, broken. Shame kept her head bowed to the pew. "You are God in every world, and in every situation."

Like the rapid flicker of images at the end of a film reel, familiar verses skipped through her mind—fast, and then faster and faster, a rolling recitation of scriptures she knew well enough to quote from memory.

Yet now, they were brand new. Swift. Sure. Sharp. They cut through every argument and all defenses.

*To every thing there is a season, and a time to every purpose under the heaven: A time to be born, and a time to die… Though I walk through the valley of the shadow of death, I will fear no evil: for thou art with me… And the peace of God, which passeth all understanding, shall keep your hearts and minds through Christ Jesus… For God hath not given us the spirit of fear; but of power, and of love, and of a sound mind. Fear thou not; for I am with thee: be not dismayed; for—*

"All right!" Karynn uncovered her face and straightened her spine. "You are God, and I am not. I trust You, Lord." She swallowed hard, but continued in a strong, unwavering voice. "In every situation, under every circumstance…even with the lives of those I love."

*Do you love me, daughter?*

"I love You, Father, with all my heart."

Soul shivers rippled along her spine, and spirit touches—like the feathery brush of angel wings—wrapped around her heart and mind. Was this really happening?

*There is no fear in love; but perfect love casteth out fear: because fear hath torment.*

Karynn managed a wry smile. "Fear has turned my entire life into torment."

The words tumbling through her soul screeched to a stop and then repeated, slowly and with powerful impact.

*Perfect love...casteth out fear. Do you love Me perfectly, daughter? Do you love Me...completely?*

"I do, Lord. I love You with everything I am."

*He that feareth is not made perfect in love.*

Karynn paused to talk herself through that one. "So then, if I love You with perfect completeness, my fears cannot survive, because..."

She caught her breath on what she should have known all along.

In that crucial moment of understanding, a ray of sunshine caught one of the stained glass windows and reflected rainbow hues onto the pew against which she leaned. Awed, she stared at the shining white cross that lay in bright splendor where her head had rested only moments before.

"Perfect love casts out fear," she whispered.

*So it does.*

Karynn smiled, even as she brushed away her tears. "So it does. Thank You, Father! Thank You!"

She leaped to her feet and rushed toward the door. She ached to find Daniel, to say what she should've said already. But he was somewhere overhead, piloting a plane full of passengers to a safe landing. *Please, God. A safe landing.* But she could wait, now that she'd decided to let God be God...and to take the high road to the future.

Outside, she crossed North Pole Bridge and hurried down the winding path to the inn. She'd been too preoccupied to notice the cold in the chapel, but now it ate at her skin, and gnawed at her bones. How long had she been out here? Savannah and Chrissy had no doubt long since gone into town without her. She passed the gardens at a run, rounded the circle drive and barreled through the glass doors…straight into a broad, warm chest that smelled of woods and spice.

# 9

**DANIEL ARRIVED AT THE INN** in time to see Savannah and Chrissy cross the parking lot. He swept his little girl into his arms and rained kisses on her face. His playful greeting drew the most delightful giggles from her, as always…and as always, he drank in the sound of her laughter like nectar from Heaven.

With the kisses over, and Chrissy clinging to his neck, he turned to Savannah. "Where's—?"

"Karynn?" She broke in, her tone both annoyed and concerned. "Good question. She was supposed to meet us in the lobby half an hour ago. We haven't seen her, but I'm sure she's OK. She didn't plan to leave the grounds."

Daniel frowned. "The grounds? That's a pretty big area."

"Trust me, she didn't go far alone. Karynn's the most cautious person in the world. Of course, she's normally the most considerate, and punctual, as well." The little crease between her brows deepened. "I'm concerned, Daniel, I admit it. But I promised Chrissy we'd have a look around Hope Creek. If you don't mind her going, I'd like to keep that promise. We won't be long. If—no, *when* Karynn shows up, would you have her call me, please?"

"Of course. She'll show up, Savannah. You two go on, and have fun." He hugged Chrissy again. "I'll get the child seat from my car."

"Daddy!" She still hadn't quite reached the weight requirement, and Chrissy hated the "baby chair." Good thing he'd arrived before she and Savannah went exploring.

"Honey, you know the drill. You wouldn't want Savannah to get a ticket because of us, would you?"

"No." She turned her frown upside down in an instant. "We'll still have fun."

"Sure we will, Chrissy-cake." Savannah was already behind the wheel. She gave her backseat passenger a smile and a thumbs-up. "Fun, fun, fun!"

Chrissy returned the thumbs up with both mitten-covered hands. "Let's go, go, go!" she trilled.

He watched them all the way down Reindeer Road North—the exit side of the split access-and-egress roads leading in and out of Christmas Inn property. Then he strode toward the inn, and pushed through the foyer doors into the lobby. Two long strides inside, he stopped, having no idea which direction to take. If Karynn were here, Savannah would have found her. She wasn't in the inn. She was outside, in the icy cold.

Daniel stepped to the fireplace to warm up, and to decide on a plan. He pulled off his gloves and held his hands close to the welcome heat. "Where are you, Karynn?" he muttered.

"You must be Daniel."

He whirled. A dark-haired woman stood behind the reception counter. She smiled, and a pair of dimples danced on her cheeks.

"I'm sorry...should I know you?"

"No, but Karynn told me about you."

"Really." He hiked a brow. "That's odd. Karynn doesn't usually share her private life with strangers."

"I'm not a stranger, Daniel. Your Karynn and I, we've known each other for a long time." Mischief sparkled from her dark eyes. "Maybe longer than she's known you."

"I see." Why hadn't Karynn mentioned knowing someone in Hope Creek? "And you are?"

"Lydia. But that doesn't matter right now. If I'm not mistaken, you're looking for my friend."

"You're not mistaken."

"She's in the chapel."

"The chapel? Across the creek?"

Lydia nodded. "I left her there..." She glanced at the big glockenspiel clock with the chasing elves that Chrissy loved to watch. "Almost an hour ago. I thought she'd be back by now. The heat isn't on out there, so…" She grimaced. "I hope she doesn't stay much longer."

"Thank you, Lydia." He pulled his gloves on and headed for the door. "I'm going to the chapel."

Her soft laughter soothed the fear mounting in Daniel's mind. "I thought you might."

He crossed the foyer to the double glass doors and placed a hand on the crossbar handle, his gaze already searching the wintry grounds.

There she was, her head down against the cold as she ran toward the inn. He grinned through a massive wave of relief. Slipping in the snow and breaking an ankle wouldn't make her less late for her meeting with Savannah and Chrissy, but Karynn being Karynn, her own safety was the last thing on her mind.

He backed away from the door and waited. When she pushed it open, he stepped in front of her and she plowed square into his chest, just as he'd expected. His arms were around her in an instant.

Sweet Lord, she felt wonderful! The damp air combined with the cold temperature had formed a thin layer of ice from head to toe, turning the woman he loved into a real, live ice maiden. Yet holding her in his arms lit a fire in Daniel's heart that would never be quenched.

"D-D-Daniel!" Despite her chattering teeth, Karynn managed his name. She raised her head, and her beautiful eyes went wide. "You're h-here."

"Let's get you warmed up." He urged her toward the lobby. "Then we'll talk."

Lydia met them at the fireplace, a heavy blanket in her arms. "Daniel, move that big chair closer to the fire. I'll get her boots off, and her jacket."

Karynn clung to the jacket with frozen fingers. "No. I'm c-c-cold!"

"And I want to warm you up. Come on—off with it! I have a

thick blanket, fluffy as a cloud, for you to snuggle into." Even as she spoke, she gently pushed Karynn's hands away so she could unzip the coat, and then eased it off her shoulders. The beanie came off next, and then Lydia wrapped her friend in the soft blanket and led her to the chair. "Sit here. I'll take your boots off. Why did you stay out there so long, Karynn?"

"I was t-t-talking to God."

Daniel blinked, but Lydia didn't. She smiled, and those dimples turned her face into something beatific. "Ahh. That's what I was hoping you'd do. OK, now just sit here with this handsome guy." She lowered her voice to a stage whisper. "I think he likes you."

"You have good instincts," Daniel supplied.

"So I've been told." Lydia was already halfway across the room. "I'll be back with hot cocoa."

He sat on the hearth, close enough to touch Karynn's face. The drop in body temperature had paled her skin to porcelain, accentuating big, brown eyes and—despite the faint blue tint around them—lips the color of apple blossoms.

"You're an ice cube, sweetheart...and still so beautiful I can barely breathe."

Karynn's gaze locked on his. A tiny crease appeared between her eyebrows, and she shook her head. "You're h-here! I thought you were s-s-somewhere in the s-sky."

"Shh...don't talk yet." Hadn't Savannah told her anything? "I didn't have to go to work. I just drove Lena to the airport."

"Was she....very angry?"

He grimaced. "That's one way of saying it." He shook his head, hoping to clear it of the look in the woman's eyes when she slammed the car door and stormed into the airport. "But she's gone now, and by the time I get home, she'll be gone from there, as well. I hope none of us ever has to see her again."

"I feel s-sorry for her."

Daniel chuckled. "Of course you do. Your heart's always been three sizes too big for that tiny body of yours."

"She's so unhappy. D-Deep, deep down." Daniel tracked the movement of her hand, beneath the big blanket, to rest on her heart. "We should p-pray for her."

"We will." He cleared his throat, moved by her concern for someone who'd shown no sign of pleasantness during their short acquaintance. "You'll make me a better man yet."

Lydia showed up carrying a tray loaded with two mugs of hot chocolate, half a dozen cookies that smelled so wonderful they had to be fresh out of the oven, and two small bowls of hot soup.

"Daniel, if you'd like, I can help Karynn with her soup while you enjoy yours."

"I can feed myself." Karynn smiled at her friend. "Thank you, but I'm doing b-better now."

Daniel studied her face. The scary blue tinge around her lips had faded, and her speech was much steadier. She'd be fine.

"Well, if you're sure…" Lydia bent to give Karynn a hug. "I'll leave you two alone."

The hot chocolate was gourmet fare, as was everything on the tray. Daniel enjoyed his soup, but kept a close eye on Karynn with hers. Her fingers shook a bit when she first picked up her spoon, but by the time she swallowed the last drop, no trace remained of the ice maiden.

Daniel laid the tray aside. He'd return it to the kitchen later. Right now, he had something else on his mind.

He knelt in front of Karynn's chair. "Are you warm enough to lose that blanket?"

"If I don't, I'll melt right through the floor." She laughed, and tossed the heavy cover aside.

Daniel drew her up and into his arms. "Don't ever do that again. You scared us all."

She smiled and cupped her hands around his face. "I'd do it again right now. God met me out there in the Christmas Inn Chapel. It was…beyond wondrous."

"Well, a meeting with God definitely trumps the warmth of this fireplace." He traced her lips with a fingertip. "I had my own

God-moment today."

"And I want to hear about it but…me first. I have something to say to you, and I've already waited too long."

"You're not going to break my heart, are you?"

"That's not in the plan." She drew his face closer to hers, and held his gaze as she touched her lips to his. Shy. Tentative.

Breathtaking.

Daniel gathered her close…close enough to feel her heartbeat against his own. The syncopation created a perfect rhythm. He responded to her timid gesture of initiation with a gentle slide of his lips across hers. Then, with a groan, he deepened the kiss to explore further, tasting the sweetness of her lips for the first time in far, far too long.

Karynn's arms stole around his neck. She responded with all the passion he'd longed for since he saw her in the dining room that first night. Whatever conversation she'd had with God out there in that little chapel had opened her to the possibility of a shared future.

His heart crashed at her feet when she stiffened and pulled away enough to fix a wide, startled gaze on his. *No, no…please, not again.*

"Do you hear them?"

How had he missed them? The musical sound of tolling bells rang through the air, loud and clear even inside the inn. Daniel held Karynn in his arms. Eyes fixed on each other, they didn't speak until the last deep peal echoed into silence.

Daniel loved the awe on her face. "I never told you about those bells, did I?"

"No, but I did," Lydia sang from across the room. Then she ducked out of sight, her low, warm laughter still echoing in the air.

Daniel laughed out loud. "She's your friend, huh? You didn't mention her."

"Because I only met her this morning."

"But she said—"

"That we're old friends? We are. We've known each other forever."

"O…K. I'm out of my league, but we'll fix that later." Right now, Daniel had other things on his mind. He drew her close once again. "Where were we?" He kissed her nose. Her chin. Nuzzled her neck.

"Uhm…I…Daniel! I need to tell you something, and I can't…think…when you…"

He chuckled. "All right, for now. You were saying?"

"I'm glad you weren't off soaring through the clouds. I'm not sure I could've waited another day to say this." A shy smile peeked through the solemnity of her expression. "My mother would faint dead away if she knew I jumped the gun and said it first, but—"

"Well, let's honor your sweet mother's memory." Daniel traced her lips with his fingertip. "Allow me. Karynn Michaels, I have loved you since before I knew you. I've never for one moment stopped loving you—there's a part of my heart that no one else could ever, or will ever claim. I loved you ten years ago, sweetheart. I adore you today. And, while it seems impossible at the moment, I know that tomorrow, and every tomorrow after, what I feel now will be stronger and deeper." He lifted her chin and brushed her lips again—a gentle, soft caress that sent a spear of warmth throughout his body. "What I'm saying, Karynn, is that I'll love you forever and always."

Her radiant smile lit the whole world, and Daniel's heart responded with a leap that didn't knock him off his feet only because the woman in his arms also held him in hers.

"Now, how am I supposed to come up with anything better than that, Daniel Sheridan? So not fair!"

"This isn't a competition, my love. Please…for my heart's sake…say *something.*"

Her sweet laughter filled all the dry, empty places he hadn't even known his soul possessed. "For your heart, then. Daniel…I think I've loved you every moment of my life. Those years between 'then' and 'now' were an eternity of waiting, and I still can't believe God gave you back to me. You are the air I breathe, the beat of my heart, and the song of my soul. I love you. I *love* you, Daniel...forever and always."

"Then and now." Daniel touched his lips to one corner of hers and held them there until she gasped. He smiled. "Forever and always." He moved to the opposite corner in a slow slide, and once again waited for her breathless reaction. Only then did he turn the playful touches into a slow lip dance.

When at last the kiss ended, Karynn laid her head against his chest. Her fingers toyed with the unruly waves of hair at his collar, sending electric tingles up his scalp. "Daniel?"

"Karynn..."

"The bells. They're ringing again."

He laughed. "So they are. Shall we try for one more encore?"

"Mmmm. Why stop at one?"

# *10*

KARYNN DIDN'T HEAR DANIEL'S NEWS about his job until late that night, when once again they snuggled in front of the fireplace. His pleasure in the telling only enhanced her over-the-top relief at the perfect timing of every event, all day long.

"I'm so glad I told you I loved you before you shared this news. I wouldn't want you to ever think I only let 'us' happen because you're not a full-time pilot any more."

"Karynn, it wouldn't matter. Do you think I'd let a job stand between us? Any job?"

"No, I don't. But you shouldn't have to change your life in that way for me. I'm glad it happened the way it did." She caught her bottom lip between her teeth, and then released it when Daniel's playfully wolfish gaze fell on the habitual gesture. "Stop that!" When, oh when, would she stop blushing like a schoolgirl? "Help me understand what this new position means. Chief Airline Flight Instructor. It certainly sounds important."

"It means a whole lot less airtime, a regular schedule—evenings and weekends off—and no need for live-in childcare. Oh, and a little less money, in case that's a deal breaker." He grinned. "Chrissy's already making an all-out plea to live in Quillpoint, not Tulsa."

Karynn laughed. "I'm all for having you closer."

"We can think about all that later, but I'll do whatever makes you happy, Karynn. Where we live doesn't matter, as long as we're together." He nuzzled her neck, and she focused on breathing.

"Oh, I meant to ask…" Daniel sat up and fixed her beneath a stern, narrow-eyed gaze. "What was Savannah talking about today? Something about…prom addiction? Frog fiction? Song diction?"

Karynn rolled her eyes but couldn't make a frown work—her lips refused to cooperate. "Promidiction."

"Ahh. Yeah, that's it. I love new words. Can I use it in Scrabble?"

Karynn finally managed to purse her lips in proper school marm style.

Daniel laughed. "OK. OK. But seriously—fill me in."

"I hoped you'd let that slide."

"Not a chance. Talk to me."

She removed the fuzzy slippers she'd worn to their 'fireside chat' and stuck both feet straight out in front of her. "My toes."

Daniel grinned. "Wowzers! Lovin' the cute little bells."

"They're not too bad, are they?" She filled him in on the whole Bells on Her Toes package. "My sister has become Miss Extravagance since she married a brain surgeon."

"Well, she did it up right with those toes." He tugged on a strand of her hair and winked. "So what was the frog fiction today? That's what Savannah was on about—not those adorable toes of yours."

He wasn't wrong.

When Savannah and Chrissy returned from their run into Hope Creek that afternoon, Daniel and Karynn still stood in front of the fireplace, wrapped in each other's arms. Chrissy's high-pitched giggle drew their attention, and they whirled to find Savannah hunkered down to the child's level, her arm around Chrissy, while they both stared, wide-eyed, across the room.

"Daddy! You're kissing Miss Karynn!"

Karynn struggled to pull free of his arms, but he refused to let go.

"I am?" Daniel made a show of noticing his arms around her. "Well, look at that. I sure am, munchkin. Know what? I think I'll do it again."

To Karynn's utter embarrassment, he pulled her into a brief, tight squeeze and touched his lips to hers. Just a peck, but heat crawled up her neck, into her face, and all the way to her hairline.

Chrissy covered her mouth with both hands, but a burst of heavenly little-girl giggles poured from between tiny fingers.

Savannah stood to her feet and lifted both beautiful, wing-shaped eyebrows. "Well, I am not surprised."

"Oh, come on," Daniel teased. "You're a little bit surprised."

"Nope. It was in the promidiction." She grinned at Karynn. "You didn't do your thing this morning, so I did it for you. Want to know what it said?"

"No!"

"Then I won't tell you." Savannah stuck her nose in the air and marched right past them, taking Chrissy upstairs to shed her damp jacket and boots.

Now, Daniel refused to let it go. "So, what did it say? That promidiction thing. I know she's told you by now."

Karynn groaned. It's so silly."

"So tell me the *silly* promidiction."

She sighed. "It said, 'Today is the first day of a whole new world. Say yes to an important question.'"

"What's silly about that? Are you going to say yes?"

Karynn wrinkled her nose. "To what question?"

"Will you marry me?"

"Now, see what I mean? That's an unnecessary question, because we both already know—"

"Will you marry me?"

"Yes. I can't wait to marry you."

"See, the promidictions are great. You should take them more seriously."

They laughed—the same way they always used to laugh, for any reason, or no reason at all. Then he kissed her, and she forgot all about crystal bells and promidictions.

****

The following week passed in a blur of activity. Now that the storm had run its course, Hope Creek became a hive of activity.

Tourists roamed the streets, and Christmas shoppers filled the malls. Santa ho-ho-hoed from half a dozen different corners. Familiar holiday tunes filled the air at every location.

Karynn and Savannah discovered they enjoyed browsing the gift shop at Christmas Inn more than any other shopping venue. Having watched Savannah drool over a couple of items and then leave them on the shelves, Karynn managed another visit without her sister. She pretended ignorance when Savannah did the same.

Daniel insisted on Karynn reading the day's promidiction with him every morning. They'd walk in the garden and choose a different bench, for a new view each day. Once she got past the mild embarrassment of answering the curious questions of other guests when she rang the crystal bell, Karynn enjoyed the fun. They made their way through a whole range of pretty sayings, from blatantly generic to a couple that bordered on specific.

*Don't be afraid to try new things.*

That evening, Daniel took her to a barn dance outside the city limits, where they two-stepped and laughed through a square dance routine. Neither of those were new to Karynn, thanks to her mother. Then he pulled her onto the floor one last time...and Mama never heard of the Boot-scootin' Boogie.

The night before Christmas Eve, they attended a holiday show at Dahlia Brewster's Family Theater. Once Chrissy discovered her new hero, Jayson Taylor, was one of the top-billed performers, the child insisted they *had* to 'go watch Jayson play.'

That day's promidiction read, "You won't regret heeding the voice of a child," so nothing would do for Daniel but that they all went to the theater.

The show proved phenomenal. Jayson played opposite a former Hope Creek native with a voice like an angel. Emilee Lancaster had come all the way from California to do the show, as a favor to her aunt Dahlia.

Afterward, in their habitual late-night spot by the fireplace, Karynn told Daniel that if the chapel bells hadn't already rang for Jayson and Emilee, they would, and soon.

"Is that a personal promidiction?" he teased.

She laughed. "Call it what you want."

"I call it pretty obvious. No way was that just good chemistry."

"Right. Those two are in love, whether they know it or not."

"And we should know, because we are now experts on the subject." Daniel laughed and ducked Karynn's playful slap to his arm. "Can you believe tomorrow's Christmas Eve? Already? After that, it'll be your Christmas-birthday."

"And you've given me the best gift of my life, Daniel. You...and Chrissy."

"Ditto, my love. So, we have the Christmas prayer service tomorrow night. I'm looking forward to that. But there's a whole day to fill in the meantime. Any plans?"

She grinned. "Yes, but they won't take long."

"Well, that's informative. Are they something I can't know about?"

"No, I guess not." She lifted slippered feet and wiggled her toes. "I thought I'd go by *Nail It* and have my toes touched up."

"Aha! More promidictions for our playful pleasure."

"No! No more of those." Karynn laughed. "I just want to brighten the bells on my toes."

"I'm surprised." He closed one eye and tilted his head to the side. "Savannah said they were a little over the top for you."

"They were, at first. But now...I don't know, I like them. They make me smile."

Daniel pulled her into his arms. "Then by all mean, go get more bells on your toes. I love that gorgeous smile."

Karynn cuddled closer. "Want to hear a promidiction right now?"

He grinned—that mischievous, crooked half grin she remembered so well...the one that melted her heart every time. "Always."

"A handsome, high-flying man will kiss me near a crackling fire. And I will smile, because his kisses really ring my bell."

"Hmmm." Daniel trailed his lips from her chin to her temple, then gently turned her face to make the same journey from temple to chin on the other side. "I like it." He stopped just shy of covering her lips with his. "So...do they really? Ring your bell?"

"Every bell on every toe."

He kissed her then, a bell-ringing, toe-curling, heart-stopping kiss.

Karynn...smiled.

# ~ About Delia ~

**DELIA LATHAM** writes Heaven's touch into earthly tales. She puts her characters through the fire of trial, only to bring them out victorious by the hand of God, His heavenly messengers, and old-fashioned love.

Delia lives in East Texas with her husband Johnny. She's a wife, mother, grandmother, sister, and friend—

but above all, she treasures her role as princess daughter to the King of Kings. When she's not writing, she designs book covers and marketing material, and edits manuscripts for other authors. See samples of her work here: **heavenstouchdesigns.com.**

Find out more about this author on her website:
**www.delialatham.net**

Follow Delia on Amazon to receive announcements about new releases:
**www.amazon.com/author/delialatham**

Or find her on social media:

**www.facebook.com/delialatham**
**www.twitter.com/delialatham**
**www.pinterest.com/delialatham**

Interested in having some fun on my street team,
and helping spread the word about my books? Check it out!
**www.delialatham.com/street-team**

# ~ More Titles by Delia Latham ~

## Coming Soon
*Radiant Rays of Grace*
*Love at Christmas Inn: Collection 3*

## Potter's House Books
*Sweet Scent of Forgiveness*

## Grace Kitchen
*One Harvest Knight (Book 3)*
See Amazon listings for titles by other authors

## Hummingbird Hollow
*Hummingbird Kisses*
*Never the Twain*
*Like a Dance*

## Paradise Pines
*Spring Raine*
*Summer Dreams*
*Autumn Falls*
*Winter Wonders*

## Love at Christmas Inn: Collection 2
*The Button Box*

## Heart's Haven Collections
*Jewels for the Kingdom*
*Lexi's Heart*

*Love in the WINGS*
*A Cowboy Christmas* (Co-authored with Tanya Stowe)
*Oh Baby*

**Pure Amore**
*At First Sight*
*Jingle Belle*
*A Christmas Beau*

**A Smoky Mountain Christmas**
*Do You See What I See?*
(See Amazon listing for titles
in this collection by other authors.)

**Stand-alone Titles**
*Treehouse* (Short Story)
*Lea's Gift* (Co-authored with Tanya Stowe)

**FREE Short Stories**
*Love Comes Lately*
(A Heart's Haven bonus tale)
*Tree of Hearts*
Find these FREE stories at
**www.pelicanbookgroup.com**

Made in the USA
Coppell, TX
14 April 2021